WHERE THE SKY CHILDREN FELL

THE MYTHS OF MAUDLIN | PART ONE

WHERE THE SKY CHILDREN FELL

THOMAS SMAK

For permission requests, contact themythsofmaudlin@gmail.com.

Published by Haus of Faun
First Edition: August 2021

ISBN 978-1-7376018-0-7 (paperback)
ISBN 978-1-7376018-1-4 (ebook)

Cover and book design by Thomas Smak
Illustration by Rachel Smak
Cover photos by Matias Ilizarbe, Jez Timms, Sirma Krustreva, and Sergio Santana

hausoffaun.com
themythsofmaudlin.com

For Tali Vega, wherever you are…

1 — Rest Stop

I HAD A SISTER ONCE—ANNABELLE AVENUE.

I'm not saying she's dead or anything like that. I just haven't seen her in a very, very long time. Eleven years and five months. I was six years old, almost seven. She was days away from turning five.

I thought I'd remember her face, but time has this funny way of rearranging the furniture when you're not home.

I wonder what she looks like now, assuming she still has a face.

My mom passed shortly before my sister vanished.

Cancer, my father said.

I don't know about that.

Maybe he's right, though. It makes perfect sense. My father was cancer or something like it. Before he disappeared, he had a way of poisoning the well-being of our family.

If you knew him, you would understand. For your sake, I hope you never do, but I don't think you ever will.

Maybe I know you never will.

In case you're wondering, my entire family is gone.

I'm the only one left.

Now, may I continue? Geez.

Before my family fell apart, my father couldn't keep a job. He lost four or five jobs in three months. Nothing was ever his fault, of course, but he didn't bother to explain. Instead, he blamed each job he lost on an "altercation." He used that word a lot.

I asked what he did for a living more than once.

Always the same answer: "You don't wanna know."

His last altercation led to several nighttime visits from the Moths. These encounters showed a side of my father I had never seen before. For the first time in my life, he seemed frightened, visibly shaken. I don't remember much else, though.

During their final visit, one of the Moths said something to my father about "breaking the code."

Whatever that means.

I kept my eyes on my mom while she kept her eyes on them.

Her eyes.

They shed more than the usual tears this time. She lost faith in my father. I watched it happen in real time.

Among everyone my father poisoned, he hit her with the hardest dose. She drank every last drop.

The last time I saw her, she was lying in a wooden box in front of the altar at Our Lady of Sorrows Church. It's hard to believe we even have a church in a place like this, but we do.

Hallelujah, right?

My father didn't come to the funeral. He went missing after my mom died—five, maybe six days. Maybe more? I don't know. I can't remember who took care of us either—my sister and me—but I know it wasn't him. I try to remember, but it's like reading a book with random pages torn out.

Something is missing.

I only remember the living room window. My sister joined me.

We just sat there, looking out the window, waiting for something to happen. That was our favorite place to sit in the house, especially in June. Fans are great, but nothing beats an open window.

I know what air conditioning is, but we didn't have it.

After five, maybe six, maybe seven days, my father came back. He seemed so happy. Maybe more anxious than happy. Somewhere between the two.

"Get in the car, kids," he said. "We're getting the hell out of here."

We had a car. Can you believe it?

Most of my memories from that day are lost, but I managed to save a few. I need to blow the dust off first. Let me take a breath.

Wow. It's hard for me to breathe right now.

Let me try again.

Bill once told me that I suppressed the days between my mom's death and my father's spontaneous trip. He insisted that I buried them deep into my subconscious, somewhere within a series of haunting dreams.

Do you know Bill Dweller?

"Your memories are sleeping demons," he said to me a long time ago. "Dream with caution."

Too bad I'm the clumsy type.

My father took my sister and me from the house; we left the city.

I remember standing in front of a massive wall of brochures and pamphlets inside an empty rest stop somewhere off the highway. I remember leaving the city, but I don't remember the ride there. All I know is that I couldn't stop staring at the wall covered with flashy pictures of places I never knew existed.

It overwhelmed me. I studied the brochures carefully, picturing myself in each one.

"I want to go there," I said to myself, gazing at a picture of some family in a giant inner tube, flying down a blue water slide.

"I want to go *there* too," I said to a picture of a husband, his wife, and their two children wearing red and white checkered bibs, eating shitloads of Alaskan king crab.

I was overcome by an unfamiliar warmth and an anxious desire to go wherever the brochures told me to go.

A pier on the beach, swarming with fishermen.

I wanted to go there.

A boy awkwardly perched next to a campfire.

I wanted to go there.

A museum littered with boring wax sculptures.

Hell, I wanted to go there too.

If you haven't figured it out by now, I had an uninteresting and borderline-neglectful childhood. I'd like to say it was all my father's doing, but that wouldn't be true.

Oh, fuck it. I'm going to blame this all on him for a minute.

And yes, I know what "awkwardly perched" means.

My mom stood in the background and watched while my father robbed my sister and me of the life we probably should have had. But I don't blame her. Fear stopped her from getting in his way, and even though she wanted to escape, she never did. The fantasy of running away remained a fantasy.

That's on me.

I may be the only thing that kept her from taking a hike.

Sometimes, I believe she'd still be breathing if I had never been born. Because I'm still here, I take responsibility.

I did find her, though, in a place between places.

A single palm tree on an empty beach.

I wanted to go there.

For twenty minutes, I spotted around seven hundred thousand different vacation brochures on the wall.

I carefully observed each one.

Unless you're lost, exhausted from the road, obsessed with travel brochures, or have some serious gastrointestinal problems, twenty minutes is a long time to spend at a rest stop. That's how I knew something was wrong.

My father didn't like to stay in one place for too long. He lived impatiently. He was the type of guy who pissed in a public restroom without washing his hands.

As soon as I snapped out of my brochure-induced trance, I looked up and saw my sister. I could tell she was frustrated after spending a small eternity struggling for my attention. She didn't have to speak; the troubled expression on her face spoke volumes.

Annabelle pointed toward the state map behind her.

"He's not on the map! Look!"

I approached her to see what the hell she was talking about.

"See, this is us," she continued, standing on her tip-toes, tapping a red dot on the highway.

You are here.

"I can't find Daddy. He's not on the map."

Poor Annabelle. I didn't know what to tell her. I didn't have the time or patience to help her understand the concept of maps. I felt relieved, though, thinking this map was the only reason why she looked at me so glumly.

"Glumly" is a real word. Just ask Bill. He'll tell you.

"It's okay," I responded. "He's not on the map, but he's here somewhere. We just have to find him."

I told her to stay by the map while I went looking for him. It would have made a lot more sense if I had her tag along instead of leaving her by herself. I don't even remember why I made that decision. I relive this memory inside my head from time to time.

The furniture doesn't move.

I wasn't afraid that my father left us—I anticipated it.

I expected this to happen ever since my mom died. It was only a matter of time. To my father, Annabelle and I were things he had to tolerate. My mom was out of the equation; we were the remainder. He never wanted us. I might as well have been parentless.

I think something happened in the car on the way to the rest stop. I'll try to remember.

Something bad happened. I know that much.

Before I reached the exit to the parking lot, I turned around to make sure my sister hadn't left the map. She was still there, looking back at me. I swear, we could communicate silently, without words. She was telling me that I shouldn't have left her alone. I should have listened. She asked me, without words, what would happen next. As her older brother, I was supposed to give her an answer.

I had nothing to offer.

I peered through the glass doors; one car idled in the parking lot. It wasn't my father's.

He left. Just like I said he would. I always knew he would disappear one day, so I can't say it scared me. I just never considered the aftermath. I wasn't prepared.

You can't blame me for being unprepared, though. Talk about an unfair advantage. He could have at least dropped us off at a park or a store or any place where we could find one decent human being. I wouldn't exactly know what to do from there, but hey, it's a start.

I had more to fear than the unknown. My sister's naivety frightened me. She didn't suspect my father would ever leave us. Her take on a father figure stood poles apart from my own.

Somehow, I loved that about her. I admired her perpetual sense of unawareness. Perhaps it's a characteristic of innocence. That's what I found in my thesaurus.

Technically, it wasn't *my* thesaurus. I borrowed it from Bill.

As we become more aware of the truth—humankind is a dark,

self-centered, unwelcoming consumer—we lose that piece of ourselves, that senseless wonder. The moment we become spectators or victims to a painful act carried out by someone dear to us is when our purity takes a dirt nap. If we're lucky, we'll still have some shred of it left by the time we graduate high school.

I'll be honest: I have no idea what high school is like. We don't have schools here. I read about high school in a couple of Bill's books.

Do you know Bill Dweller?

Did I already ask you that?

My nervous system was shot at the sight of an empty parking lot. I could feel Fear putting its hands around my body, molesting my sense of security. Being six years old while having the capacity to feel *everything* is both impressive and disturbing.

I couldn't figure out what to tell Annabelle. There was no way around this, no comforting explanation behind my father's abandonment. Her biggest fear was getting lost. She feared it more than death. If she thought getting lost in my mom's closet was tough, then this was going to destroy her.

In her defense, my mom had a huge closet.

When I returned to give Annabelle the worst news of her life, I realized that I wouldn't be able to tell her anything.

She was gone too.

I investigated the map, hoping to find something—an answer. I don't know. It's what Annabelle did when our father disappeared. I gave it a shot, but I couldn't find her. I couldn't find anyone.

Everything stopped making sense.

Despite her size, Annabelle's presence was always apparent. Whether as a whisper or a song or a fake airplane sound, her mousy voice demanded attention. It's like she was always there, everywhere.

That's how I knew something terrible happened.

Her voice was absent.

I spent a minute or two running around, shouting her name every five seconds, hoping to find her.

I charged into the women's restroom—nothing.

I even ran outside to where they keep the vending machines.

No sign of her. She was gone.

Don't let my expectations fool you. This scared the shit out of me. Thankfully, denial is a hell of a drug, and I started it very young. I waited for her to pop up out of nowhere and laugh and make fun of me for freaking out. For a five-year-old, she was a master in the art of practical jokes. This wouldn't have been her first.

I forgot about my father as soon as Annabelle disappeared. She was the only thing on my mind—well, almost. As I returned to the wall of brochures, one of them caught my eye. I must have missed it the first time around.

It had a very peculiar headline:

Disappear Into Your Dream Destination

The cover featured two men wearing yellow hats with flashlights on them. They were underground somewhere. Maybe a cave or cavern. I have no idea what they were doing.

Reading the headline inspired me to think about what it means to disappear. I started to say aloud anything that seemed synonymous with it.

"Leave."

"Go away."

"Die?"

Something dark floated past the corner of my left eye.

At first, I thought it was smoke, but by the time I looked at it directly, the whatever-it-was had materialized into a tall, thin man with a pale face.

He was dressed entirely in black: fedora, trench coat, pants, boots, suspenders, everything.

His dark wardrobe absorbed the light around him.

He had grey skin.

I found him standing with his back against the map. The only thing more startling than his out-of-nowhere appearance and black-hole wardrobe was that he was looking at me, staring with a crooked smile.

For just a second, his teeth were broken glass.

He was very excited about something. The anticipation on his face reminded me of how my father looked whenever he was about to go out for the night and come home three days later.

I averted my eyes, but I could still feel the stranger staring at me.

Seconds went by like lifetimes. With each passing lifetime, I felt more scared to death.

Being as young as I was, I had a hard time identifying emotions beyond joy, sadness, fear, and anger. I have my father to thank for the latter three. Thank you.

I know, I know. I'm overdoing the whole my-dad-was-a-monster thing. I get it.

Moving on.

This unknown feeling, whatever it was, started to grow. It felt as if someone held my head underwater, and all the oxygen in my blood had gone bad. I needed to lift my head; that's exactly what I did.

I looked up and into the eyes of the stranger.

His eyes—I recognized them.

A few nights before, I had a strange dream. It felt so real. One might say it really happened, but there's no way.

When you're dreaming, the part of your brain that uses logic takes a break. That's why the dreams where you're fighting eight-headed zebras seem real at the time. When you wake up, logic reactivates.

You realize what you just experienced was nothing more than rapid eye movement cycles and dancing neurons. There's no way you were playing a game of chess in outer space with Charlie Chaplin, but in the dream, you sure as hell believed it.

That's the beauty of belief. If you believe something happened, does it matter whether it *really* happened?

Once in a while, you might come across a dream that looks, sounds, and feels like your everyday waking life. Trees are trees. Buildings are buildings. Zebras only have one head. The best example of this is "waking up" into a dream. That's what happened when I saw the pale man; I fell out of one terrible dream and into another.

My subconscious can be a real asshole sometimes.

I woke up in my bed, but I wasn't really awake. My eyes were open—they *felt* open—and I could look around and everything. Nothing out of the ordinary except that I was lying in my bed the wrong way. I usually faced the closet, but now I faced the window. As soon as I realized this, it appeared: the blackest shadow I had ever seen—a shadow with red eyes. It stood over me at the foot of my bed, smiling with that same broken-glass smile. It growled at me.

I couldn't speak. My body was paralyzed, but my eyelids were somehow still in the game; this only made it worse. Every time I blinked, he moved closer to me. I saw the train coming, but I couldn't lift myself from the tracks. That sort of thing.

For the life of me, I can't tell you what happened next or how I pulled myself out of that demonic nightmare. I just wanted to point out the similarity between the dream and the reality that followed.

It was the same deal at the rest stop: I wanted to say something, but I couldn't speak. Maybe it was fear stopping me, but it felt involuntary, beyond my control. All I could do was stand there and wait for him to advance.

I believed I was going to die. The thought was comforting.

After my mom died, I lost all fear of death. After you see it, it's not a big deal anymore. It's rather fascinating. I developed an interest in death and the things that come after it.

Okay, so that part still frightens me—the "after" part.

The only thing I know for sure about the afterlife is that it has a waiting room.

I've been there.

I closed my eyes and opened my arms, inviting the pale man to take my life. As I stood there, staring at the insides of my eyelids, he took three steps toward me. After allowing one more moment of silence between us, he spoke to me.

"My dear child, is that *you*? Are you finally here?"

His eyes burned a hole into my being. He looked for the answer to a question he'd been asking himself for a very long time.

Something about our interaction didn't make sense to me. He's not walking toward me, I thought. Why isn't he coming closer? I didn't understand. It was as if something was preventing him from getting too close. But I know he wanted to. Oh, he wanted it. He was a rabid dog, chained to his post, wanting to bite my face off. But the chain didn't snap. The leash didn't break.

He relaxed his neck, appearing to have found the answer he was looking for, the answer he wanted: I had finally arrived.

"My boy! Oh, how long it has been. I have waited and waited and *waited* for you, marking the walls in the wake of your arrival. I've anticipated you to the point of total exhaustion. I've spent an age thinking that hope was in an unreachable place. And lo! Just as I am about to surrender, you show up *here*: an extraordinary child in a most ordinary place."

This guy talked really weird. I don't think he considered the age of his audience before using big words.

"Among all places, I find you at a rest stop," he continued.

Somehow, I found the nerve to speak.

"Sir, did you take Annabelle?" I asked.

He rejected my question.

"Do you not care for your dear old dad? Where is *he* in your question, boy?"

I can't give him credit for pointing that out. His observation wasn't a magic trick or some extraordinary psychic power. I've always been terrible at hiding my feelings about my garbage father.

"Where am I?" I asked.

Yes, we were at a rest stop, but it could have been three or three hundred miles from home. Regardless, this person wasn't exactly the type you'd ask for directions.

"*We* are in transition," he replied. "Don't let my excitement fool you. For now, we are merely crossing paths. If it makes you feel better, you are welcome to forget this event, or you may celebrate. It all depends where your heart lies on the spectrum. Do you understand what that means, child? Are you hearing me?"

He paused, expecting a response.

"Give me my family, please."

My mom taught me manners.

He put his smile away and dropped his shoulders.

"I don't have your family," he said in a guttural tone.

All I wanted was to go home.

I took another hit of denial and convinced myself that none of this was happening. I waited for the man to laugh and say, "Gotcha!" followed by people carrying cameras over their shoulders, pointing their lenses at me. Then my father and Annabelle would come back to me and tell me to smile because I was on TV. But this was not TV.

I don't have time to explain hidden camera TV shows right now.

The strange man put his smile back on, raised his shoulders, and spoke to me once more.

"I've taken nothing from you, boy! While I do not sense their beating hearts around us, I promise you: I took no one. Their hearts have left, still beating. I suggest you be gone yourself. This is your life now—on with it!"

In a frenzy, the pale stranger turned away and bolted toward the glass doors. Before making a dramatic exit, he came to a sudden halt and faced me one more time.

"One day—maybe not today, maybe not tomorrow, maybe not a thousand years from now, but one day—we will be together again. When we do, there will be others. Your world will not appear the same. Neither will mine. I have a plan for you, Elliott. I will see it through. Mark these words."

He parted the glass doors and walked away.

I'm not sure what happened after that. There's a hole in my memory. Everything went black. I've checked the archives in my mind. No record exists that shows what followed that day. I don't remember the next day either, or the next, or the next.

But a paper trail exists. I've read the reports. It's like someone wrote a book about my past without my consent.

The Incredibly Unauthorized Biography of Elliott Avenue.

Thirty-seven days later, I woke up to a new family.

2 — The Book of Alexander

MAUDLIN IS A STRANGE, SMALL PLACE.

Even when it gets quiet and no one's around, the city is still alive, still breathing. This is something I want you to remember. Don't be fooled. Even in the silence, Maudlin sings a sinister song. Behind its closed doors, both literal and otherwise, unfortunate things are always happening. Unfortunate and otherworldly.

Very few people are aware of this. They only believe in a physical world. But I know the truth: there's so much more to our reality than light, sound, and matter. If you only focus on what you can see and hear, you turn a blind eye. Some part of you will stay asleep. Not many humans bother to wake it up. Even less believe in its existence. The rest are oblivious altogether.

A lot of people die on account of this non-believing.

What you see might be what you get, but what you don't see will get *you* in the end if you don't acknowledge it. I'm not asking you to understand. I'm asking you to believe, at least, in its possibility.

Trust me. I feel like a piece of garbage for asking this.

Blind faith is a buzzkill.

I just hope you aren't like them—the ones with their parts turned off. People love to turn their parts off.

With all this talk about a breathing city and nonliteral doors, it would be easy to assume that I'm some crazy eighteen-year-old with LSD swimming under his tongue. You might think I'm making some weird attempt at discussing ghosts or Jesus or shapeshifters. Maybe you have all three on your mind. I don't know. I admit I'm being somewhat cryptic.

I'm not crazy, but that doesn't matter. I'm not the one you should be worried about here. It's the rest of them that pose a severe threat. There's no pretty way to say it, so instead of going on with all this babble that you don't understand, I'm just going to come out with it.

We live in the worst place on Earth.

But you know this already. After all, you're here, aren't you?

From time to time, I see new faces around. Fresh blood on the streets. A part of me feels incredibly sorry for them, but I'm also impressed by them. It's not that this place is hard to find or anything like that. From what I've heard, the entire world is watching us. What's impressive and hard to figure out is how these new faces got here in the first place.

We're surrounded by a hundred-foot wall of steel, concrete, and hysteria. It kinda sounds like a prison and definitely *feels* like a prison, but it's not that simple.

From what I've read and have been told, the ones who built the Wall wanted to make sure no one could ever get in *or* out. Both ways. The people are not allowed to leave. Most of them don't care, though. Stay or leave—it's all the same to them.

They found a home in suffering.

I was born inside these walls. After eighteen years, I'm still here. I've only seen the outside once. You already know that story. Well, part of it, anyway.

For years, I dreamed about the outside. Sometimes, I asked questions about it, but I couldn't ask just anybody. Only those alive before the Wall's construction have a story to tell, and there aren't many left. Maudlin's death rate is ridiculous. Most of us get murdered. The rest usually die from diseases and overdoses.

We have a hospital, if you could call it that, but most patients get thrown in a dumpster. Some are still breathing when they get tossed.

Gertrude Morton told me everything I know about this place and some things about other places.

At first, I couldn't believe the things she said. It sounded made up. She was a crazy old lady—her name alone is a nod to her age—but I learned to trust her. I had to trust her.

In Maudlin, good people are a dying breed, but Gertrude had a heart, which was far more than I could say about my family.

My sister's heart went missing.

My father never had a heart.

My mom's heart stopped beating.

If anything, Gertrude Morton was nice. Nice is good.

Still, as nice as she was, she tested my patience.

Oh my god, she was the worst when it came to that.

She didn't tell everything all at once. Her methods were tailored for the long-suffering; I found out slowly.

Her fragmented storytelling began the night of my eleventh birthday. After that, she didn't say anything about Maudlin's history for an entire year. On the night of my twelfth birthday, she picked up where she left off. Same thing for my thirteenth birthday, fourteenth birthday—you get it.

After my seventeenth birthday, she told me the story would conclude the following year. For reasons I don't understand, she separated the story into eight chapters. The final chapter would be revealed the night I turned eighteen.

"It'll all make sense on your next birthday, my dear," she said.

"Can't you just tell me now? Why do you keep doing this? What's the point?"

She just smiled.

Gertrude had a way with facial expressions and quirky gestures. Most of the time, she didn't need to speak. She was a wizard when it came to silent communication.

"I can just ask someone else. Have you ever thought about that?"

"No, you can't, Elliott."

"And why is that?"

"Because I am the only person who knows everything."

I decided to go for broke.

"It can't be *that* big of a deal if you're the only one who knows. Maybe none of this even happened. You have no witnesses. Nothing to back you up. Sounds like bullshit to me."

I have moments of believing and not believing. I'm a duality.

"You're pushing it, boy," she fired back.

"What if something happens before my next birthday? What if you get hit by a meteor or something? How will I know the ending? I don't get this whole once-a-year story thing. How can you be so sure that we have time?"

She fell silent—very still. I watched her intently. She stared at something above us. I looked up, but I only saw the sky. I think she was looking at her mind, staring at a thought or memory. Her eyes turned glassy.

"Gertrude?"

We were on a first-name basis with each other at this point.

I couldn't see whatever she was staring at; it disturbed me.

I saw a Hitchcock movie once, but I can't remember the title. Sometimes, the movie wouldn't show you the horror that took place. Instead, the camera focused on someone nearby who witnessed it.

This deliberate denial left my imagination to fill in the bloody blanks.

Everything is far more frightening when you can't see it.

I just stood there and let her stare into space. It took about ten minutes, but she came back. After scanning the yard, her eyes found me again. She took a step toward me and put her cold, pale hands on my shoulders. She looked worried.

"Listen to me, Elliott. I would never mislead you. No matter what happens in the future, whether yours or mine, the answers will find you. I promise. But you must be patient. You must. Please."

In my stupidity, I interrupted her.

"I get what you're saying, but I still don't understand why you're doing this. Why can't you tell me everything *now*?"

She looked at me with crushing intensity.

"You are not ready."

She walked away.

I know better now: never test or question the wisdom and wit of old Gertrude Morton. Just don't do it. Even if you wanted to, you'd never get the chance. She's dead.

She died twenty-nine days before my eighteenth birthday.

I never heard the end of her story, but that didn't stop her from finding a way to show me. It took some piecing together, but I figured it out. The funny thing about it all is that the end was not really the end. It was merely the first act. Now, here we are. We're living in the second act right now.

Before the sun descended on my seventeenth birthday, she had one more thing to say:

"Remember what I say to you. Keep it alive. Write it down. Put the words in your pocket. Let them follow you between places. Whatever you need to do. Just don't forget them. Remember, Elliott. Remember everything."

You're probably wondering what type of person does the things that she does. I wouldn't call her crazy. She's more shrouded in mystery than madness. Well, she used to be. I'm sure by now, she's more shrouded in maggots than mystery.

I'm going to tell you everything. Well, not *everything*. More like the abridged version of everything.

This is where it all began. All of this.

Here we go.

Once, there was a man. He called himself Alexander. As far as where he came from, that's up for debate. If anybody asked him, he would just say, "West." He didn't elaborate any further. He said very little about himself.

Still, Gertrude knew a lot about him.

At first, I thought she was making this story up, but then I found Alexander's journals in her bedroom. But who knows. Maybe she was the actual writer. I wouldn't put it past her.

On my eleventh birthday, Gertrude began the story by revealing pieces of Alexander's childhood. She picked a weird place to start.

"Alexander was thrown down a well."

"What?"

No context. No proper introduction. She just dropped right in.

When Alexander was younger, maybe eight or nine years old, a group of kids jumped him on his way home from school because they didn't like him. They didn't have any other reason. They didn't need to have one either.

Kids do the worst things to each other. All the time.

They didn't fish him out. They didn't tell anybody what they did. They just threw him in the well and left.

It took three days before someone found him. *Three days*. A farmer spotted him down there after being sent to inspect the well. Why was he examining the well? Well, the town made complaints about the groundwater. It had gone bad, and boy, were they right.

The farmer notified the police. The police notified Alexander's foster mother. His foster mother didn't give a damn. I guess she never liked him. It sounds like nobody did.

The police brought a coroner to the well. They assumed Alexander would be dead, and they assumed correctly—sort of. He was dead when they found him. No pulse. No heartbeat. Eyes fixed and dilated. But on the way to the morgue, he woke up.

Perhaps he fell into the shallow end of the deep sleep.

They skipped the morgue and drove him home. I get skipping the morgue, but why take him back home? His own foster mother didn't bother looking for him when he didn't come home from school. She didn't report him missing. She just kept going about her business. But yeah, sure, just drop him off at her house.

It was one thing after another for that kid. You'd think he would catch a break after dying and coming back to life. I guess that's not enough for some people, but I digress.

I do that a lot, by the way. My tangents have tangents. I'm sorry.

After falling down the well, Alexander wasn't the same, and he knew it. But he couldn't pinpoint what changed. In his journal, he often noted that he was drawn to something, somewhere. But he didn't know what it was. He documented his feelings about the town he lived in, stating that he was "above this place." However, a part of the old Alexander still lived inside him. It allowed self-doubt and disapproval from his foster mother to keep him in his cage. For a long time, he stayed where he was, but with each passing day, something ate at him from the inside. He had a drive, a longing, an unidentified thirst.

This inner mystery plagued him well into his teenage years. His foster mother had him put in a mental hospital because of it. Alexander had become so obsessed with "nothing" that the town labeled him socially unacceptable.

Years passed. The calendar pages ripped and ripped and ripped. He felt it: the weight of time. He learned patience. He called this stretch of time his personal Advent; he knew something was coming. The old Alexander started to fade.

One day, he woke up, took his fake mother's abuse, and gave it right back. Some say he murdered her.

Gertrude used that phrase often in her story: "Some say…"

What does that even mean?

Did she make up those parts? Were they rehashed and recycled by many mouths to the point of obscurity? Am I the newest mouth in this long line of mouths to regurgitate her story? I'm trying here, but sometimes I can't help myself.

I'm just going to shut my mouth and tell you already.

I don't know where I was going with that.

I don't feel well.

When Alexander reached his early twenties, it was time to go.

Fortune, Fate, and Doom knocked on his door and told him to get the hell out, so he left. He didn't have a destination. All he knew is he had to travel east. Something pulled him in that direction.

All along the way, he walked. No cars, buses, trains, nothing. This made it very easy for him to connect with strangers. After a while, a few of them became his travel companions. Then a few more. Then a few more. The further he traveled, the more followers he acquired. His sense of purpose had become their sense of purpose. They felt one with him without explanation or reason.

Two months after leaving his hometown, Alexander reached the Midwest with twenty-six followers. Twenty-six lost humans who wanted to feel like they were doing something with their lives. That's what happens, I guess. You feel so lost and depressed that you put your fate in the hands of a stranger.

Sure, why not.

They followed him in a single-file line through forests and other undeveloped lands during the day. He wasn't too crazy about walking along roads and preferred to stay out of sight.

At night, they slept on the ground. But not Alexander. He remained standing. Most nights, he paced around the trees. In time, he stopped sleeping altogether. It didn't affect his physical well-being. He didn't need sleep anymore.

This went on for a few months. They would spend days at a time in a single place, usually a forest. The followers slept. Alexander paced. After a while, he started talking to himself, or someone, or something. It was hard to tell in the dark, but his followers could hear him. Alexander's voice flipped like a switch, back and forth, between assertive and insecure.

One night, he started speaking in Latin. No one questioned him about it, but they noted some of the words he said:

Capti.

Porta.

Silva.

Meridiem.

Sub terra.

The following day, he stood above them and pointed at the mountain range way off in the distance.

"Wake up. We're going south. I know the way."

Despite his confidence and sense of direction, he failed to account for the indifference of Nature. If you're climbing up her mountains in February, she might kill you, and she won't care. Not that I know anything about nature. I've only read about it in *National Geographic.* I've also seen a documentary about wolves. It was on a VHS tape labeled "Wolves." I found it at the hotel.

I wonder if they think I still work there.

Probably not.

I hope not.

Didn't I get fired?

When Alexander cut across the Appalachian Trail, he didn't write in his journal often. Two weeks, no entries. He didn't write again until they reached the other side.

Seventeen of his people didn't make it.

Nine froze to death.

Six died of starvation.

One succumbed to a ruptured appendix.

One went missing—someone Alexander referred to as "the little one." She walked off in the middle of the night and never returned. They waited a day before moving on without her.

The remaining followers ate the dead bodies to survive. But Alexander didn't eat. He didn't have to. He stopped feeling hunger. It never came back. He didn't understand why.

By mid-March, they crossed the mountain range and returned to sea level just in time for spring. Their eyes needed time to adjust to the green after weeks of seeing white, but it was a welcoming sight. From there, they headed southeast, just shy of the Savannah River. By then, it was late spring in the third year of Alexander's travels. He covered twenty-five hundred miles on foot since he left home.

Fun fact: the Savannah River cuts through Georgia and South Carolina. I know this because I've seen a map before. It was a real map too, made with a printer and everything.

Alexander and the Nine didn't enter either state. They slowed their pace near the southern border of West Carolina. After crossing into undeveloped West Carolinian lands, Alexander came to an abrupt stop.

Typically, when he stopped like this, he would give a motivational speech or recite poetry or tell them to set up camp for the night. He did none of these. Instead, he held a blank stare toward the east.

Then he looked below, staring down at the ground beneath his boots. Then he looked east again. His eyes played tennis. The Nine stood behind him in silence and waited until he fell from his trance.

He pointed east.

"The coast is one hundred fifty miles that way, more or less. I can hear the shearwater birds. I can smell the salt in the air. But I've never been to that coast before."

He fell back into silence. His followers stared at each other, quietly communicating their collective confusion.

He looked at the grass beneath him. His head swayed with the movement of each blade. Before he continued his address, he placed his left hand over his chest. He experienced something called heart palpitations.

The Bible doesn't mention anything about Jesus having heart palpitations, or maybe it does. I guess it depends on which translation you read. There are so many.

Once his heart returned to a normal rhythm, Alexander turned around and faced his people.

"When I started the walk from my childhood home on the other side of the country, I was in a much different place. Not just physically, but in other ways—ways I don't quite understand. It has been two years since I left my old life, and along the way, I have met a great number of people and have seen a world both benign and hostile. But that no longer matters. All I need is right here. All we need is right here. I am so blessed to have you as my friends."

He was about to cry, but he quickly stifled his tears with anger. Classic move, if you ask me.

"If we keep walking this way, we will find the ocean. We will find civilization. I love the ocean, but I cannot say the same about people. It might be the reason why I left my home. It has been so long, though; I forget why I left.

I don't know what happened to me. I just knew that I had to go. And now, here I am.

"It is unusual for a man to leave his entire life behind in pursuit of unknown desires. But they are desires nonetheless. Remember, I am only a human being, and such creatures are well known for their stupidity and spontaneity. But even so—"

He fell to one knee and touched the earth. His voice changed.

"There is a force at work among us. I feel it. And I regret nothing. Despite what I want—what I've *ever* wanted—and despite my heart and the way it seems to aim so carelessly, our journey was always meant to lead us to this place. *This* place. *This* land. *This* ground beneath us. It is here. You are all here. Together, we are going to do the impossible.

"I would like to dedicate a moment to the men, women, and child who perished and are now forever lost in the unforgiving wilderness. Close your eyes. Let us be still."

I laughed when Gertrude told me this part of the story. This Alexander guy liked to stop himself from speaking, but he couldn't shut the hell up.

Allow me to speed things up a bit.

"You are all being given a choice," he continued. "By morning, you must decide your fate. I am not the one asking you to choose. You see, we are at the end of a path, and where it ends, three paths begin. One path leads to the past, another to the present, and a third to the future. For many months, you have substituted your roads for mine, but we are now at a fork. So this is it, my friends. Before you choose, I can show you a glimpse of what lies beyond each road."

His followers were heartbroken; they feared their time with Alexander would be over by morning. They weren't ready to feel lost again. It's the reason why they walked with him in the first place.

Alexander just smiled.

"My friends, this is not a time for sadness. Quite the contrary. Embrace this change! You've not even seen the roads that lie ahead. How do you expect to progress? Progression is life. It's the forward line. Without it, we are all dead."

Silence fell over the group. They waited in anxious anticipation for him to reveal the three paths. He shared his revelation after yet another moment of silence.

I hate silence.

I'll just paraphrase. Trying to remember everything he said, exactly how he said it, is giving me a headache.

This is taking much longer than I anticipated, and we just started.

Okay, three choices: stay with Alexander, keep moving east, or go back west. Past, present, future. The glimpse of each road was more of a threat sprinkled with something Jesus could have been credited for saying in the Bible:

"Leave and die. Stay with me and live forever."

Jesus may not have had heart palpitations, but he sure loved to talk about living forever. Once again, I'm sure this varies depending on what translation of the Bible you read.

Bill told me there are hundreds. It's like humans are playing a game of telephone with monotheism.

Something inside Alexander shifted again.

He looked at the ground with scornful eyes and spoke about his disgust and loss of faith in the human race. This was the first time any of them saw Alexander this way—dark, negative, ominous. No one saw this coming; he gave no hint that a shadow grew inside him.

Some say they saw him exhaling smoke.

That night, he recounted in his journal that he wasn't sure why he chose this place. But he could feel something. A deep grave of loss, as he put it. He lost something, somewhere, somehow. This sense of loss was met with confusion.

He didn't know what it was; he just knew that it was there.

I wish I could have crushed the stars, he wrote.

I had to stop Gertrude here. Her story had taken too many sharp turns. I wanted off the ride.

"Hold up a minute. How can a guy act so charismatic around people and yet have so much hate for them? This doesn't make any sense. Did he hate *all* people? Did he hate himself too? Is this guy still around? Do you know him? Is he an asshole? Can I meet him?"

I stood there, waiting for all the answers. At the same time, I didn't want to know. But Gertrude didn't respond. At least not right away. Her eyes turned into glass. She had gone back inside her head, staring at her mind again.

For a moment, she became a statue of herself. It terrified me.

Still, I somehow slept that night.

I can always sleep when I feel scared.

Maybe that's why I feel so tired now.

Sometime in the night, I woke up and found Gertrude sitting at the foot of my bed. When she looked at me, I closed my eyes and pretended to be asleep. I was scared and didn't want to engage her anymore. I didn't want to hear her story.

Eventually, she got up and made her way toward the door.

After she walked out of my room, I had a feeling that she would come back. My intuition proved accurate. The sound of footsteps entered my room and slowly crept toward my bed. When I opened my eyes, I saw her standing over me. She whispered to me.

"The good ones will always be drawn to the light—just like you, Elliott. But keep a wary mind. Some shine for the good in this world, and some shine for the dark. Without a third eye, you can't tell them apart. They are clever. They use light just like the good ones do, but they use it differently. It is not their instrument. It is their weapon.

"This light may blind you; it won't be by chance. They mean to draw you in. They seek to gather the world. Those who follow the false light become blinded by it. This is how they hide the evil that lives inside. Their guise is a cunning thing, and they want to ruin you.

"All I ask of you, Elliott, is that you follow your light. *Your* light."

She walked away.

The Nine unanimously agreed to stay with Alexander and live forever. They built a city together—this city—and then they all died.

But not Alexander. He kept on living.

3 — 251

I DISAPPEARED.

Nothing made sense.

My life became a foreign film with no subtitles. I've never seen a foreign film. Just trying to make a point.

Over five weeks of my life went missing. I don't know what happened to me during that time. I can only say where I ended up. The in-between is a mystery.

They kept happening from that day on—these jump cuts, or blackouts as I refer to them. They still happen. Hours, days, weeks of my memory get spliced out of time, out of mind. It's hard to explain. One moment, I'll be somewhere. Then I'll be somewhere else in both space and time. I can usually feel it coming on like a sneeze.

The sensation of slipping into a blackout is on a par with falling asleep and entering a dream that I will inevitably forget.

Maybe that explains my interest in oneirology.

It's a real thing, I swear. Just ask Bill. He's in the woods.

If you find him, ask if you can borrow his copy of *An Experiment with Time* by J.W. Dunne. If what the author says is true, I'll soon leave the fixed spacetime landscape, escape the bonds of mundane time, and pass into the fount of all consciousness.

Yeah, it's probably a load of crap, but we all need something to get through the day.

When you're six years old, the past and future don't exist. You don't give them the time of day; you're too busy living in the *now*. You're not watching old VHS tapes of your life. You live without a VCR stuck inside your head. Everything is a moment. Life happens within a blink. Nothing before or after it exists. So when you blink and end up miles and weeks into the future, what the hell are you supposed to do?

Oh yeah, that's another thing: video cameras.

Did you know you can record a movie of anything you want? There are these VHS tape cameras that let you record things. It's all real. I've used one before, I swear.

Thirty-seven days later, I woke up in a bed that didn't belong to me in a room I had never seen before.

I could tell the bed wasn't mine. The mattress was too soft.

But I wasn't afraid. Thanks to the power of imagination, I tricked myself into thinking I had slipped into a boring dream about a boring room where nothing fun ever happened.

Most of the time, my dreams have a blurry background and a strange white noise that doesn't go away.

As I scanned the room, I made a squinty face and hissing sounds.

Denial is a hell of a drug.

It looked like no one had used or lived in the room for a while. It was neat and seemingly untouched, like a guest bedroom. There were two twin beds, two identical dressers, a small yellow desk, and a double-door closet—also yellow.

Many drawings hung on the walls. Most of them were scribbles, but some had simple, familiar shapes: houses, cars, cats, people. They were done in crayon and evenly spaced apart, stretching across the perimeter of the room, beginning and ending on either side of the closet. I figured someone my age drew them. It made me feel better. I didn't feel so alone.

My eyes caught something moving in the hallway. It flew past the doorway three times in a matter of seconds. After a pause, it crept up to the doorway and revealed its form. I stopped my hissing and squinting. We stared at each other for a small eternity.

The boy looked about my age and height. Maybe slightly shorter and younger.

He wore a red-and-white striped knit sweater that was way too big on him. It's like this kid found Waldo, killed him, and took his sweater as a trophy. The thing was stretched out, speckled with stains, and ripped along the collar.

His pants were way too short. Both his shoes were untied.

I think I would have freaked out if his shoes *were* tied.

His hair threw me off. It almost didn't look like hair. It was all one color—yellow blonde—and perfectly parted to the side. No variations or subtitle changes in color. I'd never seen hair like his before. I didn't understand it.

Something else: he wore a scarf. Depending on the time of year, this wouldn't be unusual, but it was summer. In my six-year-old brain, I concluded that he was a weirdo. All because of that scarf. Even the way he wore it looked weird, covering his chin and lower lip. It had beautiful colors, though: countless shades of yellow, orange, and red. Each pigment blended flawlessly with the next.

I couldn't stop looking at it.

If I squinted my eyes hard enough, it looked like he wore fire around his neck.

After having a staring contest with his scarf—I lost—I started wondering what I was wearing. Since I had no idea where I was or what day it was, I figured I'd be wearing something unfamiliar. Maybe I ended up in some alternate reality where we all dress like weirdos.

To my relief, I had the same clothes on as I did at the rest stop.

I always wear the same thing: black jeans, a plain white t-shirt, and a black zip-up hoodie. The same thing you see me wearing now. As far as I can remember, it's the only thing I've ever worn. I came out of the womb this way. Just ask my mom.

I knew he'd be the one to break the silence between us. My social anxiety wouldn't allow it.

He pointed at his drawings on the wall.

"I made them all, but Nini says I have to keep them in here."

"What?"

I could tell he wanted to talk about something else. His drawings were just an icebreaker. I tried to get up and run, but he was blocking the doorway.

"Are you one of them?" he asked.

"What?"

"Do you do bad things too?"

"What?"

"Did they find you in a trash can?"

"What?"

If someone you've never met before approached you and asked if you were found in a trash can, how do you respond?

All you have when this happens is confusion, and too much confusion sparks fear. It's all I had at the moment. I wanted to be alone again, at my actual house, in my real bed.

"I want to go home."

The boy tilted his head the way a dog does.

"You *are* home," he replied.

"What?"

"Are you like the boys outside? Are you going to put mud in my hair? I *hate* mud."

"I'm not home! I don't live here! Daddy took me and my sister on vacation! I got lost and fell asleep! *I want to go home!* I'm ready to go home—*now*. Oh, and also, I hate mud too."

He just wouldn't quit with the questions.

"Who's Annabelle? Is *she* one of them? Where is she?"

"How do you know about Annabelle?"

"Nini told me things."

"I'm going to punch your dumb face."

It was too much, way too much. I threw the blankets over my head and assumed the fetal position on the foreign bed. For a second, I felt a touch of relief, but then I imagined the boy creeping his way toward me.

Remember: Fear doesn't always grow from what we can see. Most times, what we can't see is far more terrifying. The imagination makes up the rest.

Close your eyes all you want. The mind's eye is always open.

Perfect example: horror movies.

I've seen a few: *Evil Dead, Jaws,* and that one Hitchcock movie about birds. Why do I keep forgetting its name?

Have you seen *Jaws*? Are sharks real? I can't see how they're real. I mean, *come on.*

I pulled the blankets off, and just as I feared, the boy stood over me with his face a few inches from mine. My scream scared him; we screamed together. I put my hand over my mouth to make it stop. After seeing me do this, he did the same.

We stared at each other again, this time with our hands over our mouths. After a few seconds, he squinted his eyes, communicating a welcoming change in his mood. They looked the way eyes do when someone smiles, even though I couldn't see his mouth. I replied with squinty eyes, but not the kind that accompanies a smile or the kind that I pretend to dream with.

These squints stayed loyal to suspicion.

These squints said, "What the hell is going on with my life?"

Then the best thing happened: he laughed. It was muffled but audible and almost musical. A rush of euphoria slowly moved up my legs, past my waist, up my arms, along my neck, and once it reached my head, I started laughing too.

Life is weird.

The last time I felt this good was two days before the rest stop. Annabelle and I played outside in the mud. We built a mud city for the ants. I remember it well.

Another voice entered the room. We killed our laughter.

"What's all this screaming about, boys? You're scaring some of the others."

An old, old woman stood in the doorway. She looked about one hundred and ninety years old. Still, there was a certain youthfulness about her, almost childlike.

Her eyes. She had very kind eyes. Old, but kind.

"Sorry, Nini," the boy replied.

He looked down at the splintered wood floor.

The weird old lady grinned. Her eyes opened wide and looked into mine. I waited for her to explain what the hell was going on, but she kept smiling like a lunatic.

"You're Nini?" I asked. "What's a Nini?"

"Charlie calls me Nini. He has his reasons. But you can call me Gertrude."

I had so many more questions, but I kept them to myself. I wasn't ready. I couldn't handle it. I wanted to go back to sleep and dream the madness away, but all the hissing and squinting in the world couldn't save me from the truth.

Gertrude locked her eyes on me and took a step forward.

"I see you're already making friends. Don't worry, dear. I think you'll do just fine here."

Her sweater looked like a cape. She wore it unbuttoned; it went down to her knees. No two buttons on it were alike. Some of them were comically larger than others. On the right side of her sweater, near her shoulder, she wore a green flower-looking thing. It was made of yarn and complemented the purple surrounding it. I called it her yarn flower.

Her eyes showed youthfulness, but her hair, a frizzy mess of grey and white, implied carelessness. It curled in some places, almost like she put curlers in her hair and gave up halfway. When I looked at her hair, I kind of felt sorry for her.

And then there was the lipstick. Yes, she wore lipstick—bold, bright red lipstick, carelessly smeared across her lips. If she believed this made her more attractive, she was mistaken. Still, I didn't mind it so much. It reminded me of The Joker.

The Joker is a character in comic books. He does terrible things all the time, but I like him. He's always the most authentic version of himself, if that makes sense.

I knew a thing or two about comic books for a six-year-old.

Before my family fell apart, my father took me to the one place in Maudlin where they had a few comic books for sale. He only took me once, but it was nice. I got to pick out one comic book.

Batman #251. I still have it.

Why don't you go take a look around?" Gertrude asked.

Anxiety and agitation surged through my body.

"I don't want to look around. I want to go home now. When is my dad coming? Tell him he left me by the bus stop."

"It was a rest stop," the boy said.

"I'm going to punch a hole through your whole life."

We bickered until Gertrude put her smile away and looked down at the floor. It drew our attention. We all stared at the ground together. My head started feeling fuzzy, but it was interrupted by a *tap tap* on the window behind me.

Someone must have knocked on it, but when I turned around, no one was there. When I looked away from the window, I heard it again—*tap tap*.

I turned around again, and there he was—my father—standing on the other side of the glass. He waved the June 1992 issue of *Batman* in front of his face.

I saw his car parked behind him. Annabelle sat in the backseat. I could just barely catch a glimpse of her dancing and smiling at me. They both had big smiles plastered on their faces. I smiled back and gave a great, big wave.

"Who are you waving at, dear?" Gertrude asked.

"Look!" I shouted.

This time, I saw a large, cracked circle driveway full of overgrown weeds and rocks. Dead trees swayed around it. I caught quick glimpses of a disheveled road behind them as their branches fought for my attention in the breeze.

No sign of life in any direction.

Still, the world beyond the window appeared to move. The wind lashed at everything in sight. My father and sister must have blown away; they were no longer there.

Neurotransmitters can be very deceiving.

I kept sipping from the pool of denial and waited for my ride.

The two strangers behind me held their silence. They waited for me to say something or see something or figure something out that they already knew.

My eyes were so fixed on finding a car or a familiar face in the dry, summer landscape that I failed to see what was in front of me.

When I finally noticed it, everything made sense, and nothing made sense. That's how it goes, sometimes.

"Do you see it now, dear?" Gertrude asked. "Can you read it? Do you understand where you are?"

Before she could throw in another question, I raised my hand, signaling her to shut the hell up. I could see it just fine.

Not far from the window, along the edge of the circle driveway, a rusted metal sign stood in the ground. The rust was painted over in white, very poorly. The embossed words on the sign were painted purple. I read them over and over again, hoping I got it wrong or that it would somehow read something different.

Eventually, the sign became almost impossible to read. The tears in my eyes blurred everything.

I joined the others in staring at the floor—again—and I cried.

My mom once told me that when I was born, I didn't make a sound. I didn't even cry at her funeral.

When I looked out that window, it was the first time I cried, ever, in my entire life.

Let me tell you: it was heavy.

Then something started shifting, like when you feel your blood move around after cutting off circulation.

I felt it coming on again—that thing that makes me black out. It came back to take me, but it was different this time. It came with pre-show entertainment. I wasn't used to this.

Let me explain.

In my first few blackouts, I didn't know they happened until *after* they happened, if that makes sense. There were never any warning signs. I wandered through this life as every child does—moment to moment.

Then I'd wake up from a darkness I had no memory of entering.

The first episode happened the day my mother died.

The next one happened at her funeral. I lost track after that. You already know about the rest stop.

This one was different.

It started at my ankles. I imagined this is what quicksand feels like, but on the inside.

I know about quicksand. It's a real thing. Just ask Bill. He knows everything.

The sand rose above my knees, each grain stretching out to form a syringe. They injected me with a strong anesthetic, stabbing my skin from the inside out, ten thousand times per second. A sudden force, like wind, shot through my hips. The needles were fingers now, crawling along the surface of my neck, squeezing. I took a breath, afraid it would be my last.

The fingers released and crawled into my brain, forming a dark cloud. The cloud carried a voice in my head that whispered, "Let go, Elliott. Just let go."

I found my hands held out in front of me—palms down—like I was reaching for something or falling backwards.

Every movement felt involuntary.

I was letting go.

Six years old and dying.

Okay, so I wasn't actually dying, but I sure thought I was, and it was the most peaceful thing ever. I accepted it. I welcomed it through the door and into my heart.

But Scarf Boy wouldn't have it.

He tried to pull me out of the impending blackout spell. Just as I nearly slipped away, I felt his tiny arms. He embraced me.

"I'm Charlie Gold," he said. "I need a friend."

I guess I wasn't "one of them" after all.

I hung there, dangled, tangled in his arms, staring at the sign in the front yard before I finally faded out.

The Amulet—that's what the sign outside read.

I had seen that sign before. I knew what this place was.

In case you're wondering, orphanages are real.

4 — The Fourth Window

MY FATHER DROVE A RED PLYMOUTH ACCLAIM.

It's a type of car.

I was never allowed to sit in the front seat. Never. Neither was Annabelle. She didn't care either way, but I made a few attempts. Every time, my father grabbed my arm and pulled me out of the car.

I asked him why he did that. Several times. He always gave the same answer: "You don't belong there."

I don't think he liked sitting close to us.

I could never get close to him. He wouldn't allow it. Sometimes, I tried to sit or stand near him, but he shut me down every time.

I don't have any memories of being held by him. I tried and tried and tried to receive his affection.

When I was *three* years old, I stopped trying.

I used to obsess over what I'd say to him if he and I crossed paths again. What would the conversation be like? Would there even be one? Maybe we'd recognize each other but pretend we were strangers. Maybe we wouldn't recognize each other at all.

The daydreams always ended the same way: I end his life.

I'm standing over him as he begs for mercy. Tears stream down his face. I give him the impression that I'll back away and show him some much-undeserved compassion. I let him believe he's safe. It's in that moment of relief when I take him out. Usually, I either kick his head over and over until it turns to mush, or I grab him by the hair and drag his face along the concrete until there's nothing left of it.

Those are my two preferred methods.

But I digress.

Inside my father's red Plymouth Acclaim, Annabelle and I sat next to each other for the last time as the world we thought we knew passed by. Of course, I wasn't aware of this at the time. My father led us to believe that we were going on some kind of family vacation. Somewhere warm and green and far, far away from Maudlin.

We've taken a few trips as a family before, back when my mom was still alive, and they were beautiful compared to the rest of my miserable life. Whenever the whole family got in the car and drove to some unfamiliar place, my life didn't feel like a pile of garbage.

The most interesting thing about these trips was the interaction between my parents. They could actually tolerate each other. Hell, I think they *liked* being around each other. But as soon as we got back home, they hated each other again.

Some part of me thought that wherever my father was taking us, my mom would be there.

I sat directly behind him in the car. The city was flying by. We were traveling so fast, well beyond the speed limit.

That's a joke. Maudlin doesn't have speed limits.

At this speed, the crumbling buildings, dead trees, and every other dilapidated detail were almost unrecognizable. Miserable concrete shapes became blurred ribbons of light and shadow. The city was melting. It never looked so stunning.

Something didn't make sense, though.

As I said, the city is surrounded by a giant wall—one hundred feet tall, ten feet thick—designed to keep any human being from entering or leaving.

But you already know this.

Certain people can come and go if the Moths allow it, but that rarely happens.

No one enters Maudlin by choice. Well, almost no one.

Death is a more sensible option.

There's only one point of entry, located at the west end of the city. We call it the Gate. If you go there, you'll find bullet-proof guards and bullet-filled civilians. Riots start and end there. Small groups of Maudlings gather in an attempt to exit the city by force. It never works. They either give up or end up in body bags.

The rest of us don't fight or attempt to escape. We accept our place. We bathe in our own filth.

Despite the Wall, the guards, and the promise of death, my father was always allowed through the Gate.

I never knew why. I was afraid to ask. The last thing I wanted was to draw any attention to myself. Sure, I was just a kid, but they had body bags in my size.

As we approached the Gate, my father started acting stranger than usual. He laughed out loud, but no one said anything funny. No one said *anything*.

I thought he was trying to be silly or playful, but when I laughed with him, he turned around, looked me in the eyes, and told me to shut the hell up.

So what if I started laughing? I was a kid. That's what kids do.

This is just one example of why I hated him so much. I'm surprised he didn't kill me in the back seat.

Thanks a lot, *Dad*.

His hands trembled on the steering wheel. He started nodding and shaking his head—switching back and forth between both movements—and letting out more nervous laughter.

We were nearly at the Gate when the car slowed down. At this point, he had my full attention.

Somehow, my sister was content and oblivious, staring out the car window, clueless about everything.

He started mumbling. Most of it was gibberish to my ears, but I caught a few things.

"It's okay, Roger. It's okay."

He said this several times over and over in a failed attempt at self-comfort. Then he went on about Maudlin, or at least that's what it sounded like. I heard "walls" and "ground" and "moth." He looked in every direction and pointed at various things outside as he talked to himself. I didn't understand.

I've spent years thinking about it.

Why would he panic if he had the freedom to leave whenever he wanted? Maudlin wasn't a cage to him like it was to everyone else. At first, I thought money was involved. There was a time when he acted like money was everything, probably because we didn't have any. But that wasn't it. Nothing is that simple, especially in a place like this.

For the longest time, we thought he had a steady job at The Complex. That's only half true. He *did* work there, but he quit a week later and never told us. Then he got a new job selling all kinds of drugs: diazepam, alprazolam, hydrocodone, oxycodone, morphine, codeine, diphenhydramine, the list goes on.

I don't think my mom ever found out what he was doing. I didn't find out until *last week*. I won't get into it right now. I just can't. Maybe later.

In the car, my father kept asking himself the same question over and over:

"Why does he want this?"

He was hysterical. I wouldn't be surprised if he had no idea where he was or what he was doing. In the past, anger and indifference were the only expressions at his disposal. This was new. This was beyond him. Something much darker than his shadow took over. All I could do was stare at him and choke on the lump of fear in my throat.

My body shook. My eyes twitched. I looked at Annabelle to see if she was experiencing the same thing.

She just stared out the goddamn window, oblivious as usual.

"Is it going to snow again?" she asked. "You never took us sledding, Daddy. I want snow."

"Why does he want this?" he whispered.

Annabelle kept going.

"You have to take us sledding. And I really want snow. I want the biggest snow. Can we make snow? Let's make snow! Snow! Snow!"

She did this all the time: When she wanted something, she would tell you, and then she would tell you again, and sometimes after she told you again, she would tell you *again*.

I was on my last nerve here. How could she be so oblivious? My father was putting on a total shit show, and all she could think about was snow.

Kids are weird. They have funny brains. When you're five, the world could be ending, but it doesn't matter. You still want to go sledding.

My father slammed his fist against his forehead three times and once again asked *the* question.

"Why does he want this?"

I started dissecting his question in my head.

Who is *he*? What is *this*? Why does *he* want *this*? Does it play a part in where we're going? What the hell did my father get himself into? I knew nothing, but I was pretty sure we weren't going on vacation.

I was about to throw up.

In full panic mode, I gave the moment a chance to redeem itself, but it failed miserably. My hiss-and-squint method didn't work.

It's fun fact time.

Roughly ninety percent of your body's serotonin begins in your gut. It enters your bloodstream, travels up to your brain, binds to receptors in your medulla oblongata, and triggers the area postrema. This is the structure in your brain that controls vomiting. Of course, vomiting only happens under certain conditions, like when you get food poisoning, when your body is invaded by a rhinovirus, or when your father runs away from something you don't understand.

I puked all over the window. It changed nothing.

"Aww, now you can't see out your window," Annabelle said.

My father was trapped inside his head.

"Why does he want this?"

They took turns talking over each other.

"Doesn't matter. No snow."

"Why does he want this?"

"Can I sled with no snow?"

"Why does he want this?"

"Can I, Elliott?"

I punched her in the chest. No idea where that came from; that's just what I did. But hey, it worked! It was also the only thing that dislodged us from the skipping record of anxiety. Sure, she started crying and stuff, but then she saw the terror in our father's eyes. She heard his distress. She felt his panic.

On the way down, her tears fell for him, not because of me.

"Daddy, Daddy! What are you doing?!" Annabelle shouted.

This was great.

Now that I had someone to share this mess with, I didn't feel so alone. It was enough to keep myself together for just a bit longer.

Annabelle might have been brainless, but I'm glad she was around. Before Charlie, she was my sidekick.

I have this thing about sidekicks. I always need one. Annabelle was the first. Charlie was the second.

There was a third.

I try convincing myself that no one came after Charlie, but the truth is the truth. I have to live with that mistake.

Sorry, Charlie.

"Do something!" Annabelle shouted at me.

The pain in her voice made me feel kind of bad for punching her in the chest, but I didn't know what else to do. I had to snap her out of it. I had to change the channel and turn off this nightmare show.

Do something.

That's what she said. I was supposed to do something.

Talking to him wouldn't work.

Screaming at him wouldn't work.

Puking in his car didn't work.

It sounds like suicide, but the only solution I could think of was punching him. If something doesn't work, just punch it. I can't take credit for this idea. I assure you: This was a learned behavior.

At six years old, I didn't have much strength to work with, so a punch to the arm or chest wouldn't do. I had to go for the face.

I raised my fist. Annabelle nodded at me with nervous approval. We knew what had to be done. This was it. Here we go.

"Annabelle, switch with me. I can't reach."

As soon as I moved to Annabelle's spot, my father stopped talking to himself. I didn't move a muscle. If I don't move, he won't see me, I thought. Like a dinosaur or something.

Roger Avenue was a dinosaur.

He turned his head just enough to find me in his periphery, grabbed my shirt collar, and pulled my face toward his face.

I stared into the eyes of a man I never knew.

Tears swelled in them. He searched for words and found the same ones as before, with one minor adjustment.

"Why does he want *you*?

That's the last thing I remember before the rest stop.

I don't remember passing through the Gate. After my father asked me that question, everything went dark. Time skipped; I was looking at travel brochures. Then my family disappeared, and I slipped into darkness again, for much longer. Time lost track of itself. I don't know where I went.

There was a police report, but it didn't say much.

Apparently, I didn't go very far. The Moths found me across the highway. I was unconscious, lying face-down, and my clothes were soaked in saltwater.

They didn't find me until five weeks *after* I went missing.

Where the hell did I go? The ocean?

I've been dying to see the ocean. I love water. West Carolina is landlocked, so the desire to see and feel a massive body of water is quite overwhelming sometimes.

Bill once said that I "clash with water bearers" or something. Whatever that means.

The saltwater mystery wasn't solved. If someone knows, they didn't tell me. Same with the missing-for-thirty-seven-days thing. They found me, and that was enough, I guess.

My father and Annabelle were both declared missing.

Everything else in the report was crossed out in black bars.

I figured my sister was either kidnapped or dead. We were right off the highway. Anything can happen there. Someone could have snatched and disposed of her.

I was positive my father went missing on purpose.

The tall, thin man at the rest stop knew the truth. He was there when it all went down. He was there when we all got displaced. He was the last connection to my family.

The Grey Man. That's what I call him.

I had to find him again.

For a long time, this was all I could think about. During the first few months at the foster home, my head spun around in a loop of uncomfortable daydreams. I thought about the car ride, the Gate, the Grey Man, and my father leaving us behind. Anything beyond these people, places, and things didn't concern me.

I was in a severe state of shock. I didn't leave my bed for three weeks. Gertrude had to put me in diapers. She placed sheets of newspaper on the bed because the diapers weren't enough. I had become a vegetable.

Hi, I'm Elliott. I'm a potato.

There were no blackouts or time jumps during this time. I remember all of it, except when I slept, which wasn't often. I just lay there, staring at the stucco ceiling. Gertrude and Charlie were the only ones who made any contact with me. When Gertrude wasn't spoon-feeding me or changing my diapers, she tried snapping me out of my mental paralysis.

"You're not alone here," Gertrude said. "I know it feels that way. Trust me, I know. I was *you* once. When I was only three years old, my mother thought it would be a grand idea to put me in a wicker basket and leave me with a group of women in the woods. I don't even remember my father. I'm sure he left before I was born. Hmm, I wonder."

She talked to me about her parents, but it sounded more like she talked to herself. It was her worst attempt to get me out of bed so far. I knew she meant well, but she was out of her goddamn mind. I couldn't take her seriously with that smeared lipstick and all that crazy hair. She just kept on talking to herself at the foot of my bed, and I kept lying there, stuck in my trance. Also—Jesus Christ—she probably came into my room every ten to fifteen minutes, day and night. No wonder I couldn't sleep.

Charlie was the only other person that communicated with me. In all fairness, I wouldn't exactly call it communication. I shared a bedroom with him, and he rarely left it, so he was just around.

I thought about him a lot; I'm not sure why. I guess some part of me wondered what he did to kill time.

When he wasn't sleeping, he drew pictures with his crayons, and when he wasn't drawing pictures with his crayons, he watched me.

He'd sit in bed, working on some pictures. Whenever Gertrude came into the room to check on me, he'd immediately stop drawing and pretend to be asleep. It was clear that he had taken an interest in me, but he had a weird way of showing it.

Sometimes, I'd find him sitting at the foot of *my* bed with his crayons and paper spread out over the blankets. He wouldn't talk to me. He wouldn't talk to Gertrude. He wouldn't talk to anyone, not even himself. He would just sit there and draw.

Half his crayons were on the floor. So clumsy.

I caught a glimpse of what he was drawing a few times. It was always the same thing: a stick figure lying in a bed with a black tornado over its head.

Once I figured it out, I wanted to puke.

He was drawing me.

Above the bed, he scribbled a window. He looked at our bedroom window and back at the picture, over and over, attempting to capture its likeness.

Each drawing had something different inside the window.

In the first one, he drew trees.

In the second one, he drew clouds.

In the third one, a car.

The fourth one was frightening, and I'm sure he would agree. He trembled as he drew it.

A stick figure stood behind the fourth window. Charlie drew it in thin, grey scribbles. He used a red crayon for the eyes. The figure looked down at me through the window with a giant grin on its face.

After Charlie finished the drawing, he held it up to my face.

"I see him too."

Charlie didn't draw him for a long time after that.

He stayed by my side throughout my entire weeks-long trance. It was comforting. For the first time since my mom was alive, I felt a connection with another human being, even if the connection didn't make sense.

In the final hour of my trance, Gertrude entered the bedroom and changed my diaper for the last time.

"Go play outside for a while, Charlie. I have to talk to Elliott."

He wouldn't budge. He sat close to me while she babbled about her life. He held my hand like I was dying or something.

"Did you know I'm not even from Maudlin?" she asked. "I'm from another place. When I came to Maudlin, the Wall wasn't even a dream yet. That makes me really old! But the Wall did rise in time. You're probably wondering why in goddess's name I stuck around. Well, there's a lot to this place. Something is happening. Plain eyes don't see it. They don't know. It's strange, I tell ya. Wacky and strange."

She had more to say, but she left it at that. I think she realized it wasn't time yet.

"Perhaps, one day, I'll tell you all about it. But you need to wake up, child."

After she left the room, Charlie started breathing heavily. He wanted to say something. It took him a while, but he finally found the courage to speak.

He squeezed my hand tighter and leaned closer to me. I felt his breath on the side of my face.

From the corner of my eye, I watched him remove his scarf.

"I'm not from Maudlin either," he said. "Would you like to know where I came from?"

At that moment, my trance broke.

"Tell me everything."

5 — Triple Promise

CHARLIE GOLD ISN'T EVEN HIS REAL NAME.

Well, it's kind of his real name. It's a mix of real and not real, much like everything.

Charles Sheldon Goldwin isn't as easy on the tongue.

Before I showed up, he was the new kid. The other kids had already established their friendships and marked their territory by the time he got there, and they wouldn't let him in.

That's why he clung to me. I was the only human being who gave him the time of day besides Gertrude.

"Are you one of them?" Charlie asked again.

"No! Who is 'them' anyway?"

He kept asking me this even though I answered him several times. He must have known I didn't fully understand the meaning of the question. At first, I thought he was asking whether or not I would alienate him like everyone else did. But his question meant something else entirely.

I was awake. Truly awake. Free from that strange, dark spell.

For a little while.

Charlie and I sat on my bed, which, to be honest, was about as comfortable as sitting on a pile of corpses. My old bed was way better. It was my asylum. I might have had a crummy family life, but damn, my bed was cozy.

"Are you going to tell me where you came from?" I asked. "How did you get here? If you tell me, I'll tell you things too."

Charlie looked at me funny.

"I know about you already," he replied. "Nini told me everything. I know where they found you."

"But you don't know if I'm one of them or if they found me in a trash can."

"Okay, so she didn't tell me *everything*."

"She never could. She doesn't know everything."

"Are you sure about that?"

Jesus, that was rude, but I figured I could use this as an opportunity to find answers. Of course, it's hard to make sense of *anything* when you're seven years old—I had turned seven during the thirty-seven days I went missing—especially when the person spilling all the beans is even younger.

"Why does she talk to you about me?" I asked.

"Because I'm like you."

"What does that mean?"

"We're special."

Charlie had a big, big smile on his face, but I shot it down as quickly as it came.

"No, we're not. I don't even know you."

Before I killed his spirit, he wanted to share something personal. But I didn't care.

I didn't like that Gertrude talked about me to this…stranger.

"Do you *want* to know me? Charlie asked.

"I don't know."

I focused on myself, but can you blame me? I was all I had.

I was everything. I was the only thing.

That's what I wanted to believe, at least.

Before my mom died, she taught me a handful of lessons. At her funeral, I heard her voice in my head echoing every word of them. I had this dumb belief that if I followed what she taught me, it would bring me closer to her.

Standing in front of Charlie, I heard her voice again. It changed my mind.

I did Charlie a favor and let him go first, but I really did it for her, for my mom, Heather May Avenue.

Put the world first, and good things will come.

These days, I can't say I'm the living embodiment of putting the world first. The last time I tried, it ruined me. But back then, I figured I'd give it a shot. Why the hell not? Moms know best, right?

Right?

"Ugh, fine. I want to know you. I do. Tell me."

My delivery could have been a bit more pleasant, I admit.

I might not have sounded sincere, but it was enough for him.

I don't remember how long we stayed in our bedroom, but it felt like days. Charlie did most of the talking; I didn't mind. He must have internalized every experience in his short, sad life until then.

If you end up in an orphanage, chances are you'll have a lot of messed-up stories to share unless you keep them all to yourself. I wouldn't recommend doing that unless you want to go crazy or kill yourself. You need to air out your shit from time to time. Keeping it inside will slowly destroy you.

Why do you think I'm telling you *everything*?

It's like that scene in *The Goonies*. Have you ever seen it?

When the Fratellis interrogate Chunk, they force him to spill his guts about where his friends are and what they're doing.

"Tell us everything," they say. Chunk interprets their demand literally and responds by telling them everything. *Everything.*

This seems like a comedic miscommunication on the surface, but let's be honest: Chunk was a tormented kid. His friends used him all the time. His parents acted oblivious to his pain. He reached his breaking point in the hands of his kidnappers.

This emotional combustion turned a child abduction into a therapy session.

Where am I going with this?

I didn't mean to forget about you. There's so much happening at once, and time is not on my side. It's funny because I keep talking about nothing.

I haven't given myself the chance to thank you. I appreciate you taking the time from your life to sit next to me and listen, especially given where we are right now. This is a dangerous place. I mean, look at me. Look at what happened to me. Look at my shirt. I'm a mess.

Still, I feel better that you're here. You could have left me to die. You're not like the rest of the world, and that means the world to me.

I have a lot to get off my chest, but there's more to it than just that. There are reasons.

I don't have time to explain that right now. Just know this: you're the only thing I have left. That means you're the one who can help me, but only if you decide to stay.

Please stay. Listen. I know almost everything I'm saying makes no goddamn sense, but it will, eventually. I promise.

Thank you for everything.

I'm sorry for everything.

I feel dizzy and light-headed, but I can do this.

I must tell you about Charlie Gold.

"What d-d-do you want to know?" Charlie asked me. Now that the spotlight was on him, he stuttered. It was just Charlie and me.

No one else was around. Charlie opened the closet door to show me that there was a bathroom inside. I heard the voices of other children beyond the bedroom.

"Just tell me all the things, I guess."

He closed his eyes and let his words fly. I couldn't keep up at first. He talked so fast, and oh my god, he stuttered damn near the entire time. So much stuttering. His mouth moved at the speed of light. I listened without stopping or interrupting him.

We sat in our separate beds. Mine was at the back of the room, under the tall window. His was perpendicular to mine, against the wall that held all his favorite drawings. He had recently started a second row along the wall; he stared at them all the time. Even as he shared his life story with me, he kept his eyes on them. I looked at him, then at his drawings, then back at him. The drawings illustrated some of the events from his life's storybook.

Instead of reiterating everything he told me, I'm just going to tell you everything I know about him in my own words. It's hard enough trying to make sense of a stuttering five-year-old, so allow me to translate for you.

Okay, here we go.

Unlike me, Charlie isn't from around here.

He was born in Salem, Massachusetts. It sounds like a beautiful place. Bill once told me they have witches in Salem, but that's nothing extraordinary. We have witches here too. We probably have more. Don't believe me? Go check the woods.

Charlie said Salem is the Halloween capital of the world. When he was three years old, he went trick-or-treating for the first and last time.

"It was like I died and went to a place where kids live forever as monsters. It was the best."

Halloween 1990 was his last decent day on Earth.

The next day, he moved away with his parents. Among all the places in the world, they ended up in Maudlin.

Remember what I said before? You can't just come waltzing into this place. You can't waltz out of here either. No waltzing allowed.

Certain people have special waltzing privileges, but it's not something you can request. You don't ask the city. The city invites you. No exceptions.

When I say "the city," I'm talking about the Maudlin Authority. They're the all-seeing eye that controls everything. They operate independently of the rest of the country. They don't belong to any state. Those who sit at the top of this organization are shrouded in secrecy. They are the government. They are the police. They are the wardens. They make the rules. We live and die by them.

I call them Moths. It's the first thing that came to mind when I heard their stupid name, and I'm all about efficiency.

The Moths asked Charlie's father, Ben Goldwin, to temporarily move to Maudlin and help relieve the city's housing crisis. In the late 80s, Maudlin developed a severe overcrowding problem. It bred all sorts of garbage: drugs, unemployment, dead bodies. Many roamed the streets without a place to call home. It led to more crime, more drugs, and more bodies.

As the city fell, the body count soared. Corpses wrought with disease brought more death—a never-ending circle. Something had to change. Someone had to come in and save the day.

The Moths summoned Ben to answer their prayers.

That's not the best expression. Moths don't pray.

Ben was Salem's praised city planner and architect. He eventually left the local government to start Gold Contracting Company, or GCC for short.

Everyone wanted to hire him. He loved what he did. His clients loved his work. He finished every job three times faster than his competition and for a third of the price.

Within one year after founding GCC, his name and work received national attention. This happened right around the time Maudlin was on the verge of collapse. As fate would have it, The Moths contacted Ben and made a deal. He was scheduled to relocate on November 1, 1990.

The contract included two building plans: a brand new 323-unit apartment complex and the renovation of a Gothic mansion for an anonymous, wealthy individual. Both projects were scheduled for completion by November of the following year. After that, Ben could return home to his family.

Ben had the option but decided not to bring his family along. He had heard things about Maudlin and decided it wasn't safe. Good call. But his wife, Lana, couldn't stand the thought of being separated from him for an entire year.

In her heart, she suspected an underlying reason why Ben didn't want them to move to Maudlin with him. He insisted it was all in her head—not her heart—but she couldn't let it go. Eventually, Ben gave in and brought his wife and son along for the ride. Charlie ultimately persuaded him.

"How did you change his mind?" I asked.

"All I did was ask if he was going to stay in a hotel. Then he smiled and told me to pack my bags."

"That's it?"

"Yeah."

"Weird."

They made the fifteen-hour drive from Salem to Maudlin, stopping only three times along the way. Oddly enough, their third stop was at the rest stop west of Maudlin. Yeah, *that* one. Charlie didn't see the Grey Man there, but he's seen him before.

Charlie's first year in Maudlin is a hazy memory.

"Every day was exactly the same," he said. "All I did was watch TV with my mom. My dad was gone. He was building stuff."

"Did he ever come back to the hotel?"

"Yeah, but not until late. He was the first one in and the last one out. Sometimes, he didn't come home until the clock showed four. He smelled funny."

"Like what?"

Charlie's father drank *a lot*. Every night, he returned to the hotel smelling like a bar.

"I had no friends. My mom had nobody other than my dad, and he was gone most of the time. So we watched TV and waited for my dad to be done."

"But you had a TV!"

"I wanted to break the TV."

"Why?"

I thought TVs were the coolest thing ever. My family didn't have one. I felt like I was missing out on something spectacular. As it turns out, I missed nothing. Maudlin only broadcasts a news channel: *their* news channel. They call it the Maudlin Authority Simulcast System, or MASS. If you don't have a VCR, your TV will not entertain you.

Everyone either watches MASS or listens to it on the radio. They might as well drive a bullet through the soft part of their skull. It has the same effect.

"She stared at the screen all day," Charlie continued. "It made her scared. There was always something. A dead body. A building fire. Always something. She shook her head all the time. She walked in circles. We never left the hotel room."

There's only one hotel in Maudlin: The 86 Hotel.

You knew that already, right?

What you probably don't know is that it's the oldest building in the city. It's been around since before the Wall was built. It wasn't always a hotel; it used to be something else.

Since the construction of the Wall, business at The 86 Hotel plummeted. No one passes through town anymore because they can't. Most hotel guests call the place home. I know this because I work there. Well, I used to work there.

After everything that happened this week, I'll probably never be allowed back there ever again. I may never be allowed anywhere ever again. Who knows. Right now, I'm not sure about anything. I just want to go home, but first, I have to figure out where that is, or what that is, or who that is, or if it is at all.

I'm relieved that you're here.

Charlie spent an entire miserable year trapped in a hotel room with his mom and a TV. They didn't leave the room during that time. Anything he or his mom needed was brought to the room by his father. This might explain why Charlie never left the bedroom at the orphanage. Trapping himself in a room reminded him of his parents. He wanted to feel closer to them. How depressing.

As the months passed, Charlie and Lana became less and less themselves, moving in opposite directions.

Charlie's glowing, Type A energy died in that hotel room. By mid-summer of 1991, malnourishment changed his weight and skin color. Seclusion and claustrophobia broke his brain. His A was replaced by a B.

Lana was once calm like a patient on Percocet. Her strings hung low by default. By mid-summer, you never would have known. Just like a seed, her mental decline grew slowly over time, infecting her Zen garden. It crept and crept until, one day, she woke up in a state of paranoia.

It never went away.

By late September, Lana talked to herself *a lot*.

"This was new," Charlie said. "She never did this before. She was the same and not the same at the same time. It made me feel weird."

"Weird?"

"Yeah. Bad weird."

For the first time since moving to Maudlin, Charlie felt something other than boredom and hunger. Lana didn't have a clue. She got lost in her mind. Her son wandered through a different maze. From his maze, he watched her. He took mental notes when she talked to herself.

"I watched her fall apart every night. I couldn't stop looking at her. It was like watching her die, really. Yeah, it was like that. I watched her die every night. She wouldn't tell me what was going on. She wouldn't tell me why."

"Did you ever find out?"

"Kind of."

Lana said things like, "It's the city. I can feel it. It's *breathing*." Charlie claims she said this aloud hundreds of times every day.

The apple didn't fall very far in his family.

"This city is *alive*, Elliott," he continued. "It's not just a place. It's much more than that. It breathes. I can feel it. Maudlin is alive."

I noted the dread and sincerity in his voice, but I couldn't help my reaction; I laughed. At the time, it was the second most ridiculous thing I'd ever heard. Officer Donners' comment about my father takes first place: "He's a great guy."

I laughed when I heard that too.

"The city breathes?" I asked. "You really believe that? Sounds like your mom was under a spell."

"Under a spell? Like magic?"

"No. You know, not herself."

"Not herself?"

"Yeah. I don't know. Sometimes, things just happen."

"Things don't just *happen*. There's a reason. Something made her this way."

"I thought you found out."

"I said I *kind of* did. Give me a break or go away."

My brain melts when I think about our conversations.

Over the years, I learned to arrange my words carefully around him. Boy, he got defensive. He always believed no one understood him or was ever on his side. In his mind, there was the world, and then there was Charlie. It wasn't in his nature to trust, but he somehow trusted me. That's why I feel bad about laughing.

I feel bad about a lot of things.

One lap around the sun; not much had changed. Charlie sat around the hotel room day after day while his mother stared out the window and went insane. He ate stale food, watched the news, and waited for something to happen. He experienced moments where he thought he was going to die. His father was gone all the time.

"Why didn't you say something to them?" I asked. "What about your dad? Why didn't you say something?"

"I *did* say something. Many somethings. He told me to hold on. Just keep holding on. Then he went to sleep. Every night, the same thing. I said something. I held on. He went to sleep. Then he went out again. Everything was the same all the time. Everything is the same all the time."

Charlie lost me at this point.

"My parents were dead already. My parents are dead already."

"Were they? Are they? What?"

"I'm still holding on, Dad."

"What?"

Charlie took many quick, shallow breaths. I think this is called hyperventilating. Then he fell silent and stopped moving. No breaths. No crying. Just the sound of nothing. Emptiness. The energy in the room shifted. It reminded me of Gertrude. I had to break it.

"So, what happened next?"

Charlie's commercial break ended earlier than expected, or maybe it didn't, and I'm just too tired to outline *every* detail *every* time someone goes catatonic on me. Maybe I'm just lazy. I don't know what I am anymore. Give me a break.

"My dad's work was almost done," Charlie replied. "Just two days away from going home. That's when it all fell apart. That's when it ended—and started."

"What does that even mean?"

Charlie gave me what I can only describe as the stink eye of death. It looks the way it sounds.

"You know what I'm talking about. Just think about it. Think about how you got here. Think about the last thing you remember before you woke up in this room for the very first time. Do you remember?"

"Yes," I answered, closing my eyes. "I was alone in the rest stop. The Grey Man stood in front of me. My life would never be the same. I never wanted this."

I opened my eyes and stared at the filthy floor for a few minutes.

"I understand now," I whispered.

We left it at that for a while. A long while.

It took several years before Charlie had the guts to tell me what happened. Don't get me wrong; we had a lot of talks. A *lot* of talks. Just when I thought we were getting somewhere, he would shut down. Literally. He stopped talking and wouldn't respond or react to anything I said.

He's gone catatonic on me more times than I can remember.

Eventually, he trusted me and *himself* enough to let it all out. If I tried to recount every conversation we had, you and I would run out of time. We have to keep this train moving.

Stop. Fast forward. Play.

That's how a VCR works.

Two days before the Goldwins were supposed to leave Maudlin, something happened.

Ben returned to the hotel room much earlier than usual, and he didn't act like himself. A manic grin stretched across his face. Bouts of laughter cut through his catching breath. He tried to speak, but the words were stuck. Most of his skin held shades of black, blue, green, yellow, and purple.

"The energy in the room was different," Charlie said. "Daddy changed it. He was under a spell."

Lana turned from the window with a nervous smile on her face, expecting some kind of fantastic news that would chase her fear away.

Charlie sat in front of the scrambled television screen, idling in his new default mode: silent, attentive, scared.

"I found something!" Ben shouted between breaths. "A door. Oh golly, I found a door!"

Lana put her smile away. She knew exactly what he found. She had waited all year for this. Ben ignored her melted joy and went on.

"I was underground, under the apartment building. You know, preparing for the final inspection."

Somehow, Maudlin has plumbing.

We have a lot of things that we probably shouldn't have.

"I've been down there before," he continued. "Many times. After all, I own the project! Anyway, I've never seen anything off-kilter in the sewers, but that changed when the bedrock beneath me gave in. Suddenly, I'm falling. I mean, I am *faaaaaaalling*. I must have fallen thirty feet. Landed on my flashlight! Ouch!"

Charlie gave him a what-the-hell-are-you-even-talking-about-right-now look. He never heard his father talk this way before. Ben was usually a key lower than low key. Sometimes lower than that. This new Ben scared him.

"The flashlight turned itself on when it hit the ground. That's when I saw it: a door at the far end of the tunnel. Not like a normal door; it didn't have hinges or a knob or anything like that. Oh no, this door was built *into* the bedrock, like it was drawn on, but it wasn't a drawing. And it *leads to something.* I know it!"

"Show me what you found, Ben," Lana said. "Take me there."

He ignored her and kept talking.

"Oh! I noticed a strange symbol *right* in the middle of the door. It kinda looks like wings or a star or something. Really pointy! But before I could get a better look at it, my guys started shouting at me from above. They must have heard me fall, but they didn't know where I was. So I climbed out and covered the hole real good. They never found it. Only I know where it is, and I plan on going back there tonight."

"Ben..."

"I'm going to open that door."

"You have to show me what you found. I need to see it first."

"What? Why? Why does it matter?"

"I just need you to take me there. Please."

"No, I can't do that."

"*Please*, Ben."

"What's this about? Why can't you tell me?"

"Because I can't. I need you to shut your mouth and take me there."

"No."

"Then I'll go look for it myself."

"You're not allowed. Authorized personnel only."

Lana exploded in a screaming frenzy. She grabbed Ben, gave him a death-grip hug, and begged him to show her the door. They spent the rest of the night arguing.

Charlie fled into the bathroom, slammed the door shut, and lay motionless in the bathtub with his hands over his ears.

The night slowly faded over him, and he fell asleep.

When he woke up, he found his mom kneeling beside the tub, now filled with warm water. She was bathing him. She smiled.

"It was like I woke up from a terrible nightmare that lasted for months. For a few minutes, everything was quiet and comfortable and warm and just perfect."

"So, what happened next?"

"I asked her if it was over."

"What did she say?"

"Yes and no. She told me yes and no."

"Good grief."

Charlie and Lana shared a moment of peace. Everything was going to change after this. Charlie looked at his mom's face and saw something. Her face told the story of a broken woman fighting something inside herself.

"Can you sing me a song, Mommy?"

Lana reached into her pocket. As she revealed the object inside, she sang.

"For want of a nail, the shoe was lost. For want of a shoe, the horse was lost."

The object had six sides that came to a point.

"For want of a horse, the rider was lost. For want of a rider, the message was lost."

It reflected every shade of purple as it dangled from a silver chain.

"For want of a message, the battle was lost. For want of a battle, the kingdom was lost."

Lana gently swung the object from her shaking hand until it stopped spinning. She sighed at its stillness and returned it to her pocket.

"And all for the want of a horseshoe nail."

The oversized, metal clock on the wall struck midnight.

"Time to get dressed, darling. We have to go."

Charlie didn't know where they were going, but it didn't matter. After being trapped in a room at The 86 Hotel for a year, *anywhere* was fine.

This was the last time Charlie felt sincerely happy.

Ignorance can be a drug.

Lana nearly got them both killed once they exited the hotel. She held Charlie's hand and led him into the crumbling street.

A car passing by lost its side-view mirror; it shattered against Lana's rib cage. She didn't even notice.

Another car flew by. The driver stretched out his hand and grabbed Charlie by his scarf, dragging him across the road for several seconds before letting go. I imagine the driver did this just because. That's what happens around here. People do bad things just because.

Aside from two skinned knees and a bruised shoulder, Charlie was okay.

Charlie and Lana forgot how to be out in the world. Sure, Maudlin is only a few square miles, but compared to their tiny hotel room, these square miles seemed endless.

Charlie couldn't handle it.

He looked up at his mom to find that she didn't share the same excitement. Her mind went somewhere else.

"Your father has the car. We'll have to walk. We're out of time."

Charlie walked faster than his little legs were able to take him. At times, she dragged him down the road. Eventually, she picked him up and carried him the rest of the way.

This was the last time Charlie was held by his mother.

Block by block, Lana drew closer to the construction site with Charlie in her arms. Somewhere along the way, Charlie heard her talking to herself again.

"I have no choice. I *have* to do this. This is why I'm here. Katerina knows all. This is my purpose. Hiving off. Hiving off."

She repeated these affirmations for a few blocks. Whatever she had to do, she didn't want to do it, but she was convinced there was no other option.

This is how it had to be. She wasn't prepared.

"Oh god, we're here," she cried. "I'm not ready. I'm not ready to do this. Why can't I have more time?"

Charlie was perplexed; they weren't at his father's construction site. That's what he thought "we're here" meant. Lana put Charlie down on the crumbling sidewalk in front of an old, grey house with a circle driveway.

He noted the rusted metal sign on the front lawn. He could read the sign, but he didn't know what it meant.

"What is this place, Mommy?"

Lana bowed her head and shut her eyes.

"I'm going to drop you off here for a little bit, darling. Your daddy is in a lot of trouble. He found something bad. He doesn't know what he's doing. If I don't help him, we're *all* going to be in a lot of trouble. Does that make sense?

"No. Where are you going?"

"I'm going somewhere you can't follow, honey. I can't take you with me. You have to stay here. It's too dangerous. It's *too dangerous*. I don't know what I'd do with myself if something happened to you, Charlie Boy. Just know that I love you very, very, very, very, very much. I'll come back for you, darling. I promise. I promise. *I promise*."

She walked Charlie up to the front porch, kissed him on the forehead, knocked on Gertrude's door, and ran off in a crying frenzy.

Charlie stared at the front door in tears, too afraid to look at his mother, knowing it would be the last time.

"You triple promised me, Mommy," he whispered to the door.

"Please don't forget me. Triple promise."

Minutes passed; no one came to the door.

"I didn't know what to do. I was cold. It was getting dark."

"*Getting* dark? I thought it was after midnight."

"This was a different kind of dark."

"What does that mean?"

Charlie looked and sounded like a different person. I don't know how else to explain it.

"A thought entered my mind. I can't tell if I was *afraid* to die or if I *wanted* to die. Maybe both. It's odd for thoughts of death to enter the brain of a five-year-old child. All I wanted to do was lay on the ground and wait to die, and that's exactly what I did. I laid there, dark and cold in this prison. Then he arrived."

The Grey Man.

"He's just as you described: tall and thin. Pale, translucent skin covered by a black trench coat and fedora. I'm pretty sure he was bald. He was smiling, but not the happy kind. Those menacing teeth. That voice. Oh, that voice. I still hear it in my head."

Charlie awoke from his deathly daydream on Gertrude's porch to find the Grey Man staring at him. Charlie doesn't like feeling vulnerable, so he got up and faced him head-on.

The Grey Man found his bravery amusing.

"Tell me, child, does your mother still carry that toy in her pocket? Does she still play pretend? I like to play too, you know. I love to play games."

He held out his hand, revealing Lana's purple, pointed object. It hung from the silver chain, spinning wildly.

"That's my mom's toy!"

"She's wasting her time, boy. I will find another way in. I *always* find a way. *Look at me*. I exist *because* of the flaws in this design."

He looked up at the sky. I figure that's worth noting.

"Your rules are broken," he continued. "Soon, your heart will be broken because her skull will be broken. Sure, I could stop her. I could save her. I have that power. I can do whatever the hell I want."

"Potty mouth!"

In the face of pure evil, he does a manners check.

Pure gold.

The Grey man smiled wider, exposing his broken-mirror shark teeth. Then, much like Lana, he started talking to himself.

"Why am I wasting my time with this speck?"

Charlie fired back without hesitation.

"I'm no speck. I'll be six years old soon! I'm *so* big!"

"You're bigger than your mother, child. I'll give you that. Just don't let it get to your head. You will both be rotting corpses in a matter of time, and no one will even care."

Charlie cried.

The Grey Man broke into song.

"For want of a horse, the rider was lost. For want of a rider, the message was lost."

He started walking away, but after a few steps, he turned around and faced Charlie again.

That was his signature move: the walk-away-then-turn-around.

"Your mom is doing the right thing, kid. She just doesn't realize it. After I leave, the crazy lady in this house will find you and offer you a place to stay. I suggest you accept her offer. There's a TV inside. Turn it on tomorrow morning. I'll take my leave now."

As we already know, Charlie accepted the offer, and there was a TV in the house.

When he watched the news the following morning, MASS reported a breaking story about a man and a woman found dead beneath the newly constructed Complex. A tunnel collapsed.

They died in each other's broken arms.

There were no witnesses.

Six hours after the collapse, the Moths arrived at the scene and recovered their bodies.

Nobody knows where they were taken.

6 — Like Vultures

TWO MONTHS FELL OFF THE CALENDAR.

Welcome to October 1992.

I finally left the bedroom, but only because Charlie wasn't in it anymore. One morning, I woke up, and he was gone.

A heads up would have been nice.

I figured something terrible happened; he wouldn't just leave me like that. He needed me, I thought.

The search-and-rescue mission had begun.

For a house full of children, it was surprisingly quiet. A little too quiet, maybe? I don't know.

When I stepped out of the room, I didn't see anyone.

My room was tucked away in the far-right end of the house.

Directly across from it, I found another bedroom.

The door to this room was painted purple. It held a wreath packed full of dead roses. A silver amulet hung at the center. It had some kind of black stone fastened to it.

Latin words handwritten in black ink surrounded the outer edge of the wreath.

The message formed a perfect circle:

Nigrum umbrae sunt non receperint in hoc domum.

I've asked Gertrude thousands of times what the words meant. For years, she wouldn't answer me. It wasn't until my seventeenth birthday when she finally told me. As to *why* the words were written on the door, I can't say for sure.

That was a promise for the following year.

"You'll find out on your eighteenth birthday, my boy."

It never happened. I mean, my birthday happened, but she wasn't around for it. Neither was I, in a way. A few weeks before I turned eighteen, the incident happened.

She didn't deserve that kind of death.

The purple door belonged to her bedroom. I felt comforted knowing she slept so close to me.

I took a dozen steps down the hallway and entered what most people call a living room, family room, or great room. Whatever. It was a big, square space with an old TV, two beige couches, and two floor-to-ceiling windows facing the front of the house. I could tell the place was very old by looking at the worn, aged, almost-tired floor. It covered every walking surface of the house, including the kitchen and bathrooms.

I don't think bathrooms are supposed to have wood floors, but what do I know?

Random objects covered the living room floor: a small, red velvet purse, a wrestling action figure with its head missing, a handful of fake blood capsules, and six oil pastels in six different shades of blue.

Oh, and there were books.

I remember three of them.

First, *Speakable and Unspeakable in Quantum Mechanics* by John Stewart Bell.

Second, *Zoologijos Skaitiniai*—a Lithuanian book about animals and insects—by Clay Statys.

Lithuania is a real place.

I picked up the third book: a first-edition copy of *The Mirror of Magic* by Kurt Seligmann. It had two demons on the cover. They smiled at me.

I opened a random page. What I read still haunts me:

> *The devil can be an actor. He can be whatever he chooses. He is everywhere.*

As I read that line for the third time, a voice manifested from the corner of the living room.

"Those are mine. The books. They're mine."

I froze. I mean, I must have been sitting on that disgusting couch for at least five minutes and didn't notice anyone in the room with me. Sure enough, I looked over my right shoulder, and there he was.

"Are you the devil?" I asked.

"No. I'm Bill. That's my book."

He spoke with a calm yet annoyed voice. Kinda like Bob Ross stuck in traffic. Do you know who Bob Ross is? I watched him on a VHS tape once. He died eight years ago, I think.

I held the book up to Bill's face. I didn't know what else to do.

"I cannot say the same about everything else on the floor," he continued. "I have no use for such things. I have never been much of an artist."

Even though he sat on the floor, you could tell he was tall—taller than most kids his age. He looked about eight years old. He seemed pretty comfortable too, as if he'd been living here a while.

I didn't understand the way he dressed: a sweater in four different shades of brown. Brown slacks. Brown shoes. Brown Glasses.

Brown. Brown. Brown.

If he were standing up instead of sitting down, I would have mistaken him for a dead houseplant.

Sometimes, people take plants from outside and put them inside. I'm not sure how I feel about that.

"Do you not like animals?" Bill asked.

"What? No. I mean, yeah. I mean, what?"

"There were three books on the floor. Now, there are two. You left the animals on the floor with quantum mechanics. I can see why you would pass on the motion and interaction of subatomic particles, quantization of energy, wave-particle duality, and the uncertainty principle. But *animals*? Color me surprised."

"What color is 'surprise?' Brown?"

Bill ignored what I said and kept talking.

"The book in your hand was written by a Swiss-American Surrealist painter. It would appear that Anna took it from my shelf and didn't care to put it back. I would like to say she *forgot* to put it back, but that would be false."

"Who are you?"

"Anna possesses a certain inconsideration in her latest pattern. Her brain persuades her to take books from my collection, not read them, and leave them in places they do not belong. I appreciate your interest in the history of magic and the occult, but it doesn't change the fact that you found my book in the wrong place. The floor is not a shelf."

"Who's Anna?"

"But what can I do? Gertrude does not believe in taking away privileges as a form of discipline. I would go further to say she does not believe in discipline at all. Her heart is too soft, Anna is remiss, and I have no power. I only have knowledge, which, as they say, is power. A contradiction, if you will."

"Where's Gertrude?"

"What is power, anyway? Have you heard of anything more unbecoming? Such pettiness. Such a human thing."

"What?"

He didn't talk like a typical eight-year-old. He didn't do *anything* typical to anyone. I thought he was an alien, and the books were his way of studying our planet, but I dismissed this over time. You see, Bill loved sharing random facts, but it wasn't an act of generosity. He wanted to study the world, then he wanted the world to know how much he studied it. He wanted to be recognized for his brain.

Validation. Such a human thing.

I have to admit, his random facts were pretty cool.

"Your body creates about seventeen million red blood cells every second," he said. "Well, not just *your* body. Mine too. Everyone's body. Well, mostly everyone. On a good day."

This was his daily ritual.

It took a minute, but I realized he wasn't making eye contact with me. Not even a sneaky side-eye glance. He kept his face buried in David M. Ludlum's *National Audubon Society Field Guide to North American Weather*. I silently questioned his choice of reading material. He must have known.

"I must be straight with you. I have acquired a sizable interest in weather patterns. Do not ask me how it happened. Dare I say, too, that *this* is the definitive guide to cloud formation in the North American skies."

He gave the book a good shake.

Maybe it was his non-threatening weather book, or the way he dressed, or the way he talked, but his presence comforted me. Everything about him felt harmless. He wasn't a predator.

In a life rife with human garbage, I found a victory in this.

A string of facts paraded from his mouth.

"Alfred Hitchcock was frightened of eggs."

"The Eiffel Tower is six inches shorter during winter."

"Most American car horns honk in the key of F."

"You are Elliott Avenue."

I never told him my name.

"Seeing that I know your name and all, I suppose it is only fair that I introduce myself. I try to keep things on a level. I have sworn an oath to maintain balance in our universe. Not the other universes, only this one. I know my limits."

He pulled his eyes from a two-dimensional mesocyclone and made eye contact with me just long enough to say his name.

"Bill Dweller."

Here's what I know about Bill.

He arrived at the orphanage back in May 1988, a few months before his fourth birthday. He's the Third Orphan, right behind Anna and Delilah. I'm the Tenth Orphan. Charlie is the Ninth.

In the southeast corner of Maudlin, there's a forest. It's the only green part of Maudlin—the only evidence we have that nature exists. I'm surprised the Moths haven't uprooted the trees yet. If you've seen the rest of the city, you'd wonder the same thing. Everything here is concrete and steel, blood and money, drugs and death, yet the forest remains. The forest is *alive*. It's the soul of our garbage city.

It has a name: Ender Forest. The Enders have claimed it as their own. It's where they live, perform rituals, and sacrifice children in an effort to stop a prophecy from being fulfilled.

Almost everyone just calls Ender Forest "the woods." We only have one forest. It doesn't need a fancy title.

Deep in the woods or Ender Forest or whatever, there's a cave.

That's where they found Bill in 1988.

I know I glossed over the child sacrifice and prophecy bits. That's a lot to unpack. Let's put a pin in it for now.

Two unfortunate gentlemen made the mistake of entering the woods in search of a secluded place to get high. The track marks on their arms gave it away. It's important to note that they didn't ground or shield themselves before crossing the tree line.

Idiots.

They stumbled across the cave, found Bill, and abducted him.

When I imagine how their interaction played out, it makes me laugh. I can see a tiny Bill carrying a casual conversation with two heroin junkies like it was a normal part of his weird life.

I don't have to imagine it, though. It's all on paper. I found Gertrude's documents. She had documents about all of us.

A *lot* of documents.

These notes, letters, reports, journals, film reels, cassette tapes, classified files, and everything else…I might need to explain them.

Jesus, there's a lot to explain.

Then again, why am I explaining *anything* to you?

Why are you even here? You don't know me. *Do* you know me? I sure as hell don't know who you are, or do I? No, I don't. I'm looking at your face right now, and there's nothing I recognize. I mean, you look red, and everything looks red, but I can still see you, and I don't know what I'm seeing. I don't know your hair or your shoulders or your jawline. I don't remember your cheekbones or your teeth. If I've seen them before, I sure as hell don't remember them. If I don't remember them, I don't know them.

I don't know you. I don't know you. I don't know you.

Do you see blood in my mouth? I taste it.

Is it coming from my head, or am I pouring blood from my eyes?

What are we even talking about?

Shut up, I'm okay.

Stop. Rewind. Stop. Play.

That's how VCRs work.

According to a Moth report that probably no one was ever meant to read, Bill and the two unfortunate gentlemen were on their way out when a Moth agent greeted them at the edge of the forest. It's noted that the agent grounded himself beforehand.

The gentlemen tried their hardest to play it cool or act natural or whatever, but it didn't matter. The agent didn't approach them with suspicion. Instead, he let out a sigh of relief and thanked them for finding the missing boy.

"Thank the heavens and the stars! We've been searching high and low for this poor, scared child! Thank you so much, boys! You are true Good Samaritans. Oh hey, do you like drugs?"

The gentlemen froze.

"The Maudlin Authority's Exploratory Solutions Division is hosting an exciting, exclusive drug trial for a few lucky Maudlings, such as yourselves. As a reward for finding the boy, we'd love to have you aboard. It's the least we can do for your act of heroism. Consider your attendance appreciated—and cordially required."

The report documenting this encounter included a nondisclosure agreement and a witness testimony.

The agreement restricted them from sharing any information about the drug trial with the public. The two unfortunate gentlemen signed it—Gabriel Salazar and Daniel Mash. They were never seen again. No one knows what happened to them. I imagine that mystery left with the report's torn-out pages.

Exploratory solutions? Yeah, right.

Maudlin is run by invisible people with the power to erase us as if we're computer files.

Do you know what a computer is?

The witness testimony described a brief encounter between Bill and the future human lab rats. To no one's surprise, Bill didn't cry. He wasn't afraid of them. He didn't even acknowledge them. His face was buried in a goddamn book—a nearly destroyed copy of *Wonders of the Invisible World* by Cotton Mather.

"Are you lost?" Daniel asked.

Bill slammed the book shut. It crumbled to dust.

"This Cotton Mather fellow makes me sad. He unleashes the fear of God in his town and has the nerve to recount this event through the lens of an unbiased informer, a *historian*."

Bill's language perplexed the gentlemen. Such articulation from such a small thing.

Gabriel chimed in.

"Hey, buddy. My friend here asked if you're lost."

Bill closed his eyes, took a breath, and primed a response.

"Lost? No, I live here. Even if I did not live here, I am never lost. You two appear lost, though, but in a different sense."

"What're you talking about? Where are your parents?"

"I do not have parents. I have books. See?"

Bill held up his tiny hand and waved at his collection on a nearby boulder.

After they took Bill from the cave and headed toward the tree line, a woman jumped down from a tree and greeted them, but I don't know what happened or what she said. Any record of their interaction is missing. The bottom half of the testimony was torn out. All I know is that the tree-climbing woman wasn't there before or after Bill and the gentlemen encountered the Moth agent at the edge of the woods.

Wait. I can't say I *know* that. This encounter is based on a report written by a human being. Who's to say it's true or accurate?

Lacuna is a pretty word, don't you think?

Less than a week later, Bill ended up on Gertrude's porch.

But why *her* porch, I wondered.

If there's anything to know about Moths, it's that they don't do *any* business with ordinary people. This makes sense; Gertrude is far from ordinary.

She did her best to dodge any talk about her connection with the Maudlin Authority, but the proof was there. The documents in her bedroom proved it. The children that were left on her porch over the years proved it too.

Anyway, that's the super quick version of how Bill Dweller ended up in my life. That's how he ended up in the corner of the living room, sharing weird facts with me.

"Charlie Chaplin won third place in a Charlie Chaplin look-alike contest."

I remembered why I left my bedroom in the first place.

"Charlie—where is he?"

"Charles Sheldon Goldwin," he replied. "You call him Charlie Gold. Today was the first time I have seen him in a couple of weeks. Ever since you started living in this house, he has been out of sight like a cat. Yes, Charlie is like a cat. A Russian Blue, if I had to guess."

"He's been in my room."

"That is not your room. You are borrowing it. This is a temporary place."

"What? What's *temporary*?"

Bill made eye contact with me again, briefly.

"Everything is temporary."

"I don't know what that means."

I'm pretty sure I still don't know what that means.

"If I am correct, which I *am*," Bill continued, "then Charlie left the bedroom upon realizing that his scarf went missing. What he does know is that his scarf is not *missing*. Someone stole it. Mark the difference."

"Who would do that? Why would they do that?"

"Charlie loves his scarf more than himself."

"But who would do that?"

Bill lowered the book from his face, set it carefully on his lap, interlocked his fingers, and looked deep into my being.

"I assume you have not met them yet."

"Them?"

"You will find out this afternoon. Goodbye for now."

He got up from his corner and disappeared down the hallway and into a part of the house I hadn't explored yet. He seemed very uncomfortable about something. Uncomfortable and irritated. He left his books in the living room. I wasn't feeling too great myself, but it didn't stop me from taking a peek inside *Zoologijos Skaitiniai*.

I had a plan: find Charlie, retrieve his scarf, wrap it around his neck, enter the kitchen, steal some snacks, break out of the orphanage, and search the city for my sister. I hadn't forgotten about her. I just got a little distracted.

I was on my way, I swear.

Before I could execute my plan, the floor and the walls slowly spun around me. It was almost like the feeling I get before one of my blackout spells, but not quite. Urges to pass out and throw up were fighting each other. I needed to find the nearest bathroom.

In my panic, I forgot about the bathroom in my closet. I ran down the unexplored part of the house in search of a toilet. Luckily, I found one, just in time. If the toilet seat hadn't already been up, I would have puked all over it.

Not much came out of me, though—just some bile and stomach acid. I didn't have much inside me in the first place. I'm not sure how long I had gone without eating. It could have been weeks.

Relief washed over me once the puking stopped. You know what I'm talking about, right? There's this calm-after-the-storm feeling that rises to the surface after you're done being sick. It can be misleading, though, as it was for me here. My body went downhill again. My knees shook. My head spun.

Round two.

Most people start praying to God when this happens to them. Such a human thing. I get why they do that, but come on.

In a flawlessly staged mutiny by several of my organ systems, I threw up again, blacked out, and fainted. On my way down, the left side of my head had an unforgiving encounter with porcelain.

Lights out.

I don't know how long I was out. Long enough to dream, I guess. I saw myself lying in a dark room. A silhouette sat close to me. It struck a match and lit a white candle on the table between us. The lashing flame revealed a face.

Mom?

I woke up staring at the off-white tiles of the bathroom ceiling. Each one had hundreds and hundreds of little tiny holes. I spent an hour or so just lying there, counting every hole in a single tile. I couldn't count past twenty, but it didn't matter.

Counting is comforting.

As I counted twenty for the twentieth time, a muffled voice sounded from beyond the door.

"The bathroom ceiling tiles are made of mineral fiber with a noise reduction coefficient of fifty-five."

Bill gave the door a double-knock and walked away.

There were only twelve ceiling tiles. Well, there *should* have been twelve—one of them was missing. It left behind a large opening in the ceiling, exposing several parallel copper pipes. One of them stood out among the rest—noticeably larger. It protruded from the ceiling, making it impossible to hide or cover.

At its lowest point, I spotted a red handle. A valve.

Turning the valve handle came to my mind, but I didn't bother. It was out of my reach, like almost everything else.

The toilet did a number on my face. A rhythmic throbbing wave started just above my cheekbone, swelling and crashing against the surface of my skin. It reminded me of the time my father came home with a black eye and bloody nose. My mom put a bag of frozen peas on his face.

As I pulled my body up from the bathroom floor, Bill's voice returned to the door.

"Aristotle originally linked throbbing pain to heart rhythm. It took twenty-three centuries, but an electroencephalogram disproved his presumption. All this time, we looked in the wrong place. The beat of this unwelcome drum does not synchronize with the heart. Throbbing pain is linked to alpha waves in the brain. So much for conventional wisdom."

"How are you doing that?"

Bill gave the door another double-knock.

"Okay, I am going away now."

His footsteps faded down the hallway.

I became painfully aware of my loneliness.

The house—empty.

Charlie—missing.

Gertrude—no idea.

Bill disappeared to who-knows-where.

Anna lurked about somewhere, but she didn't leave a trace.

I stood in the center of the house, imagining a lifetime of dead silence. It reminded me of my mom. I wanted to feel closer to her, so I walked into the kitchen in search of frozen peas.

There's not much to say about the kitchen. It had all the usual kitchen things: a stove and a refrigerator, some counter space between them, a sad-looking coffee maker, and a table and chairs.

Nothing exhilarating.

This space could have used some color. Aside from the old, tired hardwood floor, everything was off-white: the countertop, cabinets, appliances, all of it.

This is only half true for the wallpaper; it was off-white, but with pale green vertical stripes. It looked ready to peel away from the wall at any moment. Humidity and gravity really did a number on it.

I found the freezer door below the refrigerator door, low to the ground. Finally, something I could reach.

No sign of frozen peas, but let's talk about the freezer for a moment.

It's hard to describe what I found inside. I mean, I saw all sorts of things, but I had no idea what I was looking at. Plant parts, I guess. Herbs? Flowers? Seeds? No clue.

I recognized the vacuum-sealed plastic bags that held the items in question, but that's it.

Each bag held a note. I remember a few of them.

My father could have used this, whatever it was:

> *For excessive bleeding at the nose.*
> *Take a few drops of the parties bloud*
> *in herds or in a linen cloth, burne*
> *alltogether: Et fecit.*

Here's one for…headaches?

> *For a scaldhed.*
> *Bray white mallowes and rootes*
> *of red docks with May butter and*
> *anoynt the Hed therwith.*

This one makes me nauseous:

> *To help the Crampe.*
> *Take a piece of Parchemint as much*
> *as will goe about your legg in the*
> *gartering place; write theron theis*
> *folowing words Gut + Gut +*
> *Egul + Getaul + and weare it*
> *next your bare leg. It will help.*

Before I could make sense of this nonsense, I heard a loud *thud* behind me, and behold, a door. A glass door. It led to the backyard.

A second and third *thud* revealed apples flying toward the door and exploding on impact.

Through the splattered apple pieces running down the glass, I glimpsed five human figures at the far end of the backyard—all dressed in black. A sixth figure laid motionless on the grass.

Charlie.

I saw something like this earlier that day.

In Bill's Lithuanian animal book, I flipped to a random chapter about scavengers. The first picture showed a wounded fawn surrounded by vultures.

As usual, I'm reminded of something Bill once said:

"Rarely do vultures prey on healthy animals. When forced to kill, they target the sick and wounded. Otherwise, they let predatory creatures do the dirty work, even if it means settling for scraps. Vultures are such vigilant creatures. They will wait, and they will wait, and when the time is right, they will gorge on the dying."

When I opened the door to the backyard, it was like walking into the book's picture. The five figures—all boys around my age—had no hair on their heads. They were bald like vultures.

They looked dangerous, wild, and evil.

Their odd appearances intimidated me. Still, it wasn't enough to keep me away. Nothing could keep me away.

Charlie needed me.

Sure, taking on five bald demons sounds pretty stupid, but when you don't fear death, it doesn't matter.

Before I marched to the far end of the backyard, I gave a quick scan of my surroundings on the off chance that someone might be around to help me.

Bill perched himself by the kitchen window.

"Do not mind me. I am only here to observe."

I didn't bother responding. Persuasion doesn't work on him. He's set in his ways.

Two girls hung out together along the fence on the left side of the yard. They were new—new to me. The girl standing up, Delilah Hayward, kept peeking at the vulture boys. The other girl, Anna Quinn, sat in the dead grass, playing with sticks and wet leaves, oblivious to everything.

Delilah shook her head as I walked toward the boys. She knew better than to get involved.

I don't have much else to say about them right now.

It was time to save Charlie.

I transformed myself for the impending fight; I held out my arms, turned my hands to fists, and put on a death stare, ready to kill.

I'm so tough, I thought.

Halfway down the yard, I pissed myself.

I got so jacked on fear and adrenaline that my bladder couldn't stomach it. I stopped in my tracks and relieved myself in the grass. Everyone stared at me.

What a nightmare.

Stop. Fast forward. Play.

All five vulture boys dressed the same: black scrubs and black hoodies. White letters were stenciled on the back of each hoodie:

> *ESD Patient 1*
> *ESD Patient 2*
> *ESD Patient 3*
> *ESD Patient 4*
> *ESD Patient 5*

As if their bald heads weren't creepy enough.

Charlie couldn't move, but he was alive. His eyes were open, his chest rising and falling. He looked up at the grey sky. To my surprise, his scarf had returned to his neck, but in a cruel and unusual way. Someone tied it very tight in a triple knot. He could barely breathe.

This wasn't a simple case of children being barbaric or whatever. I mean, you could call them bullies, but bullies don't typically try to murder people.

Or do they?

Although they all looked the same, one of the vulture kids gave off different energy than the others, and he was slightly taller. I almost pissed myself again when he spoke to me.

"Why are you here?"

"You're hurting Charlie," I replied in a trembling voice.

Not my proudest moment.

"That wasn't my question. Why are you *here*?"

"Same as you. My parents didn't want me. Well, my mom died—"

"No, no 'same reason.' You're not like us."

"But can we still be friends?"

Imagine a scared child with pee all over his pants making a last-minute switch to cowering diplomacy after failing to be a superhero.

Hi, I'm Elliott. I'll be here all night, assuming I don't bleed out.

Apply more pressure.

"No, no friends," the boy replied.

"How am I not like you?"

Christ, Elliott, shut up.

"We didn't lose our parents. We never had parents."

"Everyone has parents."

"You know nothing!" he shouted. He took several steps toward me and looked up.

"We fell from the sky."

I laughed at him. I couldn't help it. Just imagine a bunch of weird bald kids falling from the sky and acting cool about it.

"Laugh again, and I will end you."

He wrapped his hand around my neck.

Something about him didn't feel human.

I didn't get a chance to process the encounter; seconds later, I was lying on the ground with Charlie. The right side of my head throbbed in tandem with my left cheekbone.

Alpha waves in overdrive.

Charlie remained motionless, looking up at the sky, but he mumbled to himself, or maybe to me. I couldn't tell. I squinted at his lips, trying to read them, trying to make out his words, and then it started happening.

"Oh no, not now. Please, not right now."

"What's wrong?" the boy asked, standing over me. "Did you piss yourself again?"

I wish.

It's not that I *wanted* to piss myself again, but I would have preferred it to another blackout spell.

Charlie's lips slowly faded away, but I could hear him, just barely.

"Speak to me. I can't see you."

"He—he's," Charlie stuttered.

He tried to find the words. I ran out of time.

As I descended into the darkness of my mind, silhouettes of scavengers towered over us. They didn't say anything, though. They just looked down at us in silence. All six of them.

"Wait a minute," I whispered. "I counted five. Who are *you*?"

A sixth silhouette appeared.

Charlie finally found his words.

"He's here. He's with them."

In my final moment before fading out, I glimpsed a touch of grey amongst the black.

7 — Lapis Lazuli

I FOLLOWED HER EVERYWHERE.

After my blackout in the backyard, I had a new obsession: learn everything possible about the Vultures.

Everything.

I had a slight problem: Gertrude wouldn't tell me anything.

For weeks, I was her shadow. I bothered the hell out of her, or at least I thought I did. She had superhuman patience. No matter how much I hassled her for answers, she wouldn't budge.

Instead of cluing me in, she just smiled and said something like, "Oh dear boy, hide your worries. Don't let your nose wander."

I hated when she said that.

Eventually, reluctantly, she shared their names, but it wasn't her idea. Bill convinced her to do it. She bought into his exchanging-information-to-maintain-balance-in-the-universe theory.

Sure.

In case you're wondering—after I blacked out, nothing crazy happened. I was only out for a few hours this time. If I had any dreams or visions or out-of-body experiences, they're lost.

The Vultures had names:

James Grave.

Johnny Wixom.

Dallas Dark.

The Phoenix twins: Devon and Darcy.

"I could introduce you if you'd like," Gertrude said.

Last I checked, I already received an introduction. It ended with a punch to the head and a sixth silhouette, which Charlie and I both concluded was the Grey Man. We saw the same things: the tall, thin shadow with the sharp-angled jaw, a trench coat flapping in the wind, that stupid fedora.

The sixth silhouette had an identity, but we couldn't figure out why he showed up with the five bald children. In fact, why did he show up at all? This question plagued me for years.

I wish I didn't know anything. To know things is to suffer.

In the years that followed, life at the orphanage calmed down. Sure, the first few months were strange and chaotic, but after that, not so much. Charlie and I spent most of the time in our bedroom, avoiding confrontation with the Vultures.

They spent most of their time in the backyard. They'd be out there from sunrise to sunset, beating the living hell out of each other for fun. James would pair two of them up and force them to fight until one of them bled. Sometimes, even when it went that far, he kept them going. I spent many afternoons watching this from the kitchen window, usually while eating a turkey sandwich.

A hundred or so turkey sandwiches later, I got restless. I figured I'd make an awkward attempt at being social. Charlie didn't want in, so I was on my own.

Options for social interaction around the orphanage left much to be desired.

Bill preferred the company of books, not people.

The Vultures—hard pass.

Gertrude spent every day sleeping. Even when she was awake, she didn't have much to say. For the longest time, whenever she woke up, I immediately approached her and demanded answers. It was like a gag reflex. But no matter how hard I pried, she kept her secrets.

Anna and Delilah, the girls along the backyard fence, were my final options. I made a handful of attempts at being social with them over the years, but I didn't get much out of it. I mean, Delilah wasn't so bad, but Anna was the literal worst.

Anna Quinn: The First Child.

In the summer of 1987, Gertrude found her on the front porch, wrapped in a red silk cloth, crying up a storm. At only three days old, she already had a full, bright blonde head of hair. You could say she knew how to make an entrance.

Gertrude found a crumpled note fastened to Anna's cloth diaper:

This is Anna Quinn. She's my baby.

My husband disappeared. I live alone in his car.

I have nothing.

I've seen you in your backyard. You seem like a nice woman.

I'm going to find a way out of here and back to my family. I'll fix this. I'll turn things around. When I do, I'll come back for her. Tell Anna her mommy will be back soon.

I have a tattoo of a red diamond on my left wrist.

When I come back, I'll show it to you, so you'll know it's me.

Thank you. I'm so sorry. I will come back for her. I promise.

Take care of my baby.

She never came back.

Maybe she died. Maybe she changed her mind. It doesn't matter. Anna didn't care why her mother didn't come back. Anna didn't care if she came back at all. She just didn't care.

I don't care either.

Why am I even talking about this?

The way I see it, Anna never met her mother. Sure, they hung out for three days, but that doesn't count. She didn't know what it's like to have a mother, so there was nothing to miss. You can't miss what you never had in the first place. That's just my take. If you asked Anna, she would have told you something completely different.

"Don't you understand? My mom *had* to give me away. She wasn't good enough for me. No one is good enough for me. No one!"

Anna had to win at everything all the time. She made the decisions, set the rules, and acted superior to everything and everyone. The floor was lava because she said so. Being the First Child only fueled her ego.

She only talked to Delilah Hayward, the Second Child. Everyone else knew better than to approach her. Hell, she wasn't even that *nice* to Delilah. One thing's for sure, though: they completed each other. They also shared a bedroom on the other side of the house. I never walked inside, but I've caught glimpses through the doorway.

Do you know what a pigsty is?

I liked Delilah, but she kind of annoyed me. Not the way Anna annoyed me, though. Quite the opposite. Delilah liked everyone all the time. It bothered me. Thankfully, she didn't say a whole lot most of the time. Her best trait was how little she talked. I liked that.

Compare that to Anna, who hated everyone and wouldn't shut the hell up.

Birds of a feather and whatever.

True opposites in every way, especially when it came to parents.

Delilah struggled on a never-ending quest to fill the void her parents left behind. They didn't get the chance to abandon her because they ended up on the receiving end of a serial killer's appetite for human body parts.

I learned three strange things about the kidnapping, death, dismemberment, and consumption of David and Ayumi Hayward.

First strange thing: only their teeth and wedding rings were found. What remains of their other remains remains a mystery.

Second strange thing: their teeth were arranged in the form of a septagram—a seven-pointed star. Their rings were placed in the center of the star.

Third strange thing: a Moth agent brought Delilah to Gertrude's door several months after her parents were murdered. The Vultures followed a similar path.

Shit.

I need to go off on fewer tangents.

I can't resist sometimes.

Stop. Rewind. Stop. Play.

Don't mind the white lines. My tape is stretched super thin from all the years of rewind and playback. Automatic tracking doesn't work anymore, but I can do it manually sometimes.

It's not easy.

I'm losing my charge. I'm designed to degrade over time.

Do you know what remanence decay is?

Tracking. Tracking. Tracking. Tracking. Tracking.

Good enough.

When I was thirteen, I felt terribly exhausted all the time, mostly because I still invested my energy into harassing Gertrude. I wanted her to explain the Vultures. Despite many attempts, though, I had nothing to show for it, so I stopped bothering her.

It's not that I gave up. Not even close. I just realized she wasn't the only key in the house that unlocked secrets. If I couldn't get the answers past Gertrude's cracked, clown-red lips, I would find it on paper. After all, she was a hoarder of documents; the paper trail began in her bedroom.

When I couldn't sleep, I stared at the ceiling and had visions of a dusty metal box lying around somewhere in there. Much like the Vultures' hooded sweatshirts, this metal box had some sort of Moth label on it. *Property of the Maudlin Authority* in big block letters or something like that. When I opened it, in my mind, I found documents, photos, cassette tapes, a film reel and several objects I've never seen before.

This vision of a metal box haunted me every night for a year.

I wasn't ready to find it; not yet. I'd like to say I waited for the right moment—whatever that means—but let's be honest. I was too scared.

I blame my mom for this.

Here I go again.

Stop. Rewind. Play.

I remember the day before she passed. She looked godawful. I'll never forget it.

Do you know what a zombie is?

The way she limped around reminded me of this horror movie my father talked about. He did this thing where he held out his arms and pretended to be a zombie behind my mom's back while she trudged up and down the halls of the hospital. He almost gave himself away through laughter, but he stayed in character.

My father never broke character.

Give this man a trophy.

Her head of hair had become reduced to thin patches of brittle, broken strands. Her lips were nearly gone. The doctor referred to it as localized necrotizing fasciitis. My mom called it flesh-eating bacteria. It started on her lips and slowly ate away at her entire face until she almost didn't look like a person.

I still thought she was the most beautiful human being.

That day, she gave me a final lesson.

"Elliott. Look at me. *Really* look at me. I'm going to recite the thought you've been keeping inside but haven't found the courage to believe."

She always spoke to me like an adult.

"I'll be gone very soon. I can't escape it. Your father—he'll plan a funeral for me. Not for love, not for honor, not for ritual. Mostly for appearances. It has to look just right. Something terrible has a grip on him, and it drives him along a road paved by fear. But I digress, and you're so young."

Around here, funerals are a luxury, a display of status, and they only happen at one place—Our Lady of Sorrows Church. One might assume this Lady of Sorrows is just another depiction of Mary, the mother of Jesus, but they are mistaken.

She is someone else.

She is something else entirely.

But I digress.

My mom paused for a moment to collect her thoughts. Sometimes, especially near the end, it took her mind a while to arrive at a point. Does that remind you of anyone?

"Maudlin is on the verge of being swallowed. Soon, the world will follow. There's a heavy negative vibration humming underground and through the air. It has us surrounded. Many are powerless to it. They give their light to it."

Light. Gertrude talked a lot about light.

"Don't get me wrong, dear. There are still a few good souls out there, but right now, their numbers are falling. *Our* numbers are falling. We're covered in darkness. It's the same darkness that built the Wall around this city. It touched you when you were born. You were swaddled in a black blanket. It left a mark I can't erase."

I failed to understand her. I loved her to death, but I started thinking the flesh-eating bacteria might have taken a dark turn somewhere and acquired a taste for grey matter, if you catch my drift.

I like to think I understand it all now. I have learned some things since then.

"Sooner or later, one way or another, you're going to lose some light. We all lose some light, eventually. There's no hiding from it. But the beauty of it is that we don't have to lose it completely. We have a choice. You always have a choice. If you fight for what's left, you can keep it. Even if it's only a single lumen, it's enough. All I'm asking from you, Elliott, is that you fight. For a time, it won't feel like a struggle, but as you grow, so will your shadow."

Imagine a young boy crying without knowing why.

Now, ask yourself how he still knows to cry.

Release doesn't require reason.

Clarity isn't a prerequisite for catharsis.

The dandelion doesn't wonder how it ended up in the field.

It just keeps growing.

"If I don't tell you all of this now, I may never get the chance. I can't trust your father to pass these words on. One day, he may come around and find his light, but I'll be gone by then. Just remember everything I told you, even if you don't understand. Someday, you may find yourself in a situation where your light hangs in the balance. When that day comes, look back on this moment. Remember it. Remember me."

She died the next day.

Dr. Faraday visited her body and confirmed her death. He claimed it wasn't cancer that took her life, but he wouldn't say anything beyond that. My father just nodded. Stubborn as he was, he didn't bother fighting for an explanation. He either didn't care or knew something I didn't.

I was left to fill in the blanks, so I made up a reason for her death.

Wild bacterial infections incubated inside her body. One day, they all exploded. By then, her immune system had already left town. The infections raged through her bloodstream, flowing toward the lake of septic shock. Sepsis collapsed several organ systems simultaneously. Her body became a filthy breeding ground for microscopic beasts. My father became a single parent.

All of this explains why I held myself back from digging through Gertrude's property for so long. I didn't want to lose my light. I didn't want to curb stomp my lumen.

I never said this would make sense. If you're confused, that's on you, not me. No one's forcing you to keep me company.

Adjust tracking. Continue playback.

A war raged inside me for the better part of a year. My mom's voice echoed within my bedroom walls at night. I barely slept. I needed a way out of this, and I found one. I felt so stupid that I didn't see it before. The answer was there the entire time.

Sooner or later, one way or another, I was going to lose some light. There was no hiding from it. But I didn't have to lose it completely. I always had the choice to fight and hold on to what's left. Even if it's just a single lumen.

So there you go. It was inevitable. Might as well get it over with. What better time than now, I thought.

That's how you bend words.

From the moment I found the Vultures in the backyard, I felt the strongest desire to uncover their past. But I never asked *why* I wanted it so much. Shouldn't it be obvious?

I don't know. Should it?

Am I talking to myself again?

Did I ever stop?

It's not that I couldn't figure out the reason; I didn't ask myself why for—I don't know—six or seven years. For the longest time, I lived in a fog, if you could even call it *living*. Ever since the rest stop, confusion was my constant. That, and the occasional blackout. I felt wide awake and dead at the same time, all the time.

Days and days and days—I followed Charlie around the house, or he followed me. Sometimes it's hard to tell the difference because we never went anywhere or did anything. We wandered like the zombies in my father's favorite movie. It didn't take long to realize we had nowhere to go and nothing to do. No purpose. We zombie-walked to our beds and sat around all day, every day. Sure, it was comfortable, but comfort isn't happiness.

I'm not sure how to fully explain my headspace in the years that followed.

My brain went everywhere, but I felt nothing. I lost everything, but I didn't cry about it. Instead, I shut down. I internalized everything. My adolescent instincts kicked in and reinforced all defense mechanisms. I put up my castle walls. To this day, they stand tall and unwavering. I keep them properly maintained at all times.

This probably explains why I'm such a goddamn introvert, but there's more to me than that.

Beneath my bashful exterior, you'll find a boiling ocean of blood.

At the bottom of the ocean, there's a monster.

In time, I narrowed down three reasons why I obsessed over the Vultures. I tend to notice things in threes. We all have our patterns.

The first reason: they were dangerous.

From a very young age, probably from birth, violence found a home in their identities. I'd say it comes standard with children given up by their parents, but these boys took it to a higher level. Gertrude seemed way too chill about it.

"Oh, don't get so worked up. They're just going through a phase. Let them feel their feelings."

Whatever that means.

Their sadistic hearts scared and intrigued me. I had to know how they became this way. Everything has a beginning, even evil things. Oh, and I've always been drawn to violence.

The second reason: they were happy—or something like it.

Sure, darkness shimmered in their smiles, but they still smiled. We all lived in the same cage, but they found excitement in the small world around them—something I couldn't do.

I wasn't happy *or* sad, though. Like I said, I didn't cry. I just couldn't. I tried crying many times. I'd stand in front of the mirror and try to force the tears out. It never worked. I felt stupid for trying.

Even now, at eighteen, I feel nothing. Well, not all the time. If the stars align, I can feel alive, whatever that means. "Alive" isn't the best word to describe me, but it used to be. It really used to be.

The third reason: the Grey Man.

He appeared in the backyard with the Vultures like he had been summoned by them. I had to figure out how they were connected.

I went a number of years without giving the Grey Man much thought. I blame it on the fog in my head. You know, the whole zombie-walking-in-a-total-daze thing. Also, time has this funny way of flooding your basement. It waters things down.

I saw him three times over a decade ago, and then, nothing. Years went by; he didn't show up.

No night terrors.

No unexpected encounters.

No cryptic monologues.

Time suggested he was a bad dream. At best, a stressed-induced hallucination.

Charlie saw him too, but maybe he didn't. Maybe I was just seeing things, and Charlie was just seeing things.

I love that phrase: "seeing things." It's such an easy way to deny a thing's existence.

When the Grey Man first showed up, it was like he materialized in the air. I didn't see him enter the rest stop or the backyard or my bedroom. He was just there. I never saw him leave either; I blacked out before I had the chance. Was it a coincidence? A side effect?

What do you think?

When the Vultures circled Charlie and me in the backyard, I saw the Grey Man's silhouette. He didn't stand next to James; James stood next to him. There's a difference.

After that, time did its thing, and I thought nothing more of those encounters. I went on with my pathetic life. Years passed, and he didn't come back around. He didn't bother Charlie either. We stopped talking about him. I lived without purpose.

Pause the tape.

I can tell you're judging me right now.

You're ripping me apart. I know this. I feel this.

It's funny, but I'm also offended. If you're going to look down on me like this, let me remind you: I didn't abandon my family.

My family abandoned *me*.

I didn't choose to be left at a fucking rest stop. I didn't sign up for an eleven-year sabbatical at an orphanage. I didn't ask for this.

I'm allowed to deal with it any way I want. So please, don't shake your finger at my decisions. I didn't forget my sister. I didn't give up on her. Things just got in the way. If you want a better explanation, too bad. I don't have one. If my choices don't meet your expectations, that's fine. I don't owe you anything. It doesn't matter.

Unpause.

On my fourteenth birthday, I was dumb enough to think that Gertrude would reveal her Vulture-centric secrets to me.

All I got was another Maudlin history lesson. After nearly eight years of getting nowhere, I finally had enough.

I thought about choking her. I know; it's not my brightest idea. I didn't do it, though, I swear. I was about to. I almost did. I was ready to cash in my lumens, but something interrupted me. Just thinking about it makes me sick.

Gertrude and I sat at the kitchen table. The Vultures gathered in the yard. We watched them for a while. It took me a second to figure out what the hell they were doing. Most days, they'd be out there punching each other in the face or whatever, but this was different.

They stood in a circle, looking at the ground. One at a time, they took turns throwing an object against the ground as hard as they could. Sharp, blue slivers danced in the air upon impact.

Every muscle in my body turned to stone.

I frantically dug my hand into my right pocket. Nothing there. I started shaking, hyperventilating. I fell to my knees.

Bill materialized from nowhere and stuck around just long enough to be a smart ass.

"You may not agree, much less understand, but I would argue that you are a living example of transitive relation."

His superiority complex did most of the driving as he got older.

The Vultures stole something very dear to me. I watched as they took turns smashing the sacred object to nothingness.

It was a gift from my mom.

She used to tell me stories about all the places she lived. I've lost track over the years. I'm pretty sure she lived everywhere at some point. The more I think about her stories, the more I realize just how little I know about her past. I've uncovered a few things, but most of it is probably lost forever.

She was an orphan like me, but our origin stories don't align. I was born with parents and ended up abandoned. She was abandoned at birth and eventually found one of her parents after years and years of searching. That's half the reason why she lived everywhere, and it half-explains how she ended up here. She just needed a little help getting through the Gate.

After a month of wandering around the Three Carolinas, she met my father. She found him at a dive bar outside of Maudlin. That sounds about right.

"I swore to myself I'd never date a guy I met at a bar," she said. "I ended up marrying one."

Funny how life works sometimes.

I took a lot of pills today.

Before my mom met my father and followed him into Maudlin, she visited a rock shop in South Carolina—Beckham's Barn. She went there to buy a gift for me. I wasn't born yet. She wasn't even pregnant with me. I was barely an idea, but just enough of one. Just enough. It reminds me of something she told me once.

"You are the best idea I ever had."

She bought me a rock for five dollars.

A lapis lazuli, or lapis for short.

Its egg-shaped form was as smooth as glass. Flecks of golden yellow pyrite danced in jagged lines across deep blue sodalite stone.

Sometimes I know cool words.

I spent entire days of my sad life just staring at the thing.

It was gorgeous, and it was mine.

"There's something really special about this little guy," she said.

She placed the stone in my tiny hands.

I'd like to take a moment to note that my mom called the lapis a "little guy." She spoke with such approachability. Even though I was a small child, she talked to me like I was much, much bigger.

"This is a stone of protection. It will keep you safe, my love. It sounds strange, I know, but I wouldn't steer you wrong. If it's okay with you, I'd like you to take care of it. Hold it in your hands from time to time. Feel its warmth. Let it protect you. Close your eyes. Believe. I love you."

The next day, I found out she had cancer.

My mom sewed a zipper pocket in my pants to keep the stone with me at all times. That's the type of person she was. She didn't just give me a thoughtful, magic-wielding gift. She got me the right pants for it too.

Somehow, my sacred stone fell into the hands of those Vultures. I'm not pointing fingers here, but it was probably Gertrude's fault. She washed our clothes every week, and it's more than likely that she washed my jeans with the lapis still in the right-front pocket. I couldn't prove that she was guilty of this, but it seemed fitting.

No fair trial here.

It used to go missing for days at a time.

I insisted on doing my own laundry after that. I hate it when people touch my things.

After I fell to my knees, my brain was like, "Let's kill them," and delivered a heavy dose of epinephrine.

The sensation was so heavy; I had to pay extra for shipping and handling.

I know how mail works.

I flew into the backyard, ready to destroy the world.

A few minutes later, I returned with the lapis.

Gertrude nearly had a heart attack. Her horrified face still lives in my memory. If you saw what happened to me, your face would have looked the same—minus the haphazardly-applied lipstick.

Two black eyes, a rack of bruised ribs, and blood all over my face. Most of it poured from my nose. I had to spit some blood from my mouth. No broken bones, though. I've somehow gone my entire life without breaking a bone. I mean, I've broken bones that belong to other people, but I've never broken my own.

The stone was in much worse condition. Half of it was still intact, but the rest of it lay scattered throughout the yard in a million pieces. It lost its perfect egg shape. It was no longer beautiful. Holding the half-destroyed stone in my hands made me want to die. This pretty much sums up my entire life.

In a flash of rage, I spit blood in Gertrude's face. I regret that.

"You see?! Do you see what I go through because of them?! This is the *only* thing I have left of my mom. This! It's all I have! Now, look at it! Look at what they did! After all this bullshit, the *least* you can do is *explain them to me!*"

That's all I could say, but it was enough. The blood helped too. I was on fire. This was my first rage episode; it wasn't the last.

My rage evaporated the moment I stormed out of the kitchen. I felt terrible, but at the same time, I kind of felt good. I mean, I felt bad for blowing up at her and spitting blood in her face, but those feelings had been festering inside me for far too long.

The weight had been lifted from me but in the worst way.

I peeked into the kitchen from the hallway. Gertrude's hands shook as she struggled to wipe my blood from her face. She started crying. I came back.

We sat at the kitchen table, again, for a while.

She kept crying. I kept quiet. I wanted to say something like *I'm sorry*, or *I didn't mean it*. I wanted to put my hand on her shoulder or give her a stupid hug. But I couldn't remove my armor. It's stuck to my skin.

"I can't help but pretend, Elliott. Especially in the presence of children—you, Charlie, Anna, Delilah, all of you. As a surrogate mother of sorts, it's my instinct to protect you from all the rotten things around us. There's no place like this in the entire world. We're surrounded by an unclimbable wall, locked in with every unspeakable horror, and we can't leave."

"My father left. Explain that."

"Your father is a man of many secrets."

"Was."

"Was, yes. Anyway, I'm afraid I can't explain his special treatment, dear. I don't have that knowledge."

Liar.

"Everything changed when Alexander Morris arrived from the West. His proximity birthed the misfortunes of this place."

"What happened?"

"We'll save that for another time. For now, let me tell you about the boys outside."

She pointed at the kitchen window. The Vultures were punching each other in the face and laughing about it.

"Are you joshing me, or is this for real?"

"I don't understand your words, child."

"Never mind."

Gertrude took a breath, rolled her eyes, and shook her head.

"Now, Elliott, before I go any further, I want you to know that parts of this story, or maybe the entire thing, will sound far-fetched. Please trust me when I say that it's all real. Everything I'm about to tell you—it happened. Everything happened."

She took another drawn-out breath.

"There's a reason why those boys believe they fell from the sky. James reinforces this idea into their heads every day, but there's a reason behind it. I admit I can't explain why things transpired the way they did. I can only say what happened. The rest lies in the hands and minds of the Maudlin Authority."

"The Moths? How?"

She responded with a grunt, seeming frustrated with herself or with me. Maybe both.

"I need to start over. Yes, let me start over."

She took another deep breath. It sounded like broken glass rattled in her chest.

"There's no beginning to this story, but I'll begin at the closest thing to a beginning."

I still have a hard time believing everything she said. You may not believe it either.

"If I'm correct, Elliott, you were born on the first of August in the year 1985."

"Yeah, I think so."

"Well, a couple of months after you were born, something happened—something nobody expected. It was sudden, it was quick, and worst of all, it happened again after that. Then it happened again and again."

She stared into oblivion.

"First, it happened at the Maudlin Cemetery on one of the quietest nights. A rare occurrence—no riots, no gunshots, not even the wind made a fuss. And it was cold. Very cold—even for October. But there was something else about the night—something you couldn't see, hear, or feel. Perhaps strange energy dangling in the air. An omen. A sign of ill things to come, and I was there.

"I stood there, for a time, waiting for it. All the while, my ears kept playing tricks on me. I thought I heard the wind picking up, but the air remained still. Still, I heard it. I heard something. Off in the distance, but not too distant, a howl pierced the silence. It was neither wolf nor wind. It sounded desperate and menacing.

"The night's chill seeped into my bones, but I refused to leave. In time, my stubbornness was rewarded; I heard something else: a voice. It was the voice inside my head. *Follow the howl*, it said. The wind picked up at that very moment. It blew my hat right off and ripped the veil from my face. As I pawed the air for my veil, the corner of my left eye detected a shadow at the far end of the cemetery. I caught it just in time to watch it dissolve where it stood."

Gertrude's eyes turned glassy.

"I'm not crazy," she said. "I know what I saw. I know what I see."

She *is* crazy but not because of this.

"The wind left with the shadow. The howl fell silent. I followed the direction of where the shadow stood. One hundred paces exactly. There, I found myself beneath a dying willow tree. Much of its bark had been removed by time. Years and years of lashing wind. I felt its pain beneath the bark."

She reached out at nothing and touched the willow in her mind.

"But there was something else: rustling, scraping, cloth and metal, movement. The contorted tree obscured my view. Something stood behind it. I peered at the other side and found a metal can for discarding waste. An ordinary object, yes, but I turned white when I saw what lay inside."

She forced her words out between the sobs and shaky breaths.

"It was a child—new to the world. As new as new can be; the umbilical cord was still attached! Oh, Elliott, I nearly fainted. I wish I had. It's hard to scream in an unconscious state. I screamed so loud, my boy. Everyone within earshot followed the sound. My scream birthed a crowd. Among the crowd stood two Maudlin Authority agents. There were always agents in the cemetery."

That's still true. There are always agents in the cemetery.

"The agents slinked through the gathering of onlookers, removed the infant child from the trash can, and slithered off into the night. I didn't stop them. I couldn't. I just kept shouting, 'I'm so sorry, sweet angel! I'm so sorry I screamed!'"

"Why couldn't you stop them?"

"They knew who I was, and I knew them. We had crossed paths before—several times. I had made an agreement with them once upon a time. It's the reason why I couldn't stop them."

"What agreement?"

She ignored my question.

"The crowd melted away. I was alone again as if none of it ever happened, but it *did* happen. I felt touched by that child in a way I didn't understand. It just goes to show you, my boy. If you're brand new to this world, even just a few minutes old—you can still change things. You can move people. You have that power."

"What are you talking about?"

"Everything."

She motioned a circle with her frail left hand.

Okay, so maybe this story does make her sound crazy.

There's some truth behind her nonsense, though. When I was born, something weird happened to me.

I don't remember it, *obviously,* but the event was documented.

It was worth writing about, I guess. Of course, you shouldn't believe everything you read, and you shouldn't believe everything you hear. Use your head or your gut or whatever.

Pick your organ of choice.

If this story was a ship, we'd be breathing salt water right now.

"That night haunted me for weeks. I bought a color television to distract myself. The distraction actually worked! It became a habit, a ritual, my obsession. Every evening, I watched MASS. I sank into its warm embrace of misinformation. It sang me to sleep."

I remember that TV very well. We used to play "I Spy" while watching the news. Delilah made us guess the object of her gaze on the screen. I always guessed wrong on purpose.

"I spy something red."

The suit's face as he fed us our daily dose of diarrhea.

"I spy something orange."

The increasing levels of iron and manganese in our water supply.

"I spy something black."

My mind.

"Another newborn was discovered in a trash can five weeks later. Umbilical cord and everything! I saw it on the news program. They didn't find it in the cemetery like the first time. This one appeared at Wixom Station. You know—that old abandoned train station at the northernmost part of town."

Once upon a time, trains passed through Maudlin. They don't anymore.

"According to the newsman, the child was safe in the hands of the Maudlin Authority. That's like claiming a lamb is safe with a lion. Lies, child! I'm livid and winded just thinking about it."

"You don't have to keep going if you don't—"

"Stop it! Yes, I do. I must finish this, boy. I *must* finish this."

I'd never seen her like this before. I understood why she bottled this up for so long. Revisiting old wounds and all. But in hindsight, I think it was good for her. You can only internalize so much for so long before it eats away at your insides.

Unsettled memories are unsettling. Something like that.

"Elliott, my dear child, there's a fine line between coincidence and conspiracy, as you'll soon find out. Something sinister is at work here. This is just a taste."

I miss the taste of blueberry pancakes and coffee.

The only thing I taste now is blood.

"I was out caroling with Henry Schroeder."

Oh yeah—Henry. Gertrude never talked about him. This was the first time I ever heard his name. He's the closest thing she ever had to a partner.

"As we passed Sacred Dark Hospital, a crowd of boisterous Maudlings gathered around the main entrance. I thought it was grand to see such a gaggle on Christmas night. Finally, an audience! Earlier that evening, for the longest time, we sang to no one. So many empty homes."

I never believed in Santa. My father told me he wasn't real from the start. You'd think my mom would have been pissed about that, but she sided with him. She felt that reinforcing a belief in Santa created a distorted line between reality and fiction. It was one of the few times I witnessed my parents bonding over a shared belief.

I guess you could say Santa brought my parents closer together.

Thanks, Santa.

Aliens are real, though.

Maybe Santa is an alien.

Oh my god, Elliott, get it together.

Gertrude deserves better than this.

"Henry and I sang 'A Boy Is Born in Bethlehem' as we made our way to the crowd. We interlocked our arms, walked in unison, and sang to each other's souls. Oh, the euphoria. It was the happiest I had felt in ages. The moment was fleeting. Oh, that moment. That sweet, sweet moment."

I didn't interrupt. I liked this tangent. She was in love.

"Oh, forgive me, boy. I'm getting all worked up. Henry was very dear to me. That's all. But I shouldn't get myself too carried away right now. No time to dawdle!"

Dawdling means wasting time. For example, I'm dawdling right now by taking the time to explain what dawdling means. And now, I'm dawdling by telling you that I'm dawdling.

"We continued caroling until we reached the edge of the crowd. No one paid attention to our performance. They didn't notice at all! Their eyes fixated on the ground beneath them. I couldn't see what drew their attention—I'm a short little lady—but I didn't have to. I already knew what they had found. Henry, being over six feet tall, could see just fine. Oh, Elliott, he was whiter than a bedsheet soaked in bleach. He vomited all over me. Others were vomiting too. To this day, I haven't seen a greater collection of bodily fluids."

Thank you, but I didn't need to know that.

"Another newborn lay in a trash can, covered in blood, barely breathing, hugging its absent mother's umbilical cord. But I wasn't appalled or afraid. This wasn't a crisis. This wasn't vomit-inducing pandemonium. Not for me! My boy, this was a chance for me to redeem myself after letting the first two infants slip away. On this night, I was Maudlin's lone heroine, protecting the unprotected against an inhumane pseudo-government of fallen men.

"I removed my overcoat and swaddled the child. Together, we stormed into Sacred Dark Hospital. I left Henry outside. As I carried the child down the endless halls of the hospital, I felt so alive, overflowing with love. Another perfect moment, just like the moment I shared with Henry. Such rarities—these moments—and it ended in tragedy."

She raised two white-knuckled fists and rattled an invisible cage.

"They took the child from my arms."

"Who?"

"Men in masks. Surgeons, maybe? Oh, Elliott, I don't remember. They had to take the child, right? I mean, we were in a hospital."

She looked to me for validation. I said nothing.

Sometimes, when I'm here, I'm really not.

"The baby needed medical attention, warmth, medication, bathing, everything. I couldn't have done anything, right? I'm not a doctor. I'm not a nurse. I'm nothing. I didn't follow the child down Sacred Dark's corridors. I thought it would be okay if I waited until morning. I would check on the sweet child then. Besides, poor Henry waited for me outside, covered in frozen vomit. He needed my feminine comfort."

Gross.

"But when I stepped outside, he was gone. I figured he had walked home to clean himself up. Henry was a clumsy fellow, but he could look after himself, so I went back inside the hospital. I sat down to decompress and gather myself. I only intended to rest my eyes for a minute. Intentions are funny like that, though. When I opened my eyes again, it was morning. I slept all night in the lobby."

It makes me depressed when people fall asleep unintentionally.

I don't know why.

"I raced to the front desk in a tizzy. Two security guards stood near the desk, watching me intently. They were expecting me. I saw it in their eyes. The man behind the desk gave me an odd look—he was expecting me too. I asked him about the infant, but I already knew the answer before he had the chance to speak. His response echoed my suspicion."

There is no child. There never was. I must ask you to leave.

"The guards dragged me out of the hospital. I walked home, but I don't remember a single step. I only recall waking up in bed several hours later. The journey home is lost on me."

Full disclosure: Gertrude had an on-again-off-again drinking problem. That might have had something to do with her memory loss. She hid it from us very well, but toward the end, not so much. In her final days, she drank herself sick every waking moment. After everything she's gone through, I don't blame her. I'd do the same.

I already have.

"Two months passed. It was February 1986. The new year and my old bones made an odd pair, like crying and laughing at the same time. I couldn't stop thinking about those poor children. I imagined all the ghastly, dreadful things they were being subjected to. Take it from me, Elliott. The Maudlin Authority do not believe in the sanctity of life. They are not here to protect us."

"What did the Moths want with those babies?" I asked.

Saying it out loud, it's a funny question.

"The Maudlin Authority is a four-headed beast. The Exploratory Solutions Division carried out the abduction and subsequent experimentation of the infants. On second thought, it would be untrue to call it an abduction. Let's call this what it is, my dear. It was a trade."

"A trade? With who?"

"Whom."

"Whatever. Just tell me."

"Your questions breed more questions that I'm not prepared to answer. My strength and stamina are phantoms of their former selves. Let them rest for now. Please."

"Then why bring it up at all?"

"Silence, boy!"

I didn't press her any further, but I got my way in the end. I eventually went through all of her stuff and found out on my own.

The Moths made a pact with the Enders. Well, not all of them. Just some of them. The good ones, or the bad ones. It depends on how you look at it, I guess.

The Moths eventually made a deal with Gertrude too, but that was a different kind of deal.

It's all connected. Everything.

I don't expect you to understand.

"My lonely heart and baffled brain led me to The Phoenix every night for weeks and weeks. I perched myself at the bar, drinking brandy wine from a snifter. This new nightly ritual of inebriation replaced the television."

Oh, The Phoenix. How I love thee.

"One night, after several rounds of brandy, I stumbled out the back door of the bar. It was the last time I ever drank, and as far as I'm concerned, it will always be the last."

Those words didn't age well.

"As I fumbled around in the dark behind the bar, I heard the cries of infant children. It was happening again! My blurred, double vision somehow spotted two metal trash cans. I thought this was the brandy's doing—playing tricks on my cerebellum—but when I lost my balance down the alleyway, I found out the hard way that there were indeed two trash cans. I tripped over one and hit my face on the other. Dear Elliott, I am a monster."

"You're not a monster."

I didn't know what else to say. What are you supposed to say when someone calls themself a monster that starts bawling? Should you even say anything? I'm convinced there are times in life when words have no power. This was clearly one of those times, but I had nothing else in my toolbox. I don't like touching people, and I don't care for awkward silence.

I told her she's not a monster for my benefit, not hers.

I'm a monster.

This is the part where you say I'm not a monster.

She ignored my selfish reassurance. Thank you, baby Jesus.

"When I knocked the trash cans over, two babies fell out. One in each! Mind you, I was about halfway through vomiting up all the brandy I had drunk earlier. Just imagine: a dirty old woman crawling on the floor of the earth, vomiting, reaching her cold, shriveled hands toward the new lives that laid beside her, and with a smile. In my poisoned mind, I was saving them. I was giving them another chance. I was given another chance. Then I blacked out.

"I woke up the next morning, in the same spot, with a dry mouth, an empty stomach, and a tempestuous headache. Oh, and the infants were gone—taken by the Maudlin Authority, I presumed. I wanted to die. I wanted to kill myself. The one thing I had, which I never really had at all, was taken from me. Do you understand?"

"No."

I didn't understand then, but I do now.

"So, did you kill yourself?" I asked.

Yes, I asked that. Maybe it was the lack of sleep, or maybe I slipped into some weird alternate reality, but for a second, I honestly didn't know the answer to that question. Still, she answered without judgment.

"No, my dear. I nearly ran myself into traffic, but instead, I walked past the man with the cart who sells odds and ends and bought some lipstick. I wanted to feel pretty."

Don't we all.

"As soon as I got home, I gathered all of my art supplies and made posters."

"What? Posters? Like movie posters?"

I've only ever had one movie poster. I hung it above my bed in my apartment shortly after I moved in. *Edward Scissorhands.* It's a movie about a guy who can't touch people.

Okay, so it wasn't *my* apartment.

"No, Elliott. I made posters—advertisements—for my foray into foster care. From that day on, my home would be an orphanage. I named it The Amulet as a tribute to someone I used to know. Someone very, very dear to me. She gave me this once upon a time."

Gertrude reached into the neck of her cardigan and revealed an amulet dangling from a thin, silver chain.

"What are the odds!" she shouted, showing me the lapis lazuli at the center of the amulet.

"Where is she now?"

"It depends on what you mean by *where*."

Her answer made me feel fantastically uncomfortable. I changed the subject.

"So, what happened next?"

"For a year and some odd months, no one responded to my posters, but everything changed in the summer of 1987 when Anna showed up at my doorstep. Then Delilah on the first day of spring in 1988. Then Bill just two months later. I must be truthful: I felt I was in over my head after Bill came to me. Looking after children is a full-time job. I didn't want to burn myself out or stretch myself too thin. I stopped taking in new children, or so I thought. So I thought.

"It was the end of November—1990. I went into town and removed the remaining posters. When I got home, I found five young boys in *ESD Patient* sweatshirts standing on my front porch. It had been nearly five years since I drunkenly stumbled upon the Phoenix twins. Now, here they all were. All five trash can kids. They looked horrible, pale, malnourished, expressionless."

"How did they get there?"

"They sure didn't come to my home of their own volition. The Maudlin Authority had no use for them anymore. Their experiments had failed."

"What experiments?"

"I don't know."

Liar.

"Okay, but who brought them to the house?"

"Henry. It was Henry. He brought them to me."

"What? Henry? How?"

"Henry was a plant."

I imagined Gertrude visiting Henry on the weekends to water him and change his soil. I laughed so hard that I fell on the floor.

You can add this moment to my list of regrets.

Gertrude left the room. That was it for her. She made no mention of Henry ever again. Of course, that didn't stop me from finding out about his involvement. He wrote her a letter. She kept it. I found it.

Let's talk about plants.

Plants are Maudlin Authority agents pretending to be ordinary people. The Moths place these plants all over the city. They have eyes on everything, and you'd never know. They're that good at faking it. Gertrude may have had a talent for spotting bullshit, but Henry got the best of her.

Henry's letter to Gertrude was dated December 24, 1985—three days after the Sacred Dark trash can baby incident. He started by confessing his involvement with the Moths. By the end, you would have thought you were reading a suicide note. You know, the whole I-can't-do-this-anymore thing. In between, he rambled about the children and how the Moths wanted them to unlock a door. He also mentioned something about an unlimited, unreachable energy source. His handwriting suggested he was in a hurry. I couldn't make sense of it all.

Gertrude insisted that Henry delivered the children to her home, but there's no way that could have happened. The day after he wrote the letter, he killed himself. Someone found him in his bathtub, bathing in blood that flowed from his wrists. The Vultures showed up *five years* later.

Someone else had to have been involved.

This matches up with the "secret friend" that Henry mentioned in his letter—another plant with a change of heart—but he didn't give a name. Gertrude didn't have any files on him either.

Very strange.

Henry promised that the children were alive and would eventually find their way home.

His secret friend must have fulfilled that promise.

For the record, that secret friend owes me one egg-shaped lapis lazuli stone.

8 — Thirty Strikes

ALEXANDER MORRIS. I HAVEN'T FORGOTTEN HIM.

His story and my story are the same.

Sit me up a little higher, please. I'm not breathing well.

What if I told you that he's the reason why all this is happening? I'm almost sure of this, but I can't be entirely certain. Gertrude died before confirming my suspicions, although she left many artifacts behind. One thing is for damn sure, though: Most events surrounding Alexander are, in many ways, connected to me.

Then again, we're all connected, stuck inside Maudlin together, forced to live a prisoner's life.

A part of me clings to the idea that none of this means anything. Wall or no Wall—it doesn't matter. We're collectively trapped—every living, breathing human being—in the same meaningless nightmare.

Please pardon my brain.

Alexander was a respected and charismatic man—a charming cult leader. I say he *was* because he's not those things anymore. He's not those things anymore because he's dead. I know this because Gertrude knows this. She watched him die.

I watched too.

Stop.

Rewind. Rewind. Rewind. Rewind.

Stop.

Play.

Too soon.

Stop.

Rewind.

Stop.

Play.

Perfect.

I didn't mean to cough blood on you. Apologies.

Let's pick up where we left off: Alexander and the Nine reached the place that would eventually become Maudlin, West Carolina. The following day, they started building.

Aside from Alexander, no one had any clue what they were doing. They didn't know where to start, so he showed them the way. He educated them about shelters and explained how to build one. He taught them how to farm. He identified which crops grow best in an 8a hardiness zone.

The Nine were amazed by his extensive knowledge. It was like he knew everything. Still, some of them were equally as frightened.

The village started as a few tents and huts. Within the first week, they dug a well. Alexander knew how to build one, which is funny since he also died in one.

At the center of their little world, they built a massive fire pit. They lit a fire, and the fire never went out. It's still burning in Maudlin Cemetery. I've seen it. I've touched it. I don't understand it.

Don't try to put it out. You'll burn half your face off.

Every night, Alexander gathered the villagers around the undying fire. He gave simple, motivating speeches. Sometimes, he shared long stories about their walk across the country. I don't understand that. What's the point? Everyone had experienced that deathly journey. They don't need to hear about it. They shouldn't have to relive it.

Some reminders go too far.

Every speech, story, and musing ended the same way; he recited his stupid prayer or whatever it was:

> *Build your homes strong. Make them last for lifetimes to come.*
>
> *Build your hearts steadfast. Make them beacons of pride and loyalty to your new city, your new life.*
>
> *This is your land, but I with great sincerity that it will not always be.*
>
> *This is a sojourn. Something much greater is coming. Bigger than the earth itself. I will bring it to you.*
>
> *Each and every one of you.*
>
> *Leave and die. Stay and live forever.*

That's how this city got its name. Originally, Maudlin wasn't Maudlin. Alexander and the Nine called it Sojourn. It stayed that way for a while, but when Alexander died, everything sort of went to hell, and now here we are.

That's an oversimplification.

Less than a year later, Sojourn transformed dramatically. For one thing, the Nine were on the cusp of multiplying. That's too bad. The Nine is a cool name. They really screwed that up when their first baby was born. Eventually, they started calling themselves Sojourners. They really messed up.

Sojourn—what a stupid name. Do you know what a sojourn is? It's a temporary stay. To sojourn is to stay somewhere for a short time, and yet here we are.

How am I supposed to get through this when I keep stopping myself?

Around the time the Nine became the Ten, a group of masons found Sojourn and made it their home. They used their skilled hands and Alexander's unlimited knowledge, replacing the tents and huts with spacious houses made of brick and stone.

It didn't end there. Everyone started showing up.

Hunters and fishermen from the east coast moved inland and helped expand their settlement. Farmers tended to acres of emptiness until the land flourished. Pipelayers and steamfitters constructed a system of pipes that connected Sojourn to the ocean. It removed salt from the ocean water, making it safe for consumption by humans and plants.

They had everything they needed to survive.

Still, despite their growth and progress, Alexander reminded his people, every evening, that all of this was temporary. This confused everyone. Myself included.

"This guy's an idiot," I shouted.

Gertrude and I sat at the picnic table in the backyard. It was shortly after midnight on my sixteenth birthday.

I loved that picnic table.

"Why put so much into something if you're just going to leave it all behind?"

"Well, my boy, you have a point there."

She laughed at my naivety while I thought I had it all figured out. When you're sixteen, you think you know everything. Eventually, you'll realize that you know nothing. What a brutal crash landing that will be.

"Nearly everything about Alexander Morris made little to no sense," she continued. "After all, he did travel clear across the entire country, on foot no less, encouraging every soul within proximity to join him, subsequently risking their lives. He told them to build a city from nothing. And after all of this, he reinforced the idea that it would all go back to nothing. So you're right, boy. You're right. It's hard to say Alexander Morris wasn't something of a halfwit."

"Obviously."

"But I find it strangely interesting, Elliott, that you waited until now to call him such a thing."

"What do you mean?"

Gertrude talked me into a trap.

"You take offense when Alexander addresses his people about the impermanence of their home, yet nothing else about his story so far has ruffled you to this extent. Now, I find that interesting."

She didn't miss a thing.

"I don't get it! Why would anyone build a city just to tear it down and leave? That obviously didn't happen. The city's still here. So what the hell is this nonsense?"

"Silence! Now, Elliott Avenue, you listen! I made no mention of anyone tearing down or leaving anything!

"Sure sounds like Alex did."

"His name was Alex*ander.*"

I had a knack for exhausting her.

"I need a minute," she whispered, hobbling off the picnic table and retreating to the house. She did that sometimes. Our conversations weren't always pleasant. She'd have to step back and take a break, but she always came back. I just had to give her time.

I sat there for about ten minutes, waiting for her to return.

I can be a bit much. I know that.

On her way back, I saw the pain in her eyes. Walking wasn't easy for her anymore. Time has its way with us all.

She plopped her sack of bones on the picnic table and took two rattled breaths.

"Now, my boy, if I ever implied that Alexander expressed a desire to pack up and leave, then I am sorry. I'm merely the messenger."

Her breathing changed.

"Alexander spoke in riddles, metaphors, and sideways talk, but he was not an idiot. He knew exactly what he was saying, doing, thinking, planning—all the time—with heavy intention and conviction. He was the harbinger of unutterable change. Not just a change in location, but something much greater."

Something much greater is coming. Bigger than the earth itself. I will bring it to you.

He said it himself.

"I'm sorry, Elliott, but I have to stop now. I don't feel very well. I must lie down for the night. We will continue this next year, on your eighteenth birthday."

"Seventeen. I'll be seventeen next year."

She didn't respond.

We shared silence until she broke it with violent snoring. I carried her into the house and put her to bed.

Sixteen was the worst year of my life.

Nothing happened. Each day blurred into the next. A dull rhythm tapped on my skull with the passing of time.

I'd wake up, brush my teeth, roam around the house for about half an hour, go back to my room, lie in bed, talk to Charlie—he rarely left the room—then I might eat something before zombie-walking into the backyard to watch the sunset. After the sun fell, I dropped myself into bed. That was it. Colorless. Uneventful. Every day.

Imagine a record skipping for all eternity.

I was depressed. I wanted to kill myself.

It's hard to grasp what someone is going through when they say those words: *I'm depressed.*

Unless you're being devoured by a dark cloud of your own, you can't understand or sympathize.

Just so you know, depression kills. It almost took me. I'm not sure how to explain it.

It is, as Gertrude would say, unutterable.

I was going to end myself with pills—Gertrude's pain medication. I know; it's not the most poetic way to go out, but when you think about it, taking an excessive amount of painkillers and listening to old records while waiting to die sounds kind of nice. Well, it sounds nice to me, especially considering the colossal mess I'm in right now.

I didn't plan on living this long.

How many times do I have to die before it finally sticks?

Bill—that hyper-aware weirdo—pointed to a bookshelf next to his bedroom door.

"I have a self-help section. It is not for me, clearly. Take a book if you must."

I didn't know what I was looking for, but I picked one anyway.

The title was a mouthful:

I Could Do Anything If I Only Knew What It Was: How to Discover What You Really Want and How to Get It.

I didn't read it, except for the back cover.

"A life without direction is a life without passion."

Okay, Barb.

Two Barbs, actually: Barbara Sher and Barbara Smith.

The Vultures stayed out of my hair that year. I barely saw them. They locked themselves inside their shared bedroom.

Some nights, I heard them through their bedroom door.

They whispered. It terrified me.

It's in their nature to be loud and obnoxious and rip the heads off of dolls. I got used to that. I never got used to their whispers.

Between those two Augusts, misery and monotony owned me. Day after day, night after night, I did nothing. My brain fired off feelings of crippling despair and impending doom.

Again, I asked myself the same questions.

Why am I still here? Just to suffer?

Why don't I just leave?

Why am I not out there looking for Annabelle?

It had been ten years since I last saw her. I wondered if she was ever real. I convinced myself that she never existed. I was not well. My head wasn't straight. It's still not straight. Time has this funny way of slanting your home's foundation.

Along with my entire family, the Grey Man made it on the list of people who disappeared from my life. He was nowhere to be found. I started to think he forgot about me. It feels weird to say this, but it really bummed me out. You'd think I'd be happy that someone like him stopped coming around, but I only felt forgotten.

He said he had big plans for me.

He promised.

Maybe this was all part of his plan, I thought. Just leave me to my own devices until I'm so lonely and empty that I crave his company.

His plan succeeded. I tried summoning him. I had no idea what I was doing, but I gave it a shot.

It didn't work.

I tried to trigger one of my blackouts just to pass the time. In my brilliant mind, the best method was to smash my head against a blunt object. I chose the picnic table in the backyard.

Did I lose consciousness? Yes, for a minute, but no blackout this time. Just a giant blue-and-purple lump on the side of my head and two different-sized pupils. I learned that smashing your head against stuff won't solve your problems.

Well, that's not entirely true. It depends on the problem.

After a while, I forgot what day it was. I never knew the time. No calendars in the house. No clocks. Gertrude's watch stopped ticking. Somehow, I made it to March, but by that time, I was ready. I couldn't take it anymore.

"I'm going to kill myself."

I lay in bed alone. No one was around.

In the deafening quiet, I contemplated deleting my existence.

Stop. Eject.

Bill stood at my doorway, materializing from nowhere.

"How's the book?" he asked.

"Oh, you mean this book?"

I still had his stupid self-help book. I threw it at his face. It hit his forehead. He didn't flinch.

"I admit that I probably deserved that."

"Could you just leave me alone?"

"That is the problem, Elliott. You have been alone too long."

"Alone? What do you mean? I haven't been alone. I've had your book with me! I cradled that literary masterpiece every night. It sang me to sleep. I have to commend your brilliance, Bill. Your self-help section saved my life. How can I ever repay you? *Please* tell me how I can repay you."

I smashed the back of my head against the bed frame five times. With each blow, I felt everything and nothing at once.

Bill kept his composure.

"Elliott, you are not in debt to me. You owe me nothing. In return, I owe you nothing. I am here because I felt your pain from down the hallway."

"You felt my pain?"

"Do not ask me about that. I am not here to talk. I am here to give you this."

He revealed a flat, bright yellow object from his messenger bag and slid it across the floor. I had never seen anything like it before.

"Discman? What's a Discman?"

"It is an electronic device that plays compact discs. Most people call them CDs. They have music on them. Unfortunately, I lost most of my collection. The boys stole them from my room and used them as Frisbees."

"What's a Frisbee?"

"It is a flying disc."

"What's the difference between a compact disc and a flying disc?"

"Not much. Anyway, there is a CD in the player already. It is not from my collection, though. I found it by chance. Please enjoy. Oh, you will need these."

Bill slid a pair of headphones across the floor. Before I could figure out how to open the CD player, he was gone. He liked to keep things short and sweet. Heavy on the short. Short on the sweet. I didn't mind. I liked it a lot, actually.

When I held the CD player in my hands, I realized I hadn't listened to music since before my mom died. I forgot what it sounded like.

I don't think I was prepared for this.

It took me a minute before I figured out how to work the thing. There were all these buttons and parts. I discovered a little half-circle button on the left side. Four raised letters rested near it: *OPEN*.

Do you know what a mix CD is?

The inside of this alien device housed a disc, just as Bill described. Its smooth, matte surface was littered with words, words, words. The words formed a list. The list had a title:

Play This at My Funeral.

The playlist was written on the CD in black marker:

> Azure Ray — "November"
> Ennio Morricone & Joan Baez — "Here's to You"
> Elliott Smith — "Waltz #1"
> Secret Zeevs — "Incoming Human"
> Bright Eyes — "The Center of the World"
> Bjork — "Joga"
> Radiohead — "How To Disappear Completely"
> Sigur Rós — "Starálfur"
> Glassjaw — "Everything You Ever Wanted to
> Know About Silence"
> Mew — "Comforting Sounds"

I hit the play button and immediately fell into a strange, euphoric trance. Heavy emotions, once buried and forgotten, swam to my surface. They collided and exploded and enmeshed to form new feelings I had never felt before.

I was alive again, or maybe for the first time.

These ten songs saved my life.

I played the mix endlessly, or until the batteries died. That's how I learned what batteries are. Thankfully, the CD player had a little hole on the back of it to plug in a cord. Then you plug the cord into a wall, and it will stay on forever. Bill left one of these cords in front of my door. He must have figured I would need it.

He thought of everything.

I'm not going to give you a track-by-track review of *Play This at My Funeral*. That's not what this is about. This was a long-winded way of saying that I wanted to kill myself, but I didn't do it—thanks to the song on this CD.

Music is medicine.

If you're dying to hear the CD, I have it in my backpack. I don't have my backpack on me, though. I left it behind. We might have to go get it.

* * *

Finally, I made it to seventeen.

Jesus.

I can't believe I made it that far, or this far, all things considered. It's amazing what you can do, even if you have no faith in yourself. Still, I have a hard time finding any victory in "making it" to another birthday. These days, it feels like everything means nothing. It's all just more of the same, and then you die.

Here's my advice to you: when you die, if you get the chance to come back or reincarnate or whatever, don't be a person again. It will only let you down. We're all so screwed up with our sadness and our phobias and neuroses, so fuck it. Be a flower. Be a lobster. Be an amoeba. Just don't be a person, if you can help it.

How about you be a cat? I'll be a cat too. We'll roam the streets together and eat from trash cans and have the time of our lives.

Why does this sound so familiar to me?

Never mind. I know why.

Gertrude and I returned to the backyard picnic table, keeping our ritual alive. It was dark out. I lay on the table, scratching at the red paint. Gertrude sat at the far end. We didn't talk for almost half an hour but for a good reason. The Perseid meteor shower would peak in two weeks; we were already looking up. If we were patient enough, the sky surprised us.

"There's one!"

That's the thing. When you see a meteor, you're always supposed to shout, "There's one!" You just have to.

"Elliott, before we begin, there's a question you want to ask me."

"How did you know?"

"I've left much unsaid. I think it's obvious, my boy, that you're wondering how I ended up here. So please, ask your question."

Her brain was always a hundred steps ahead of mine.

"Were you—are you—one of the Nine?"

"I know you think I am because I know so much. You've believed this for months now."

Maybe two hundred steps.

"How else would you know so much about Alexander? How could you know all these details about his hike across the country? How could you know about his followers and his weird speeches? How could you know *any* of it if you weren't there?"

Gertrude gave me the most serious of looks.

"I wasn't there. I'm not from the West. I'm not one of the Nine, or Ninety-Nine, or any of those numbers. I didn't find Alexander and follow him here. It's quite the opposite, actually. You see, Elliott, Alexander Morris found *me*. I was already here.

"Oh, and Alexander documented everything in his journal. I'm not exactly sure why he had a journal, though, given his nature."

"What does that mean?"

"He just doesn't come off as the journaling type. That's all."

Yeah, okay.

She held Alexander's journal in her hand and spoke to me like she had memorized every single word of it. Either that or she could read with her eyes and the journal closed.

About a year after Alexander and his people settled down in West Carolina and founded Sojourn, they started running low on space. Housing was at full capacity, yet more and more people showed up from all directions, looking for a new life. Alexander started a movement, and everyone within earshot wanted in.

Sojourn responded by expanding vertically, adding upper floors to homes, converting attics and cellars into living spaces, and building bunk beds. This worked, for a little while, until they ran out of resources. People kept coming in. Babies came out of the people. It was a whole thing.

"Fertility and childbirth bloomed in great abundance," Gertrude said. "I've never heard of such a thing happening so aggressively, and I've been around for a very, very long time. Ninety-nine infants were born in the first year alone. For a new town only half a square mile in size, it was both wonderful and devastating."

"Wonderful?" I asked. "How is that wonderful?"

"Childbirth is a beautiful thing, Elliott. All life is sacred."

"I disagree."

"What, may I ask, is your basis for this feeling?"

"On the basis that humans are trash and nothing good happens."

"Oh, dear. We have a lot of work to do."

"Agree to disagree."

"Have it your way, boy. Agree to disagree, for now."

I still feel that way, depending on who I am when you ask.

Let's talk about Samuel Ross.

Samuel Ross was an architect. Alexander found him conveniently camped out near the Savannah River shortly after Sojourn was founded.

"You haven't mentioned this guy before," I said. "What's his deal?"

"Alexander encountered old Samuel along the river and asked if he could join him for a night. The next day, Samuel walked with him back into town. He adopted Sojourn as his new home, became its city planner, and sparked a series of events that led to my eventual entrance into this story.

Samuel could build anything, but not without materials. He needed wood. He needed trees. Luckily, there just so happened to be a massive, old forest located near the town's eastern border.

Remember Ender Forest? That's the one.

All they had to do was cut some trees and get to work, right?

Wrong.

"Samuel stressed the importance of expanding eastward, but Alexander shut him down. Not a single Sojourner stood at Samuel's side in support of the expansion. They all refused to challenge the *brilliant mind* of Alexander Morris."

I rarely witnessed Gertrude use sarcasm. I found it refreshing.

"We must stay here," the people chanted. *"Something much greater is coming. Bigger than the earth itself. Alexander will bring it to us."*

Samuel wasn't a subscriber to Alexander's prophetic speeches. He only cared about keeping the people safe, even if they valued their leader over their own lives. His daily plea to cut down the forest fell on deaf ears and into the hands of a leader who blocked the way in. There was no getting through to him.

"Did Alexander explain why?" I asked.

Gertrude licked her thumb—gross—and flipped to a page in Alexander's journal.

"Look at this," she said, holding the open journal in her shaky hands. "You'll have to bring your eyes to the page. I can't hold my arms up like I used to."

Alexander had perfect handwriting. I didn't like it.

"Read the last section here," Gertrude said.

> *I feel your energy pulsing beneath the roots, vibrating through the stone. Your chrysalis calls to me.*
>
> *We will be together again soon. I must first carve a way past the entity. I must find you before they do.*

For now, I shape them, the restless people. They help me
without knowing why. The village is theirs, but the
forest is mine.

I know who I am now.

"I thought this was a journal," I said. "It sounds like a letter."

"Indeed!" Gertrude replied, letting out a laugh-cough.

She did that a lot toward the end. It made me depressed. I tried to act normal when it happened, but it's hard to act normal even when someone isn't laugh-coughing.

"What does all of this mean?" I asked. "What was he saying? What was he doing?"

You're asking the same questions, which is why I asked them.

You're welcome.

"We're not there yet, Elliott. In time, in time."

Oh, how I loved when she threw "in time" at me.

"Well, you can't just show me this and not tell me what it means. Not cool!"

"As the storyteller, I get to choose how I tell the story. However, if your curiosity must be satiated, I can say this: Alexander's entire purpose for existence dwelled in the forest, but fulfilling that purpose wasn't a straight line. Many obstacles lay before him, and he wasn't ready. He needed time to solve them. That's why he forbade entrance into the forest. He wanted to go in first, alone, to seek and destroy an entity in the woods. However, he also feared the very thing which he sought to destroy."

"What's an entity?"

"You already know the answer to your question."

"I don't understand anything you're saying."

"No one ever does, dear. It's okay."

Every night, Sojourners gathered around the fire that never goes out. Alexander continued to say the same words:

Leave and die. Stay and live forever.

"Live forever!" the people shouted. But not Samuel. He stayed quiet amongst the crowd; it didn't go unnoticed. His silence bought him a reputation as an outsider.

He wanted to save their lives, and they hated him for it because he refused to bend the knee. Even when the town turned to shit, they cursed him.

Their plumbing and sewers weren't built to handle a town that size. What was meant to go down came back up. Human waste flowed in the streets. Bacteria in the waste made everyone sick. Many died, and still, despite all of this, the people gathered every evening and chanted about living forever.

Instead of confronting Alexander, they swallowed their desperation and waited for the great, bigger-than-the-earth-thing to come and change their lives.

"So that's it?" I asked. "Did Samuel stay quiet?"

"It likely depends on who you ask, dear. Old Sam was quite the conversationalist—an absolute delight. I thought so, at least."

"Wait. You *met* the guy?"

"Elliott, please, your fingernails," Gertrude said with a cringe.

She made me go inside and wash my hands. I had red paint from the picnic table caught beneath my fingernails. All that scratching. She wasn't very fond of it, but I loved it. I couldn't help it. It felt so good. I must have scratched half the paint off the picnic table that summer, but I didn't care. It filled my soul. Even in my current state, I can smile about it.

Luckily, I didn't smash my face on anything in the bathroom, but

I hit a roadblock when I noticed the towel was gone. Jesus Christ, wet hands are the worst. Have you ever washed your hands and didn't have a way to dry them? I mean, yeah, you can always dry them on your clothes, but not me.

The only thing worse than wet hands is wet pants. I could have wiped them on my hoodie, but I don't treat my hoodies that way. I have standards.

And besides, I wanted a *towel*.

I could really use one now, but I think the blood on my hands dried up already. It's hard to tell, though. I still see red.

A memory of Gertrude folding laundry in her bedroom flashed in my brain. I ran down the hallway and snuck through her door. Sure enough, a fresh stack of clean towels rested on her bed.

Crisis averted.

This isn't about wet hands and towels. It's what I found that makes this memory a real conversation piece.

Conversation piece—what does that even mean anyway? I once heard someone say "conversation piece" at the hotel not long ago. If it was up to me, I'd call it a conversation *slice*. It sounds more appealing.

Here's a slice: Let's talk about eyeballs.

Your peripheral vision detects light much better than your focal or central vision. These are real things, I swear.

A faint star may disappear when you stare at it, but as you turn away, it'll pop up again in the corner of your eye. Photoreceptor cells in your eyes are concentrated at the outer edges of your retinas. They're called rods. Cones detect color.

Fascinating!

That explains why I stopped in my tracks after snatching one of Gertrude's towels. I wanted to get out of there, but the shiny silver watch on Gertrude's dresser had a different idea. Naturally, I couldn't help myself. I had to investigate.

It was some kind of antique pocket watch—the kind that dangles from a chain. There's not much else to say about it, but the hands were stopped at 12:34.

Strange.

For a while, I woke up every night at 12:34. That eventually stopped, but only because I started staying up later. Much later. Then I got a job working the night shift, but that's a story for another time. I hope I live long enough to tell it. It took me a small eternity just to get this far.

Storytelling is hard.

The watch rested on a withered, weathered book, *The Lesser Key of Solomon.* Just looking at the book nearly crumbled it to dust.

These objects fought for my attention, but the unassuming envelope lying next to them ultimately won.

Its surface held two words scratched in blue ink: *New Admit.*

Was Gertrude about to foster another child? Was I getting a new roommate?

The contents of that envelope held the answer, but I respected Gertrude too much to open it. As a human who values privacy, I kept hers intact. Still, it weighed on my mind.

I can't remember what I did with the towel after I dried my hands. I sure as hell didn't put it on a towel rack. Nobody ever did.

I walked back outside with my hands in the air, waving them around like an asshole.

"Quit bein' a smart apple!" Gertrude shouted. She never cursed. Needless to say, it wasn't the first time she called me a fruit. I've also been a bad banana. Whatever. She was a fruitcake.

"See? No more paint. So, where were we?"

"Old Sam."

Samuel Ross was an older man. Older than Gertrude at the time. Mid-to-late-sixties, if I remember that right.

"He knew *everything*," Gertrude said, "but not in the way that Alexander knew everything. Samuel's knowledge came with age, curiosity, and hard work. Alexander's knowledge came supernaturally."

Rewind.

"What was that you said about *supernaturally?*"

"No time for the weeds, child."

Another one of Gertrude's sayings: something about digging in the weeds.

"Sam was a peculiar man but equally as delightful. I enjoyed many things about him, especially his voice. A mere exchange of words in passing eased even the most tachycardic heart. If mountains could talk, they would sound just like him."

Tachycardia means your heart is beating fast.

I know things.

Thanks, Bill.

"The first time I heard Sam's voice, it came from afar. I remember it well. Not a single breath of wind exhaled from any direction. All was still as ever. I can still feel the sun's warmth cutting through the cold air of that late winter morning. I can see the trees lending their arms, creating shafts of light on the forest floor. Nature wrote poetry that morning."

My eyes lit up.

"Wait—you were in the *forest* that morning? What were you doing there? How did you get there? *Why* were you there? Did I miss something?"

"Shhhhh."

Had I known she'd be dead before my next birthday, I wouldn't have submitted to her shushing. I turned eighteen the following year. She meant to complete this story on my eighteenth birthday. Of course, that never happened. She said the final chapter was the most important part, and that's what kills me. I wondered how important it really was since I had to wait nearly a decade for it.

Doesn't matter anyway. She's dead now. You already know this because I told you, and I'll probably tell you a few more times.

My memory is like an old friend who never calls you back.

Her death was no accident. I watched it happen. Then I ended up in a coma for twenty-eight days. Her death and my coma were caused by the same thing.

The incident.

"Don't spoil the moment with your tongue, my dear."

"*Fine.* So, the forest wrote poetry, eh? What kinda crap did the forest write about?"

She didn't like that question.

On that early winter morning, Gertrude heard Samuel mumbling to himself near the edge of the forest.

"I heard the voice of a man frustrated by circumstance. The repetition and meter of his words suggested a rehearsal. He practiced a speech, unaware of his audience. I wanted to reveal myself, but I knew better than to leave the forest. There's a funny little thing about knowing things, Elliott. The heart doesn't always listen. It doesn't speak the same language as your brain. That's why I walked in his direction. No matter, though, and probably for the best. He turned around and walked away without sensing my presence."

Samuel caught everyone's attention when he began his march to Alexander's house, which stood at the top of the hill in the center of Sojourn.

Some followed him along the way.

Some threw trash and cursed him.

Some already stood at the base of the hill in nervous anticipation.

"The entire town panicked, and they didn't even know why."

"They didn't know why? What does that even mean?"

"I have a book about that!" Bill shouted from the window.

"Bill! How are you everywhere?"

He set a book on the windowsill and scurried away.

Gertrude kept talking, unaware of Bill's interruption.

"It's sad, really. The folks in town didn't have minds of their own. When the hard times came along, not one soul left Sojourn to find a better life, let alone a *safe* life. They stayed and suffered for a man who promised greatness, though no greatness was to be found. And then they condemned the only person among them who saw the world with open eyes. Trust me, Elliott. When I first heard about all of this, I was just as perplexed as you are right now."

The hill swarmed with people covered in dirt and human waste as Sam reached the base of it. Their hair was falling out. Impressions of bones showed through their clothes. Many of them had jaundice. It made their skin and the whites of their eyes yellow.

Jaundice is a symptom of hepatitis.

A mix of fear, anger, and disillusion flickered in the yellows of their eyes.

"I don't mean any harm!" Samuel cried to the crowd. "I just want to talk to him."

And so he did.

Samuel reached the top of the hill and gave two soft knocks on Alexander's red door. His knocks silenced the crowd. While they waited for the door to open, two people died. They just straight up collapsed. As they lay on the ground, waiting for salvation, their bodies gave out; they moved on. No one did anything to help them.

I wonder what they saw in their last moments, assuming they saw anything at all. Gertrude used to say that our dead friends and family come to us during our final moments and help us cross over to the other side or whatever.

Too bad. When she died, none of that happened to her.

There were so many times when I wanted to bleed myself out just to see my mom. But I could never do that. Not to myself, at least. That's not how I'd want her to see me.

If I don't stop bleeding, she just might show up.

I mean, come on, look at me.

"When Alexander opened the door and let Sam inside, things started getting…weird,"

"Oh, so *this* is when it gets weird, because nothing you've said so far sounds weird at all, like the trash can babies or the fire that never goes out or the Exploratory Solutions Division. Yeah, all that sounds pretty normal to me."

Gertrude kept talking as if I said nothing.

"Despite every watchful eye on Alexander's red door, no one can say for sure just how long Sam was on the other side of it. The town's perception of time had become lost. I'm not sure how else to explain it. A collective confusion rose amongst them. Some thought they had been standing there for days. To others, that same stretch of time felt like an instant. There was an unnatural force at work. Everyone's mind went dark. Then the storm came."

Gertrude didn't need to rely on Alexander's journal for this part of the story. She recalled it from memory.

"Through the treetops surrounding my home, I saw clouds moving in from every possible direction, converging at a single point in the sky above me. This was no act of wind, my boy. At first, I thought I was seeing things, but then a large mass of blackbirds screeched above me and took off. They saw what I saw: clouds shifting from heather grey to jet black."

Gertrude's eyes danced, following a memory. She extended her arms, reaching for something I couldn't see.

"I'm back there," she said in a deep voice. "We're back together."

This disturbed me. I mean, she'd done this before—the whole staring-into-space-flashback thing—but never like *this*. She thought she was back there again, in that place in Ender Forest.

I followed her lead and extended my arms, but only to keep her from falling. She got up too fast and zigzagged around the backyard.

"Take me to the cellar!" she kept shouting.

I cried out for help, but no one responded.

"Bill, this would be a great time for you to come out of nowhere and help me!"

Nothing.

"Charlie! Wake up!"

Nothing.

The Vultures watched me from their bedroom window.

I marked their faces with my eyes.

The Phoenix twins laughed in unison.

Johnny Wixom and Dallas Dark whispered to each other.

James Grave just stared at me. He didn't smile or laugh. I can't say for sure what he felt at the time. Something was on his mind, though. Gertrude's bizarre episode wasn't a joke to him.

All I could do was carry Gertrude into the house before she hurt herself. When I laid her on her bed, she still flailed about in her trance. If I didn't know her as well as I did, I would have thought she took some kind of psychotropic drug.

There's always the possibility that James drugged her or something. I wouldn't put it past him—that piece of shit. I confronted him about it days later; he denied any involvement.

That doesn't mean anything.

Does anyone tell the truth anymore?

I was about to leave the room, but she started talking to someone.

No one else was around.

You're right. None of this makes sense.

"Lock the cellar door behind you," she said. I thought I'd play along, so I shut her bedroom door. She appeared satisfied, slipping slurred mumbles through a half-smile.

"Are you having a stroke?"

That's always a funny thing to ask someone when they're having a stroke. I asked my mom the same question the day before she died. I know the signs: sudden confusion, inability to speak, difficulty understanding speech, facial drooping.

Do you know what 9-1-1 is?

We don't have 9-1-1 here. We only have the Maudlin Authority Public Order Division, and they never help.

In a medical emergency, you have two options: drag yourself to Sacred Dark Hospital or handle it yourself. I prefer the latter. I guess I'd rather rely on myself than seek help at a dirty, makeshift hospital.

But sometimes, you have to choose the former.

I could see Sacred Dark from the orphanage, but I had to climb the roof and use Bill's binoculars.

Some watch birds. I watch body bags.

Over half the patients leave the hospital in body bags.

Aside from the illusion of safety, Sacred Dark has very little to offer. You can trust me on this.

Gertrude thanked me for closing the door, but she called me by a different name.

"Thank you, Darwin."

Her eyes changed. She looked frightened and relieved at the same time, blinking a thousand times and scanning the room. As soon as her eyes found me, she exhaled.

"Oh, I'm here," she said.

I felt her heart sink.

"Forgive me, Elliott. I was back there again. Was I there? I could have sworn I just returned from the forest. I saw everything. Oh, and the lightning. Thirty strikes. I felt each one."

She spoke faster than her lips could handle; her words became unintelligible. She lost me.

"Who's Darwin?" I asked.

Just like that, she stopped. I felt her energy drain from her body. She looked away from me and muttered a single word.

"Nobody."

The clock struck. Two in the morning.

Eight hours passed since she started telling me this story in the backyard.

My birthday ended. Gertrude fought a losing battle against sleep.

"Are we done?" I asked.

She answered my question with loud, obnoxious snoring. As much as I wanted to, I didn't wake her. After everything she went through that evening with the flashbacks and whatever, I'm surprised she wasn't dead. I let her rest and recover, but it wasn't a selfless decision. I took it upon myself to do some snooping around. My head exploded with unanswered questions.

What happened between Samuel Ross and Alexander Morris?

When did Sojourn become Maudlin?

Why did Gertrude live in the forest?

Who was Darwin?

Where is he now?

Oh, and then there was the envelope labeled *New Admit*.

I had to know what was inside.

It always bothered me when Gertrude kept things to herself. Was she trying to hide this? Why leave it on top of the dresser where I could find it? Was she testing me, or did old age finally get the best of her?

So many unknowns.

For about an hour, I stood in the darkness of Gertrude's room while she made snoring sounds that could be easily mistaken for a diesel engine or a baby seal being clubbed to death. I got caught up in my head, trying to rationalize what I was about to do.

"I'll just pretend I'm a secret agent on a mission to recover classified documents."

Not the greatest rationale, but it would do.

My secret agent mission had two objectives: acquire the contents of the mysterious *New Admit* envelope, and locate any documents about Maudlin's history.

This wasn't the first time I've done reconnaissance in Gertrude's room. I knew where she kept her journals—all sixty-six of them. They were locked in an oversized suitcase beneath her bed. I just needed to find the right ones.

Removing the lock was the easy part. Nothing two bobby pins couldn't handle.

Over the next three nights, I cracked the lock and read through her journals. Eight journals contained both personal and objective accounts of Maudlin's history. They lined up perfectly with the story she shared with me on my birthdays.

The first six journals covered everything she shared with me up until the night she called me Darwin. The eighth journal had half its pages ripped out.

I never found those pages; some questions remain unanswered.

Regardless, the seventh and eighth journals are a trip.

If I focus hard on my breathing, keep my eyes open, and slow the bleeding, I think I might be able to share what I found, including the contents of the envelope.

Gertrude was taking in someone new at The Amulet:

Autumn Vester.

Oh—the book that Bill left on the windowsill was *Psychology of the Unconscious* by Carl Jung.

9 — Votum

WHY ARE YOU EVEN HERE?

Are you with the Moths?

Did Marlowe send you?

Anything like that?

Forgive me for being so suspicious. I just can't imagine anyone stopping to help someone around here.

Not in a place like this.

Everyone here is trash, including me.

Until I figure you out, I'll stay suspicious.

But please. Don't leave. Not yet.

The night I found the envelope and the journals—everything changed.

I spent night after night in Gertrude's room, flying through her journals, saving the letter for last. Don't get me wrong; waves of guilt coursed through my veins as I invaded her privacy. No one on this planet—living, dead, or otherwise—is more deserving of respect than Gertrude Morton.

But I don't know.

Maybe a part of me knew she'd be gone before my eighteenth birthday. I learned so many things that she never had the chance to tell me. I like to pretend that she'd be glad I did this. It helps me sleep at night.

I haven't slept in three days.

After everything that went down this week, you'd understand.

Eight of Gertrude's sixty-six journals mentioned Sojourn and its evolution into what we now call Maudlin. Let's call them *Sojournals*; it's a lot shorter than calling them *The Eight Journals about Sojourn and Maudlin*.

Whatever. Moving on.

The *Sojournals* matched up with Gertrude's annual stories, so I have good reason to believe the remaining untold entries are accurate. But despite their accuracy, they were pretty hard to read. Gertrude had atrocious handwriting. It's like she wrote them with a blindfold and a hangover while riding a roller coaster.

I've seen a roller coaster on a VHS tape. You wouldn't believe it. They're insane.

After two nights of meticulous reading, I found patterns in her writing. Her G's looked more like A's. It gave me anxiety.

The first five *Sojournals* were not firsthand accounts of Gertrude's experiences. She started playing an active role in the sixth journal. She had a way of gathering detailed information. Quite the historian, although, it definitely leaned more toward obsession.

She might not have been there when Sojourn was founded, but she wasn't very far. She lived in Ender Forest.

Her cabin was "quaint and only slightly uncomfortable," as she described it. I'd guess that the discomfort came from the detached outhouse behind the cabin, or maybe the fact that she had to share such a small space with someone else.

Remember Darwin?

He was Gertrude's younger brother. He built the cabin by himself when he was only sixteen. Apparently, finding the place wasn't easy. The *Sojournals* claim that it "moved around the forest." Seems like a stretch, but sure.

A few days after Darwin was born, Gertrude hid him from her people. As a "child of the prophecy," it was Darwin's destiny to be sacrificed for the greater good. But during Gertrude's attempt to keep him hidden, he disappeared. Twenty years later, Gertrude found him in the forest. He reappeared in the exact place where he went missing. After their reunion, Gertrude moved into his cabin, and they had a few good years together before everything went wrong.

I know; you're confused about Darwin's disappearance. Let's put that on hold for now. I'm mentally placing it next to the child sacrifices and prophecies.

Gertrude described her brother as a stick: tall, thin, and organic. He desired to be as close to the earth as possible.

As I read about him, he felt familiar to me. I didn't know why.

Like Bill Dweller, Darwin was a tall, skinny lover of nature with dark brown, unkempt hair and thick glasses. He was also legally blind. His glasses gave him bug eyes. How fitting.

Although the Morton siblings spent decades apart, Darwin insisted that he built the cabin for both of them. He knew they would find each other again. He insisted it was their destiny.

You're probably wondering what the hell all of this has to do with me. It will come together, I swear. Just stay with me. Keep me awake.

Are you a paramedic? Did you call the police?

That was a joke.

I know a guy who entered the Moth's police academy, or at least their version of a police academy. Not sure how they do things out in the real world.

We worked together at The 86 Hotel. He'd been working the

front desk for a while and got me a job after my coma. I didn't quite care for it, but you don't have a choice when you have to pay rent.

I'm pretty sure I've been fired.

After a few years of solitude in Darwin's cabin, Gertrude noticed a growing presence to the west of the woods. The eastern border of Sojourn rested less than half a mile away, but that's debatable if the cabin moved around all willy-nilly in the forest.

Am I right?

I am right.

Gertrude felt drawn to Sojourn. She admitted to curiosity and expressed a naive interest in the "place beyond the trees."

She heard the playfully shrill voices of children off in the distance. And horses—she listened as they trampled the ground near the outskirts of the forest. Over the months that passed, she paid frequent attention to these unfamiliar sounds. It eased her loneliness. Despite her temptation, she didn't make contact; Darwin wouldn't allow it. Staying away from Sojourn was a house rule. This, of course, only sparked more curiosity.

At night, she would sneak out of the cabin and walk to the edge of the forest, but she didn't go any further. Curiosity aside, she stressed the stupidity in disobeying him.

Nobody knew these lands better than Darwin.

If he told you to stay away from somewhere, you stayed away.

He had good reasons.

Gertrude made six nighttime visits to the edge of Ender Forest before her brother found out. The first five visits were surprisingly quiet and uneventful, but during her sixth visit, she spotted a little girl wandering in the woods. She looked to be around five years old. Gertrude found her spinning in circles, speaking gibberish, and waving a stick.

"What are you doing?" she asked the girl.

She obliged Gertrude with a cryptic answer.

"Casting a spell."

A voice cried out from somewhere beyond the trees.

"Abigail Harris, where are you?!"

The girl froze when the voice called her name. She pointed her stick toward the sky, spoke more gibberish, and disappeared.

Gertrude stood there for a while, paralyzed with fear.

> *I heard that name before—Abigail Harris. The Enders believed she would birth a powerful hedge witch when she came of age. I longed to set her free from their lust of prophecies.*

Through the pillars of trees, Gertrude spotted a gathering of silhouettes—hundreds of them. A tall, thin shape stood at the center. It paced slowly, back and forth, while speaking. Sometimes, it raised its voice, extended its arms, and pointed to the undying fire.

This was the first time Gertrude saw Alexander Morris.

It wouldn't be the last.

Gertrude nearly had a heart attack when she felt a hand snatch her wrist. The faint flickering glow of Sojourn's undying fire revealed Darwin's emerald eyes. She felt like a child again, being sent home for bad behavior. All the way back to the cabin, they bickered over right and wrong. They each saw Sojourn in a completely different way.

Initially, Darwin was furious. He didn't yell, though, because he didn't want to draw attention. He was *that* afraid of being discovered. Gertrude didn't understand why her brother was so scared. She had never seen him like this before.

"Did anyone see you? *Anyone?*"

"No."

Darwin went back to bed as soon as they returned, but Gertrude confronted him before he had the chance to fall asleep.

"Tell me why you're acting this way. What are you so afraid of?"

"I would rather not tell you," he responded. "It's a burdensome explanation. But I can show you. Just not tonight. Never at night. We're safer in the daylight. Now, go to sleep, sister."

Who calls their sister "sister?"

Gertrude couldn't sleep. Her mind went wild with possibility and "the thinnest thread of fear."

> *Will we sneak into the town?*
> *Why must we be so discrete?*
> *Why not an open, peaceful visit?*
> *Why not live there?*
> *So many unknowns.*
> *Tomorrow feels so far away.*

Her handwriting was much harder to read in future entries.

Lines appeared more jagged—a sign of distress.

Spacing between words shrunk—a sign of impatience.

Sometimes, she only wrote half or part of a word. I'm not sure what this means.

I didn't have to continue reading to know that something terrible happened.

These fragments of words and broken paragraphs were a telltale sign. I spent an entire night studying her ink scratches, looking at her paragraphs like pictures. Every fifteen minutes or so, I had to take a break. If I stared at them for too long, I started feeling nauseous.

Her "thinnest thread of fear" had woven itself into a tragic death sweater. Plausible turned into obvious when I read the words as words, not pictures.

I was blown away.

Absolutely stunned.

After scratching down her list of questions, the storm arrived.

> *Darwin is the heaviest sleeper. Lightning struck near our cabin thirty times in the past five minutes, yet his snore remains. Somehow, the cabin is intact. I don't see fire or smell smoke. What is happening?*

The next morning, she awoke to the sound of clanking metal. Darwin stood at the foot of her bed, holding two shovels in his left hand and a kerosene lantern in his right.

She didn't need a clock to know that it was four in the morning.

Darwin was notably tense and apprehensive.

Wait. Why am I talking like this?

When do I ever say, "notably tense and apprehensive?"

I don't talk like that.

Pause.

Rewind.

Play.

She had never seen her brother like this before.

> *He was a sweaty, shaking mess overcome by a fear I did not know or understand. This foreign behavior made him nearly unrecognizable. For a moment, he wasn't my Darwin. I did not know the man who stood at the foot of my bed.*

That's how I felt about my mom. Before she died, she started acting really weird.

Darwin raced out of the bedroom and into the kitchen. Gertrude heard both shovels crash against the bare wooden floor—it's a good thing she took the lantern—followed by the sound of silence.

She exited the bedroom with her left arm outstretched as the lantern guided her in Darwin's direction. She found him leaning against the countertop, his hands wrapped around a mug of hot coffee. He held the mug up to his nose. Upon inhaling the scent, his fear dissipated. Gertrude recognized him again.

Darwin loved coffee. Gertrude wrote about it for damn near six pages. I have to admit that I share the same love for it. Next to opiates, it's my favorite thing. My brain loves black gold. I've had some rough nights at the hotel. Coffee made them better. But I'm not bleeding out just to tell you why I like coffee and which kind is the best—Sumatran.

After reading Gertrude's six-page coffee essay, she mentioned the shovels again, wondering what they were for. My guess was that they were for digging.

I know; I'm not really funny, but I can make myself laugh.

That has to count for something.

After the shovels, Gertrude wrote about her conversation with Darwin in the kitchen.

"Did you hear the storm last night?" she asked.

"A storm? I didn't hear anything, but that doesn't surprise me. My mind goes to deep places when I'm dreaming. Oh, my mind. Lately, it has been so very preoccupied."

"By what?

"I can't keep this to myself anymore."

Darwin nervously gripped his mug.

"What do you mean?" Gertrude asked. "What have you been keeping from me?"

Darwin took a deep sip of coffee.

"I found the thing your people speak of in their prophecies."

Darwin's confession flooded Gertrude's head with curiosity, but mostly, she felt offended.

Very, very offended.

"They're not my people. Never say that again."

"Apologies, sister."

"What do you know about the prophecies anyway? You have been alone all these years, and I have said nothing. How do you know so much? Who told you about them?"

"You did. You told me."

I hate to admit this, but I couldn't read her handwriting on the rest of the page, only a few words. She mentioned something about a "place between places" and something else about being really old.

I don't know.

That's all I could decipher.

Her handwriting calmed down on the next page, but by then, she had moved on. The rest of her kitchen conversation with Darwin remains lost in her scribbles.

Gertrude wrote about how she and her brother would become "entranced" from time to time. It was usually triggered by stress, and when it hit them, all they could do was wait for it to pass. Memory loss frequently followed.

I know the feeling.

I'm guessing that's what happened to Gertrude in the backyard on the night of my seventeenth birthday. It also explains all the times I found her staring off into space, mumbling to herself.

Gertrude and Darwin exited the cabin, each carrying a shovel. Gertrude held the lantern. Darwin brought his coffee for the journey.

"I need more hands," he said.

He placed his coffee mug on his head—very impressive—and fumbled through his coat pockets in the early morning moonlight.

Seven pockets later, he pulled out a square-shaped piece of leather.

He held it in his hands, but it did not belong to him. In Darwin's world, this map was a discovery, not his creation. The legend, scale, grid, and directions were penned by another hand. Its designer, a mystery.

"Light, please," Darwin whispered.

Gertrude walked forward with the lantern until he reached out and grabbed her shoulder, stopping her at the perfect distance from the map.

He looked at her with a great, big smile.

"Try to keep up with me, if you can."

He buried his head in the map and took off.

His pace quickened with each step. Gertrude struggled to match his speed and direction, blaming it on hunger and sleep deprivation. It didn't help that Darwin was zigzagging all over the woods.

Zigzagging.

Gertrude expressed frustration with her brother's movement, but at the same time, it impressed her. This particular area of the forest was very dense. Trees stood less than an arm's length apart from each other in every direction.

Darwin kept his eyes fixed on the map, moving sporadically while dodging the oaks, elms, and firs. Somehow, the mug on his head didn't fall or spill a single drop.

As Gertrude struggled to keep up, she wondered how she got to this point in her life. If I found myself in a forest at dawn, chasing a man with a coffee mug on his head, I'd wonder the same thing.

"Do you even know *where* you're going," she asked, but Darwin didn't answer.

She asked a second time. Still, nothing.

The light from the lantern revealed an intense concentration in Darwin's eyes. Beads of sweat rolled down from his forehead and into his eyes, but he didn't blink. His hands shook. His legs wobbled and buckled as he walked, but he didn't stop.

Gertrude suggested that he remove his coat, but it was no use.

After ten minutes of zigzags and bewilderment, Darwin came to a sudden stop. He threw his shovel like a javelin, piercing the forest floor. He stood like a statue and blinked his eyes a hundred times.

"There!"

Gertrude insists that the only thing her brother had in his system was coffee.

I have nothing clever to say about that.

"Now what?" Gertrude asked.

"Now, we dig, but first, I must do something."

He fumbled through his pockets again, patting himself rhythmically until he felt a hard, rectangular object through the fabric of his jacket's left breast pocket. Reaching inside, he pulled out a brilliantly polished chrome lighter.

With a flick of the flint wheel, a flurry of sparks gave birth to an orange and blue flame.

Darwin held the dancing flame under the map. He watched with bright eyes as red and black ink bubbled up from the map's surface, evaporating into the chill morning air.

The map curled and shriveled, sending glowing embers of dead animal skin up into the sky.

"What was that for?" Gertrude asked.

Darwin threw the scorched map to the ground and stomped it out. He took a moment to dig a small hole and bury the ashes so no one would discover them.

"We don't need it anymore. I'm never coming back here. Neither are you. Not again. Not ever. This is the last time."

Gertrude noted her reaction to Darwin burning the map.

I felt something bittersweet, like reading the last page of a good book. Finality fell upon us, and nothing could disturb her resolution. Whatever she wants, she gets.

But the passing of time has taught me that nothing ever ends. I'm on the last page, but I hold the entire book in my hands, starting at the front cover again.

"Okay, sister. Let's dig."

The top layer of the forest floor was very soft. Of course, most things in life aren't as they appear on the surface. The supple soil hid the rock-hard clay and webbed tree roots beneath.

Gertrude was not pleased.

She detested all forms of manual labor, mainly due to her back problems. If I remember correctly, she had a herniated disc between her L1 and L2 vertebrae. This often meant frequent shooting pains in her back that radiated up her neck and down her legs.

She didn't mention any of this in her journals. Let's just say I might have accidentally come across her Sacred Dark medical files one night. They "fell" out of her bedroom closet. I couldn't believe just how much she had going on inside her body.

I'll keep the rest to myself.

No offense, but it's none of your business.

It's none of my business either.

"Are you sure we're digging in the right spot?" Gertrude asked. "The ground appears untouched. So many roots. This doesn't look right."

Darwin stopped digging.

"No one—and I mean *no one*—knows this forest better than I do.

We're right where we're supposed to be. Besides, I followed the map."

"Oh, you mean the map that you *set on fire*?!"

"You're so naive, little sister. You don't understand."

"Then why don't you explain yourself? Last night, you dragged me away from the edge of the forest. Now we're digging a hole in the ground. What does your fear of *them* have to do with *this*? Tell me!"

Like an angry rabbit, Gertrude stomped her foot against the ground. Digging was no longer necessary; she kicked the ground in just the right spot, with just the right amount of force, causing it to break apart and cave beneath them. In a matter of seconds, she went from arguing with her brother in the forest to lying on her back somewhere underground.

The fall knocked the wind out of her. She coughed up clumps of dirt and clay that had fallen in her mouth. It got in her eyes, and her hair, and her ears.

Her ears rang, but only for a few seconds. The ringing faded into an unwelcoming silence. As she waited for the sound of her brother's voice, she wished they had never found each other after their twenty years of separation. She regretted their reunion.

This regret nearly consumed her, but when she opened her eyes, she became herself again.

She looked up at the hole in the earth and couldn't believe she survived the fall. Surprise gave way to disbelief when she felt the ground with her fingertips. It wasn't made of dirt, clay, or tree roots. Through the corners of her eyes, she observed a floor made of soap-stone, smoother than glass.

Somehow, the lantern beside her remained lit and unbroken.

Like the lantern, her bones were intact, but every muscle in her body ached. The flickering light of the lantern revealed new bruises, slowly developing like a Polaroid photograph. Fresh blood seeped through lacerations on her arms and legs.

This fascinated her.

It's so neat how we bleed inside our bones. I always thought of bleeding as something that happens on the surface, but we bleed on the inside too.

There is so much happening inside me, so much I am not aware of all the time. My body struggles to adapt and survive every second of my life. It fights to maintain homeostasis, and the details go unnoticed.

I have roughly two hundred trillion cells in my body. Each one faces millions of chemical reactions. By the time I finish writing this sentence, trillions of chemical reactions will have taken place inside of me.

What is it all for?

She was a scatterbrain like me.

We get sidetracked so effortlessly.

Our mutual habit of tangents brought us closer together, but they also kept us from getting too close. I don't expect you to understand this, but that's okay.

We weren't always this way.

I blame humans.

The forest floor had become a ceiling that hung at least thirty feet above her. There might have been a way to climb out somehow, but she wasn't a skilled climber—not like her brother.

She gave herself two options: lie there and wait for Darwin to show up, assuming he wasn't dead, or head down the dark cave corridor revealed by the lantern's flickering light.

Gertrude has always struck me as a play-it-safe person, so I was shocked by her decision.

> *I chose the dark path, even if it meant walking into the*
> *open arms of danger. I wasn't supposed to wait. I've*
> *tried that before—waiting. The mere fact that I'm*
> *writing this is a testament to its futility.*

The lantern provided scant visibility—a faint sliver of light in the underground.

Again, why am I talking like this?

Pause.

Rewind.

Play.

The lantern gave off very little light, but it was just enough to find her way forward in the dark. She could only see the next three steps ahead. Everything else rolled into shadow.

No sign of Darwin.

Unlike the forest floor, the soapstone tunnel wasn't soft. It didn't hold footprints. Gertrude relied on her instincts and the lantern, but as luck would have it, the lantern's light died along the way. The fuel chamber ran dry.

She followed her gut and moved forward, but her mind made other plans.

> *What in heck's name am I doing, I thought. I wanted to*
> *turn around. Darwin might have been up there wait-*
> *ing for me above ground.*
>
> *Such is the way of denial.*

I found myself at an impasse, crippled by dismay and apprehension. That's when the sweats and shakes hit me. It felt like my blood sugar had hit the soapstone floor. I fell to my knees and let my tears follow. It lifted the weight inside.

It felt good to cry.

Down the heavy darkness of the corridor, Gertrude saw a light.

It danced at first, moving and stretching unconventionally, but only because the tears in her eyes had distorted her vision. As soon as she wiped them away, the light shifted and flickered like the flame from a book of matches.

Darwin.

Her mind and gut shook hands, agreeing to chase the light at the end of the tunnel.

See what I did there?

Just kill me already.

I shattered the world record for fastest running speed by a human being, but no one will ever know. I broke it underground, in the dark, and with no witnesses.

I think this was Gertrude's idea of being funny, or maybe she was serious. I don't know. With her, you can rarely tell the difference.

She reached the end of the tunnel and found two things: a dead end and Darwin. Although she swelled with relief, she wasn't cool with the fact that he left her by herself after the ground caved in.

"I thought you were dead!" she shouted. "You had me fearing the worst, yet here you are without a scratch—and smiling! Why are you smiling? How did you get here before me? I didn't see you fall in."

Darwin didn't respond. He just stood there, facing the dead end of the tunnel with a look of euphoric anticipation. Something seemed off about him. Gertrude looked into his eyes and felt as if she was looking at someone else.

"You're not Darwin."

Saying those words broke the spell that entranced him. His smile fell, and he fell with it.

"What's wrong, Darwin?"

"My whole body. Everything hurts. What happened? Did we fall through?"

Darwin kept his sentences short, breathing heavily between them.

"We fell. How do you not remember that?"

"I don't know. I don't know anything."

"When I realized where I was, you were nowhere to be found. I thought you were hurt, maybe dead, maybe worse. But I found you just in time! The lamp died down the tunnel. I had no light, but then I saw yours."

"But how—how did I get *here*?"

"You tell me, brother. I found you here, standing, smiling. For a moment, you weren't you. I don't know how to explain it. But that's over now, and that's all that matters."

"For now."

"Hmm?"

"It's over, *for* now, sister. You missed the preposition."

I appreciate Darwin's attention to words.

"This is all part of it," he said. His eyes stared at nothing, shifting back and forth. Gertrude knew that look.

"What are you building?" she asked.

"Words, faces, events, and every connecting thread."

"Where do they all lead?"

"Here. All threads lead here."

He pointed at the dead end, ignited another book of matches, and handed it to Gertrude.

"Hold this."

"But there's nothing there. It's just a wall."

She placed her hand on its surface and pulled it away.

The wall burned her skin.

"Do you really believe that?" Darwin asked. "Is that what you tell yourself?"

He removed his coat and used it to clear the dirt and dust from the wall. Gertrude held her hand in discomfort.

"This isn't a wall," he said.

He took a breath and blew the remaining dust from the surface.

"This is a door."

Upon closer examination, Gertrude found a razor-thin indentation that framed a section of the wall, indicating the possibility of a doorway.

"I don't see a handle."

"It's not that kind of door."

Gertrude spotted some markings at the center.

"What do these mean?"

She wasn't familiar with Latin. Not at this point in her life. By the time I met her, it was her second language. I'm guessing this event had something to do with it.

A single Latin word was carved in the stone.

Votum

"It means 'vow' in Latin," Darwin explained.

"What about this?" Gertrude asked.

She pointed to a symbol carved above *Votum*.

"It's a septagram. See the seven points? 'Septem' is 'seven' in Latin.

That's where September gets its name. It was originally the seventh of ten months on the ancient Roman calendar, but I digress. This septagram is upside down."

"I don't understand. What is all of this?"

"Your people haven't told you yet?"

"They're *not* my people!"

Gertrude's voice rumbled and reverberated down the soapstone corridor.

"Stories, cult behavior, mass hysteria," she continued. "That's all they have. That's all it ever was."

"Apparently not." Darwin pointed at the door. "I'm shocked they haven't found this place yet."

"Who says they haven't?"

Darwin stood there defeated.

"Nothing makes sense anymore," he whispered.

They stood there in silence, but they didn't stop talking.

Are you confused yet?

Here. Let Gertrude explain.

> *Darwin and I had a way of communicating with each other without saying a single word. We always have.*
>
> *As we stood there, staring at that ugly door thing, I felt his fear. He wanted to turn around and fly out of there. He feared the next event. He knew something I failed to understand. He saw things I couldn't see.*
>
> *This was it.*

"The people beyond the forest—they answer to one person," Darwin explained. "They follow his every word. He doesn't care about them, though. It's all an act, a facade. He only cares about one thing. He exists for nothing else."

"How do you know all of this?"

Lightning flashed at the other end of the tunnel. The walls around them shook from the sound of heavy thunder. Then, nothing.

"Are we expecting another storm?" Gertrude asked.

"In a way, yes," Darwin replied. He closed his eyes and pressed his fingers against his temples, rubbing them in a circular motion.

"You didn't answer my question."

"I just did."

"No, my other question."

"I've been studying him for a while now. He wanders through the forest at night. About a week ago, I followed him in the darkness. He carried a shovel with him and dug a hole after hole in the forest floor, searching for something. Every time he pierced the ground with his shovel, he recited a Latin word. They all began with the same letter: vaco, vado, veritas, vigilo. But he always went back to a certain word: votum. I heard him speak it thirty times. Then he dropped his shovel and fled back to his people."

"Did he come back?"

"No. I haven't seen him since. A couple nights later, though, I spotted a little girl in the forest. He must have sent her."

"Abigail."

Darwin looked at her with wide eyes.

"You saw her? The little girl? When?"

"Last night. Before you found me at the tree line."

"So you lied to me."

"I'm sorry. No more lies. I promise."

"What was she doing?"

"She pretended to cast a spell."

"*Pretended* to cast a spell or *actually* cast a spell?"

"What's the difference?"

"Gertrude! What was the spell? You have to tell me."

"I don't remember."

She was lying.

"None of that is real anyway," she continued. "Spells, curses, hexes, prophecies. It's all a bunch of hogwash. I believed in it once. It cost me everything."

Gertrude never opened up to her brother, or anyone, about her life with the Enders. She kept that door closed until now, but Darwin was too distracted to listen.

"The spell," he whispered. "Now he knows."

"Knows *what*?

Another flicker of lightning flashed down the tunnel, followed by a crackling wave of thunder. Brighter, louder this time.

Through the thunder, Darwin made a disturbing statement.

"You should have killed her when you had the chance."

His words shook Gertrude down to her soul. She never heard Darwin speak such a horrible thing before. But it didn't stop there. He grabbed her by the shoulders and started shaking her.

"Why did you lie about Abigail?" he asked. "What are you not telling me? Are you protecting her?"

Fear and confusion consumed her.

"I don't know what's happening. Please, you're hurting me."

Darwin didn't let up.

"Did they send you here to spy on me? They did, didn't they? How could you do this to me? I trusted you!"

He spoke the three words that killed her spirit.

"You ruined everything."

Gertrude started crying, sobbing, balling her eyes out. She reached out to her brother and grabbed his shoulders, attempting to embrace him before collapsing to the ground.

Darwin didn't catch her.

"I don't want to be here anymore," she cried. "I don't want to be me anymore. I can't keep doing this."

Lightning struck a third time. It shook the soapstone corridor. Gertrude's skin vibrated from the thunder. It took her mind away from the fact that she wanted to die, but only for a second.

"Please don't leave me," she cried.

Darwin ignored her plea and fled down the corridor.

The part that really gets to me is that Gertrude had just been left for dead by her own goddamn brother, but she still wanted to make sure that he got out of the tunnel safely. After all of this, she still looked out for him. As he ran away from her, she kept her eyes on him and writhed in agony.

How depressing.

Every few seconds, a bolt of lightning revealed his form and position. His silhouette grew smaller with each flash until he began his ascent to the surface.

I wish I could say that Gertrude didn't see him again after he climbed up and out of view, but that's not how it went.

Darwin fell on his way out.

Lightning struck him seven times and shot him back down into the tunnel. He fell thirty feet and landed on his back. The sound of his skull cracking against the soapstone floor echoed down the corridor. Gertrude wasted no time running to his aid, but she couldn't do anything other than hold him in her arms.

Most of his clothing had disintegrated. The rest fused to his skin. His dark, shaggy hair melted, revealing a charred scalp. Whatever skin he still had left was covered in red streaks. His eyes were bruised.

He was still breathing.

Gertrude had never climbed anything in her whole life—not even a tree—so she remained trapped down there with her dead brother, rocking his body back and forth, kissing his melted forehead, and talking nonsense, or at least that's what it sounded like.

"Why do we keep failing like this, Darwin? I tell the tales so you can learn from them, but we always fall apart at the door. Do you leave it behind when you wake? What will it finally take? Each time, I try something different, hoping it will alter the path, yet here we are again. Now, it's their turn. Nothing changes."

Hours passed. Day fell into night.

As the moon rose over the opening in the forest floor, a silhouette appeared above her.

"Don't be afraid, my dear. I am here to save you."

The adrenaline in her body dissipated. Before passing out from shock, she heard the silhouette speak once more.

"It's so very nice to meet you. My name is Alexander."

10 — My Silver Medal Winner

I AM GOING TO DIE.

I mean, look at me. I'm a mess, and I'm getting it all over you.

Wait a minute.

You saw it happen, didn't you? Yeah, I bet you did. You showed up right after they left. Not a second later. You must have seen what they did to me.

What else did you see?

What else do you know?

How long have you been following me?

You know what? Don't answer those questions. Time is not my friend right now. I may not last the next five minutes. As long as I'm still breathing, let me do the talking.

I want to talk about the envelope.

Let's talk about the envelope.

The envelope.

Whenever someone gets a letter with the Maudlin Authority's insignia stamped in the top-left corner of the envelope, it's not a good thing. My father had one hanging out of his back pocket the day he took my sister and me away from the city. I didn't get my hands on it, though. I was six years old and had no idea what was going on. I didn't know anything about anything.

I kinda still don't know anything.

A few years later, another Maudlin Authority envelope surfaced. Gertrude walked through the living room with the mail. As soon as she noticed it, she put the rest of the mail down and locked herself in her bedroom.

Hours later, she re-emerged, looking sick to her stomach.

In the days that followed, she only got worse.

I never found that envelope. I can only guess that she destroyed it. Maybe she was instructed to do so. I can only assume.

Imagine my surprise when I found yet another Moth envelope on her dresser the night of my seventeenth birthday.

I entertained the idea that the envelope contained a letter about my father. It matched the one I saw in his pocket on the day he disappeared.

Maybe they found him, I thought. Maybe he had a change of heart and wanted to take me back. Maybe they found my sister too.

Annabelle.

I miss Annabelle, but I probably wouldn't recognize her if I saw her. I forgot what her face looks like, and that face is eleven years and three months older now.

Did we talk about this already?

Stop. Rewind. Play.

Yes, we did.

Stop.

Fast forward.

Punch the floor with your fist.

Stop.

Play.

You're probably wondering how we get mail around here.

I hear the rest of the country has something called the United States Postal Service. Yeah, we don't have that. The Moths handle mail through their Unified Communications Division, the same division that runs the Maudlin Authority Simulcast System.

The mail, the TV, the radio, the newspaper—the UCD owns them all. It controls the flow and consistency of diarrhea in this city.

It's not hard to tell what the Moths do and do not own. They aren't discrete about it. Take the cops, for example. Every cop uniform comes with a *Property of the Maudlin Authority* patch sewn on the right shoulder. Such arrogance.

Don't let this Moth charade fool you. They have their secrets, just as you have yours, and I have mine. All humans have them.

Every cop's uniform also bears a *Public Order Division* patch.

If you ever hear someone refer to the cops as "pods," now you know why. I still call them "cops." It feels like a dirty word. Just calling a spade a spade or whatever.

Just to keep score, I've mentioned three Moth divisions so far.

The fourth one isn't known to the public, but I've heard things.

Am I stressing you out? Do you feel overwhelmed? I know I'm a lot to handle, especially in large doses. It's written all over everyone's face when they're near me. I talk a lot. I repeat myself. I'm a terrible listener. I know, I know, I know.

You win the bronze medal. Only two other people in my life have ever sat with me and listened to me as long as you are right now.

My mom was one of them. She gets the gold medal.

Gertrude wasn't one of them, believe it or not. Don't get me wrong. She was a great human, and I had a strong connection with her, but man, she had the most abysmal attention span. I'm sure you've noticed. She was more of a storyteller than a story listener, if that makes any sense.

Charlie isn't one of them, unfortunately. I don't blame him. He had potential, but he was a little too preoccupied with his demons to handle my brain. He gets a pass. I'm okay with it.

I gave my silver medal to someone I didn't expect.

Isn't that how things go?

We're still talking about the envelope. Try to keep up.

My silver medal winner's life was printed, tri-folded, and stuffed into the envelope I found on Gertrude's dresser. The Maudlin Authority's insignia rested prominently at the top-left corner. By the way, whoever came up with their stupid logo—an "M" with a line through it—could have done better. I mean, I'm all about minimalism, but come on. Try harder.

Anyway.

One thing separated my silver medal winner from the rest of the orphans at The Amulet, including me. We all showed up there as kids. Four, five, six years old. Delilah was only a year old when she showed up. Anna was just days old. We arrived at very young ages.

But not my silver medal winner.

Okay, stop.

Since we're making sure spades are correctly identified, let's eighty-six the metaphor.

Autumn Vester is my silver medal winner.

Elliott Smith's "Everything Reminds Me of Her" started playing in my head just now.

Can you hear it? Do you hear it too?

Listen with me.

One of the first things I learned about Autumn is that she had already turned nineteen.

She was born on October 11, 1983.

How does a nineteen-year-old end up at an orphanage?

Based on everything inside her envelope, her age exceeded the

Moth-imposed requirement for transferring to The Amulet. Oh, and both of her parents were very much alive.

On the day she was expected to show up, she went missing.

The envelope contained a one-page letter addressed to Gertrude from the Moth's Public Order Division. It claimed that Autumn had been "misplaced."

You know, like how someone misplaces a sock or a pair of glasses.

Except they misplaced a human being.

The letter also assured that she would be recovered quickly and put under Gertrude's care once her misplacement had been resolved. It ended with a reminder that Maudlin is only a few square miles, so Autumn couldn't stay missing for long.

The letter was dated July 21, 2002.

I met her on June 20, 2003.

It took the Moths *that* long to find her.

That's one of the great things about this place. It may not be huge, but if you're creative enough, you can disappear.

The day before I met Autumn, I was very upset. In six weeks, I would be eighteen. Technically, I was supposed to leave The Amulet after my birthday.

This is how I learned what a double standard is.

"I can probably get away with keeping you here a little while longer," Gertrude said. "I'm not sure for how long, though. If it was up to me, you could stay forever, but I don't make the rules."

"Are you saying you never thought this out?" I asked. "What am I supposed to do? Where am I supposed to go? Do you not have a plan for me?"

She just kinda looked at me and shrugged her shoulders. I felt a stabbing pain of rejection in my stomach.

"What about Bill?" I asked, pointing at him. "He turned eighteen last fall, and he's still here! Explain that!"

I decided against bringing up Autumn and her age.

"I have to leave too," Bill chimed, "but I am okay with it."

"We're all doing the best we can, Elliott," Gertrude said.

Fun fact: Gertrude didn't make arrangements for us because she knew she wouldn't have to. She sensed the impending trainwreck coming for us all.

I had no goddamn clue what to do with myself. I spent many sleepless nights wondering what I'd do with myself after my time at The Amulet came to an end. I failed to realize that I'd be leaving one confinement and entering a larger one with just as little opportunity. A box inside of a box, if you will. Like nesting dolls but not as fun.

For the first time in my life, I worried about money. What a terrible, stupid thing to worry about. It wasn't just about money, though.

We were never allowed to leave The Amulet. We could watch the world around us from the backyard or the rooftop, but that was it.

The obvious reason: Maudlin is a death trap.

During my time at the orphanage, I didn't know the full extent of the Maudlin's darkness, but I had an idea. I saw some things, thanks to Bill's binoculars. I stole them and climbed onto the roof to get a better view of the city.

Sacred Dark Hospital's back doors caught my telescope eyes. That's where orderlies exit to dump bodies and take smoke breaks.

From what I saw, I don't think anyone liked those doors very much. They collected rust and looked hard to open. Sometimes, they would get stuck. This created a challenge for the orderlies whenever they had to drag a body outside. But once they got past the doors, it was a piece of cake. All they had to do was walk fifteen steps to the dumpster and toss the body inside.

Some orderlies resorted to sliding the bodies down rather than throwing them. They did this in pairs. Each pair had a unique style of body disposal. Some took an approach that maximized efficiency.

Others just wanted to have fun with it.

I'm trying to have a sense of humor about this, but I'm mortified. Seeing those bodies tossed and slid and dropped and flipped into a dumpster like unwanted trash disturbs me to this day. They weren't even covered or wrapped in sheets. Some of them were naked. That was the worst. I could never throw someone's naked body into a dumpster, even if I didn't like them very much.

Maybe that's not true. I could think of a few people.

A woman ran to the back doors of Sacred Dark with a little girl in her arms. Possibly her daughter, unmistakably unconscious. They were both covered in blood.

They entered the hospital as people. They left as bodies.

The woman was carried out by her limbs—one orderly on each side. After they disposed of her body, one of them went back inside and returned with the little girl's body. He tossed it one-handed by the hair into the dumpster. After taking out the trash, they lit up their cigarettes and played dice for money.

Talk about being desensitized.

After spending one night watching lifeless humans pile up in a dumpster, I realized the binoculars were a bad idea. There's something to be said about the horror that blooms from seeing bodies bend and move in ways they shouldn't. You can't unsee that.

It came with side effects.

I puked my guts out, slipped on my vomit, and fell off the roof. I'm surprised I didn't break anything, aside from the binoculars. I landed right on them. The lenses shattered.

"I had big plans for those binoculars," Bill said, emerging from the shadows.

"What do you mean? I don't follow."

"Exactly, and neither do I. We're not followers, Elliott. We forge our own paths."

"No, I didn't mean—"

"We will be leaving soon—out and on with our separate lives. I have most certainly overstayed my welcome. No matter, though. I know my calling. Even in a place like this, purpose awaits."

His words triggered me.

"Well, Bill, you probably won't need those binoculars after all. I did you a solid and used them to look at the world out there. I saw what waits for us out there, and it ain't purpose. Purpose waits for no one *in a place like this*. Only death awaits, and if we're lucky, it will be quick. That's it. That's all there is."

"Wrong."

"What?"

"I said you are wrong. You know it too. You know you are wrong. Do not pretend to be like them."

"Excuse me?"

Ignoring the fact that I just fell off the roof, Bill sat next to me and proceeded to talk more than I ever heard him talk before.

"I have never been a people person, as people say. It is apparent to me that you are not one either. This creates a separation between us, on several levels, in several ways.

"You and I—we do not see eye to eye when we view this world, or any world, but we align on one truth: Something intangible and ferocious lives among us. We may align on other truths as well, but I do not have evidence of those yet."

Bill removed a quarter from his pocket and stared at it.

"For a moment, imagine Maudlin as a coin. Fear and death haunt both sides.

"Heads: climb the Wall, or dig beneath it, and greet death on the other side.

"Tails: stay inside the Wall and accept the fear, dismal landscape, and the ever-looming possibility of being tossed into a dumpster."

He pinched the quarter and held it up to my face.

"The universe flips this coin in the air and asks you to choose: heads or tails. What do you choose, Elliott?"

My fight-or-flight response kicked in.

On the surface, this was a silly, hypothetical question. A harmless coin toss. But I reacted like Bill had a gun to my head. I couldn't remember the last time someone asked me to make a choice. I never really had choices back then. All of them were made for me. It made heads or tails feel more like life or death.

"You must choose, Elliott."

Bill shook the coin at my face. I studied it, hoping it would help me decide, but all I found was the year 1955 and something about trusting God, which sounds like an interesting idea.

Think about it: Some higher being rips you from non-existence into a life you didn't ask for. That alone is intrusive and entitled. But wait, there's more! If you don't follow the rules, you'll spend eternity in a state of extreme pain and suffering. But sure. Trust him, or them, or whatever.

Studying the coin didn't help me; I focused less on the coin and more on the person holding it.

Bill is a strange one, but not in the straitjacket-and-padded-walls sort of way. More like the Mariana Trench sort of way. His depth goes deep. I don't expect you to understand what I'm saying. All you need to know is that I figured out what Bill was trying to do with that coin. He didn't force a decision between two choices. This was a lesson, a teaching moment. As soon as I figured it out, I felt like Neo from *The Matrix*.

The Matrix is a movie. I don't have time to talk about it.

"I choose neither," I said.

Bill's eyes lit up with approval and respect, but he tried not to get too excited. He wanted me to elaborate.

"Why do we choose no side, Elliott?"

I grabbed the quarter from Bill's hand, fell to my knees, slammed it against the concrete, and when I lifted my hand, the quarter was standing straight up. Vertical and balanced.

"Because we walk the edge."

Bill picked up the quarter, stood up, and shook my hand.

"You passed the test."

"What test?"

Bill's energy changed. He looked tired and pale, even in the dark.

"I must lie down now. Maybe I'll read a book about worms. Leave me alone, okay?"

When Bill was done, he was done.

I didn't try to get anything more from him.

He made a request before slipping away.

"When you find me out there, bring a pair of binoculars. I will wait for you."

This has been my greatest tangent so far.

I'm sorry.

Before Autumn showed up in my life, I already knew so much about her. More than I should have. It's not my fault. I blame the envelope; it disclosed many of Autumn's secrets. All I did was open it.

The envelope held a picture of Autumn's mother standing next to a man with his face scribbled out in black marker. I assumed it was her father. The attached documents mentioned him, but like the picture, parts were blacked out. His identity hid behind black bars on the page, courtesy of the Maudlin Authority's Public Order Division.

Some things about her father were left visible, though. For example, he was referred to as "the man of very high status."

The same can't be said for Autumn's mother, Joan Vester. The Moths treated her like Hester Prynne from *The Scarlet Letter*. They plastered her past all over their stationery.

When Joan got pregnant with Autumn, the man of very high status tried to abort the child himself with a coat hanger, baseball bat, turpentine, and gunpowder. Somehow, all his attempts failed, so he kicked Joan out and disowned his unborn child.

The Moths divulged little about the nature of their relationship, but it sure as hell didn't sound like love. I don't even think they were married. Joan was described more as a prostitute than a wife.

I'm sure some people are both.

Homeless and desperate, she walked the streets of Maudlin, selling herself for sex. She conducted all of her business at The 86 Hotel, and she didn't let her pregnancy stop her. Some of her "clients" had a thing for it. This became a selling point.

I didn't like reading this, and I don't like talking about it. I'm not sure why it was relevant to Autumn's placement at the foster home, but whatever. I wouldn't expect anything less, I guess.

As if that's not messed up enough, Joan continued conducting her business at the hotel after Autumn was born. She locked Autumn in the bathroom until she finished for the day. Eventually, as Autumn got older, she would sneak out of the bathroom and walk around the hotel by herself.

This went on for over ten years. Then, for a time, they found a way out of that depressing mess.

Autumn caught a break when Joan and one of her clients fell madly in love with each other. It sounded more like a shallow, hollow infatuation, but Joan settled for this guy because he had money. A lot of money. It was the only reason Joan accepted his marriage proposal. Plain and simple.

Yes, even in a place like Maudlin, people get married and have weddings. Kinda funny.

I'm sure you know about him already. Everyone knows Ethan Sellers, the richest man in Maudlin.

Well, he used to be the richest man in Maudlin.

Autumn and Joan moved into Ethan's mansion after the wedding. How conventional. It was the same mansion previously owned by Alexander Morris—the one at the top of the hill. Ethan bought the place after Alexander died.

As far as I know, Alexander didn't share blood with Ethan. He didn't have heirs. The Moths possessed the mansion and eventually sold it to the highest bidder.

Joan never received any Mother of the Year awards, but she finally had a chance to give Autumn a somewhat normal life. Of course, it didn't last. Good things never stay good around here.

Three months into living the mansion life, Mr. Ethan Sellers died in his sleep. Joan inherited the mansion, the money, everything. She won it all.

The autopsy report blamed Ethan's death on a heart attack, which raised suspicion. Heart attacks aren't super common among people in their late thirties.

Speaking of autopsies, they don't happen too often around here. Almost everyone ends up in a dumpster after they die. You only get an autopsy if the Moths think you should have one.

For a while, everything stayed quiet for Autumn and Joan. They didn't bother anybody. Nobody bothered them.

This era of peace ended last year when Autumn heard a knock on the door. She opened it to find three Public Order Division cops with their guns out.

"We're here for Joan Vester."

Joan didn't come to the door; she saw the cops from the balcony. During her attempt to flee, she fell from the balcony and broke her legs. The cops dragged her away. Autumn saw the whole thing.

Autumn's Moth file claimed that a "young man pretending to be a detective" linked Joan to her late husband's death.

This guy just goes around town solving murder mysteries for fun. Strange hobby, if you ask me.

The file didn't reveal the lone detective's real name, just his alias: McMike.

After the arrest, the Moths sent Joan to prison without a trial, seized the mansion, and took custody of Autumn.

Let's talk about prison.

Technically, Maudlin has two prisons. Most prisoners end up at Wixom Station. It's an old train station built back in the early days of Sojourn. It's where Johnny Wixom got his name.

Gertrude was very fond of that place.

"Once upon a time, Wixom Station was the busiest, loudest part of town," she told me. "All the traffic, the loading and unloading of train cars, the sounds of engines and fast conversation. I must admit I hold a bit of nostalgia for that place."

After the Wall went up, trains no longer passed through Maudlin. They shut down Wixom Station and repurposed it as a prison. Freight cars are used as holding cells.

My father spent a few nights there, or I think he did. He'd been taken to prison before, but Maudlin has two prisons. I can't say for sure which one he went to. He didn't specify.

Depending on who you talk to, the second prison doesn't exist. But I've been around long enough and talked to enough people to know it's real. The Moths have a separate prison for "special cases." They keep it below the surface of the city.

The Maudlin Underground.

It's where Moths hide.

It's where they experiment on people.

It's where they kept the Vultures.

It's where Autumn's file came from.

It's where Autumn ended up after the Moths took Joan away.

Even though Autumn was eighteen, they still took her in.

A few days after being in The Maudlin Authority's custody, she escaped. The Moths made plans to hand her over to Gertrude, but as you know, she disappeared for a while—almost a year.

I feel weird for saying this, but after I found the *New Admit* envelope and read her file, I thought about her every day. I hadn't even met her, but I guess that didn't matter. After reading her file over and over, I felt something for her.

I learned so much about her, yet there were so many things the file didn't disclose.

I didn't know what her voice sounded like.

I didn't know what she smelled like.

I didn't know the color of her eyes.

I didn't know how tall she was.

I didn't know if she cut her hair or let it grow wild.

I didn't know if she listened to music or watched movies.

I didn't know if she had ever broken a bone or flown a kite.

I didn't know if she had ever fallen in love.

I didn't know anything.

After months of waiting and wondering, I started to think she might have died during her disappearance. Some girl I had never met in my entire life might be super dead, and I was very upset about it. It makes me sound like a lunatic, but I don't mind.

Sometimes these things just happen.

I don't expect you to understand.

I came to terms with the fact that she might not show up or that she might be dead, but that didn't make me think about her any less.

Gertrude acted like nothing ever happened. She just went about her business as if Autumn didn't exist. She didn't bring her up to me or anyone.

It made me angry. I didn't take it very well.

I had to say something.

"I found the *New Admit* envelope on your dresser. I know about Autumn. You're just gonna forget about her? You're just gonna act like everything is fine and wonderful? Bullshit! Why aren't you out there looking for her?"

Gertrude didn't say anything.

I should have stopped there, but I pushed her over the edge.

"You have connections with the Maudlin Authority, don't you? I bet you have a file on me too. What does it say? Do you have me figured out? You must know everything, right? How about you use your inside connections, classified documents, and whatever other secret bullshit to find her!"

She didn't say anything.

I had to throw in one last punch.

"Be useful for once."

I still can't believe I said that. It felt like the words came from someone else. Regardless, the damage was done.

She didn't say anything. She just looked at me in painful silence, then she stormed out of the house. I followed her to the back door and watched as she stumbled to the far end of the backyard, dug a small hole in the ground with her hands, and removed a crumpled pack of cigarettes.

She stayed in the backyard all evening, chain-smoking. I never looked at her the same after that. She had become a different person. Until then, I had this idea that Gertrude Morton was, in her own way, perfect. It's hard to explain. In my mind, she embodied the greatest example of what a human being should be. She stood firm among us as a tree among many trees, unshaken by the wind as the forest shook.

I know what poetry is, but I'm not good at it. Give me a break.

Seeing her desperately reach for a vice disturbed me.

She shook. Just like the rest of the forest. Just like the rest of us.

Stop.

Fast forward.

Stop.

Play.

Months passed; nothing exciting happened. Everyone moved on with their miserable lives.

Autumn Vester was reduced to an idea, so I idealized her.

Maybe it's the other way around.

Strings of thoughts like strands of hair grew from my head, and I refused to cut them.

There I go again.

In my mind, she was everything I ever wanted, even if it was all make-believe. I simply filled in the blanks with my own answers. As I got to know the idea of her, a fondness and a longing bloomed.

She existed. And yet, she did not exist.

She wasn't here. And yet, I talked to her all the time.

We went for walks around the house and the yard all the time.

This caught some attention.

"Are you alright?" Charlie asked. "I've never seen you talk to yourself like this before."

"I'm not talking to myself."

"Oh. Who are you talking to?"

"You wouldn't get it. Just leave me alone."

After a while, everyone kept me at a distance.

Maybe it's the other way around.

Most of the orphans already avoided me—Anna, Delilah, James, and the other asshole kids—but Charlie joined the club. Gertrude and Bill still talked to me, but our conversations were few and far between, and I acted like a complete asshole to them.

I had never become this fixated on a person before. Autumn

wasn't even real. Well, she *was* real. You know what I mean.

She just wasn't *here* here, if that makes sense. It messed with my head. Eventually, I started talking to myself in between talking to her. I narrated my life to an audience of zero. I had no one else to talk to besides the girl who wasn't there.

Fast forward.

Stop.

Play.

June 20.

The last day of spring.

I got out of bed super early and decided to spend some time, or the rest of my life, on the backyard picnic table. It's where I found the most clarity. Sometimes, finding that clarity felt so effortless. All I had to do was lie on my back, dig my fingernails into the painted wood, and look straight up. The rest happened automatically.

The summer solstice always meant something to me; it was my mom's favorite day of the year. Just like someone who goes outside at night to watch a meteor shower or fireworks, my mom went outside to watch summer begin.

"You can tell the difference," she said. "When summer comes, something special happens. Everything feels different." I smiled at her words, but I had no idea what she was talking about. At least not at the time. Everything felt the same to me. After she died, nothing felt the same. Summer didn't feel like summer anymore.

In my own little way, I celebrate the summer solstice to reconnect with her. I try to see the world as she once did. I look back on her words and still smile, if smiling is even possible. But I want to do more than smile. I want to understand. She died so young. I barely got to know her.

Want to know what's a real drag? I can't think about my mom without thinking about my father. I couldn't help it then, and I sure as hell can't help it now. They're forever linked in my mind.

I hate it so much.

My mom welcomed change. My father fought with an unrelenting stubbornness to keep his world the same. I say "his world" and not "the world" because he only lived for himself. Nothing else mattered. I'm not saying he loved himself or even liked himself. He put a lot of energy into protecting a part of himself, though. He barricaded his heart behind castle walls.

Now you know where I got it from.

I remember the last thing my mom said about him, maybe a couple days before she died. Skin fell off her face. Her teeth turned black. She didn't have lips anymore. I wiped the saliva from whatever was left of her chin. She shifted her gaze as my father zombie-walked behind me slowly. I could see his shadow.

"He just might surprise you," she said.

Even in death, she bled optimism.

Annabelle joined my mom at the summer solstice picnic table thought parade inside my head—the closest thing I had to a family reunion. I stopped thinking about them for a while; it hurt too much. I couldn't handle the reminder of their absence. Granted, there are people—*a lot* of people—who choose to torture themselves and relive traumatic or heart-breaking events over and over. The motion picture never stops in their heads. But I am not one of those people.

I always walk out of the theater.

What can I say about Annabelle? By last summer, I had gone two-thirds of my life without her. If I could describe her in one word, it would be "there." That's what I remember about her. She was just there, everywhere.

But that doesn't mean we were close.

As siblings, you'd think we played together all the time, but nope. We both acted like the only child of the family. After my mom died, we each reluctantly acknowledged the other's existence for a few days until my father drove us to the rest stop, and everything went to hell.

I'm not sure where I was going with that.

I don't remember how long I was lying on the picnic table. If you haven't figured it out by now, losing track of time is sort of my thing. The same goes for daydreaming.

My summer solstice family reunion thought parade could have gone on much longer than it did, I'm sure, but someone shook the picnic table and pulled me out of it.

He's here, I thought. The Grey Man is finally here for me.

It had been years since he last showed his sunken face. My memories of him faded with time; I started thinking I made him up.

He had returned to remind me of his existence, I thought. After all, he once said he had big plans for me.

At this point, I was ready. Big plans sounded great. I didn't have any for myself.

Before I could get too excited, I heard someone light a match. It must be Gertrude, I thought. She must have come outside to have another smoke and blame me for it. After all, I had recently pushed her to the point of digging in the backyard for her cigarettes. She kept some distance between us since then.

Whatever.

I do this thing where I convince myself that I don't care when someone gets upset at me, but the truth is, it kills me. It almost doesn't make sense because I've been a jerk to people my entire life. Maybe it's one of those things I got from my father.

He had a way of making me feel bad about everything.

I care deeply about how other people feel about me and how I make them feel.

I hate myself for it. I hate myself for it. I *hate* myself for it.

Keep this between us.

Please.

I heard the match ignite into a flame. The smell of cigarette smoke quickly followed. It was time. I had to confront Gertrude. I needed to make amends. After taking a few deep breaths and counting backwards from ten, I sat up to face her.

But it wasn't her.

A girl leaned against the edge of the picnic table with her back facing me. I couldn't see her face, but I could tell she was staring at the far end of the yard, concentrating on the brick wall she had just climbed to get inside.

She looked like fall. Her hair was this reddish, coppery color. She wore an oversized, dark brown knitted cardigan, similar to what Gertrude used to wear.

She smelled like fall too. Through the cloud of cigarette smoke, I noted hints of vanilla, sandalwood, and dead leaves. Perfectly proportioned. Balanced. Just the right amount of each.

I kept staring at her. I couldn't do anything else. I didn't want to do anything else.

She knew I was there, but she didn't acknowledge me. Not right away, at least. I watched her head move as she surveyed the yard. Her shrugging shoulders spoke volumes; her surroundings didn't impress her. After all, it was just a yard—an overgrown lawn, a picnic table, and a brick fence. Not much to see.

As I watched her survey the scene, I wondered why she came here or if she even knew where she was. Maybe she was lost, I thought, but then everything hit me. She wasn't lost. Not at all.

She knew exactly where she was.

"You smoke?" she asked, still facing the brick wall.

She waved the cigarette in her left hand so I could see it. I didn't know what to say. I had never smoked before, but I wanted her to like me. My brain glitched out as it often does.

I didn't answer her question, but she kept talking as if I answered her question.

She placed the cigarette between her lips, looked me in the eyes, and set it on fire.

"Good answer, kid. These things'll kill ya."

Her blood-red lips demanded attention against her pale skin. Her eyes were big, very big, I mean *massive*—and light brown. She smiled with straight, pearl-white teeth. No stains from cigarettes or coffee.

Oh yeah, that's another thing. She casually held a ceramic mug of coffee in her right hand like it was normal. The mug had a cartoon rabbit on it. Just beneath the rabbit, I noticed the word "rabbit."

She held the mug closer to my face so I could see it better.

"This is my rabbit-rabbit mug."

"Okay."

I felt so stupid.

Under her unbuttoned cardigan, she wore a black Led Zeppelin shirt. It reminded me of my mom, a fellow lover of Led Zeppelin. I never liked them when I was younger, but they grew on me over the years. When I saw this girl wearing their shirt, they became my favorite band of all time.

We shared awkward silence for what seemed like centuries. She kept looking at me. I kept looking at her, then away, then back at her, then away, over and over.

I'm not great at the whole making-eye-contact thing. I'm sure you can tell. I keep looking through the window at the gas station across the street. I was just over there. Now, here I am, lying on the floor at The Butterfly, wearing a red shirt that used to be white.

I'm not stupid. I know I'm dying.

She leaned over the picnic table and squinted, looking at me up and down, examining my being.

I didn't realize I was holding my breath until she looked away.

To my relief, her attention shifted toward Gertrude's house. She pointed her cigarette at the back door.

"So this is where I'm supposed to be."

She spoke in a raspy, low voice. I liked it, but let's be honest, she could have talked like Oscar the Grouch, and I would have liked it.

This is called romanticizing.

Take my advice: Don't do it. Ever.

Oscar the Grouch is a weird green puppet-thing that lives in a trash can. That's all I have to say about that.

The girl sauntered through the yard, taking in the view and several breaths of smoke. Without thinking, I got up and walked behind her, following her steps.

"Looks like I haven't missed much," she continued.

I didn't respond, but oh my god, I tried so hard to come up with something witty or charming to say. That's not my thing, though. It never has been.

"Not much of a thrill, but it will do. Besides, it sure beats where I've been. I'd stay out of the sewers if I were you, kid."

"I'm not a kid."

That was my big opening line. I know; I'm a smooth talker.

But it worked. She laughed.

"I know, kid, I know."

"Why are you here?" I asked. "It sounds like you could go anywhere or be anyone.

"If we're speaking truths, I'm still figuring that part out. For now, let's say curiosity got the better of me. Curiosity leads me everywhere. Life is a boring picture show without it."

"You make it sound so easy."

"That's because it *is* easy. Just take a step forward."

She looked at me, then at the ground, then back at me.

"Like right now?" I asked. "I'm supposed to take a step forward?"

"You're supposed to *want* to."

"I don't understand."

"Have you ever slow danced before?"

"No."

"Would you like to dance?"

"What?"

"Would. You. Like. To. Dance."

"There's no music."

"We don't need music."

Her confidence towered over my apprehension.

She placed my hands on her hips and rested her arms on my shoulders. Her cigarette almost set me on fire, but it wouldn't have made a difference. I was already on fire.

I could have died right there. I mean, come on. This girl shows up in my backyard. Ten minutes later, we're slow dancing to silence.

It felt like oxycodone binding to my opioid receptors.

Before I could sink my entire being into her arms, she pushed my hands away and ran to the end of the backyard.

"Hey! Where are you going?"

Like a cat, she leaped to the top of the brick wall. Effortlessly.

"What's your name, kid?"

"Elliott. Elliott Avenue. Where are you going?"

"You have my curiosity, Elliott Avenue."

I envied her for doing what I could not. I wanted to join her on the wall. I wanted to explore the other side. But I couldn't. I was still a good boy back then. I feared what waited beyond the boundaries of Gertrude's backyard. I wasn't ready, but no one is ever really ready.

I'm weakened by my own excuses on a daily basis.

"Autumn! Wait a minute!"

That got her attention.

"I guess the secret's out."

She squinted at me and straddled the wall.

"Will you come back? Will you return?"

She tilted her head and looked up at the sky, giving my question some thought, or at least pretending to. Something tells me that she already knew the answer.

"You will never see me again."

My heart sank into her trap.

"Kidding! I'll be back soon."

"Hey! Don't do that to me!"

"Sorry, kid."

"When is soon?"

"It depends on when the Moths drop me off. But first, I have to pretend to get caught."

"I don't understand."

"Au revoir, Elliott Avenue, until our next encounter."

She blew me a kiss and disappeared behind the wall.

A half-lit, lipstick-stained cigarette rested on the picnic table.

That's when I started smoking.

11 — The Consciousness Hotel

I SHAKE ALL THE TIME.

Violent tremors rip through my body.

Fear stomps on my trachea. I talk to myself, begging for it to stop, but it doesn't stop. It never stops.

All these things—fear, anxiety, tremors, pain—they're not the real problem. They're just symptoms of the disease. When the stars align, they give way to something else. Some other part of me vibrates. It looks back on my life and smiles an evil smile.

It breathes in the noxious fume of self-destruction and exhales in wild laughter.

It wants this. It lives for this. It kills for this.

I've killed before.

I ended someone about half an hour before you showed up.

Are you afraid now? You should be.

I'm kidding. I don't know why I said that.

The pills are talking.

I'm not thinking clearly.

This is awkward.

I'm not sure how to segue back to what I talked about earlier. I have nothing clever to say. Why does cleverness matter to me right now? What's happening to me? I feel my sanity evaporate with each breath. I taste it every time I cough. I keep coughing blood on you.

Not the best segue, but given my current condition, it will do.

In Bill's dictionary, the word "incident" has multiple definitions:

> *A violent event.*
>
> *A hostile clash between two forces.*
>
> *The occurrence of dangerous or exciting things.*

They all apply to what happened at the orphanage last July.

Stop. Rewind. Play.

June 22.

Eleven days before the incident.

Two days after I met Autumn.

Forty days before my eighteenth birthday.

Six months ago.

I think I got that right.

Numbers are hard sometimes.

I spent the morning staring out the living room window. The cold, wet, and grey outside covered every inch of summer. Mud and water glazed the broken concrete. Busybodies walked beneath umbrellas. For such a dreary day, Maudlin felt so alive.

I felt alive too.

For the first time in forever, I felt like a real person.

There's something about spending mornings by a window, watching the world happen, and finally feeling ready for it.

It didn't last long.

Someone knocked on the front door. Two knocks. The entire house heard it. Everyone ran into the living room, except Gertrude. She was nowhere to be found.

No one ever comes to the door. Maudlin isn't that kind of place.

Neighbors don't drop by with a Jell-O mold to see how you're doing. A delivery man doesn't come to your door with a box containing whatever you ordered on the Internet.

We don't have Jell-O or delivery people or the Internet here, but I know what they are. I'm just trying to make a point: When someone knocks on your door in Maudlin, it's serious business.

Rain fell on umbrellas from beyond the door. I peered through the window, catching a black umbrella resting on a stocky shoulder. Before I could think another thought, I ran to the door, or I tried to, but I didn't get very far.

Someone tied my shoelaces together. Gravity took care of the rest.

My face slammed against the hardwood floor, knocking me out cold for a few seconds. When I came to, I heard laughter fill the room as blood filled my mouth. I bit my tongue very hard on impact. When I looked up, I found all the orphans standing around the living room, indulging in my accident.

The rage monster inside me woke up.

Three more knocks fell on the door.

No one bothered to answer. Everyone stared at me as I lay on the floor and oozed red from my lips.

I'd like to thank my rage monster for giving me the strength to pick myself up from the floor. Thank you.

My mouth tasted like metal. A painful throbbing crawled over the entire right half of my face. My nose bled. The laughter stopped once everyone got a closer look at me, but five faces in the room kept their smiles.

Those Vultures.

I didn't know which one of them did it. None of them were going to talk, but I already knew that. Either way, I didn't care. I said to hell with the detective work and went straight for the Vulture I hated the most—James Grave.

He wasn't all that different from the other boys, but he took it upon himself to be their alpha dog. I'm not exactly sure how that happened, but it happened. They followed his every word, all the time. I blame his false sense of entitlement and need to intimidate.

I admit that I've been intimidated by him before, and for that, I hate myself.

Oh, and James was crazy. I mean, absolutely batshit crazy.

"Who thinks Elliott should lie back on the floor and bleed for a while?" he asked.

Who says something like that?

Johnny, Dallas, Darcy, and Devon raised their hands.

My ribs throbbed. My face swelled. I think I sprained my ankle. I held my left hand over my rib cage and limped toward the couch where the Vultures sat. Several thundering knocks hit the door.

"Maudlin Authority! Open the door!"

I didn't let that stop me.

The orphans turned their attention to the door, but James and I kept our eyes locked on each other. I didn't speak because of all the blood in my mouth. He confused my silence for fear.

"That's what I thought."

I spit a mouthful of blood all over his face. He didn't even flinch.

I thought he'd freak out or try to kill me or something, but he stayed calm, wearing my blood with a straight face. He didn't wipe it off or anything. He just stood up and faced me with that crooked smile and those yellow eyes. Small pupils too, like they always took in too much light.

"Someone's here to see you," he added.

At six feet tall, he had a height advantage. On a good day, I'm five-foot-seven. My slouch doesn't do me any favors.

"Coming! Coming!" a voice shouted behind us. Gertrude summoned herself, right on cue, oblivious to what just went down.

She hobbled toward the door, almost slipping on the blood, and placed her skeleton hand on the door handle.

I remembered who waited for me on the other side.

With my bruised, maybe-broken ribs and bloody, maybe-broken face, I followed Gertrude to the door. Everyone else stared in silence, unaware of the extraordinary day ahead. But I knew. I wished they would all go away, back to their bedrooms or the other side of the world. Anywhere but here, any time but now.

I wanted this moment to myself.

This was all for me.

This was mine.

Mine

Mine.

Mine.

Gertrude half-turned the handle and stopped herself. She looked at me with wide eyes and leaned toward the swollen half of my face.

"We have an unwelcome visitor," she whispered.

After taking in a million-year-long breath, she opened the door.

This didn't go the way I imagined.

Not even close.

I created a fantasy where I opened the door. Autumn waited for me on the other side. Nobody else existed. The world around us faded away. Time forgot itself. We had always known each other. She didn't feel anything but my energy. I wasn't broken.

Ideas are dangerous.

In the real world, two tall, emotionless figures in Public Order Division uniforms stood on Gertrude's front porch. They matched in every way possible: height, build, posture, facial expression, everything. It made me wonder what factory they came from. I swear, they were both copies of each other.

Perfect clones.

Their raincoats, collared shirts, pants, boots, badges, umbrellas, sunglasses, and side-parted haircuts were all black. I might have been a little more intimidated if they didn't try so hard to be bad boys.

When people try hard to look or act tough, it doesn't usually work on me. If anything, it works against them. Their forced, fear-based charade reveals the insecurity that lies beneath. There are exceptions, though. I learned that the hard way. But the Moth statues at the front door didn't fool me.

I found Autumn huddled between them. Her hair and clothes were soaked. She looked at me, greeting my gaze with a smile—the kind laced with sympathy at the sight of pain.

"Are you okay?" she mouthed. I answered with the slightest of nods. I didn't want anyone to know that we already knew each other.

It felt like we were the only five souls in the world—Gertrude, me, Autumn, and the two Moth statues.

Gertrude waited for them to speak, but they stayed quiet. I didn't understand. You'd think this would be a simple here's-the-girl-have-a-nice-day scenario, but something lurked beneath the surface of this interaction. Gertrude and the clones were on edge with each other.

I didn't know why.

I remember the scent of alcohol. Someone smelled like whiskey. It wasn't me, I swear. I hadn't started drinking yet, but these days, I can't live without it.

One of the Moths lowered his jaw, but before any words came spilling out, someone in similar attire exited a car down the street and came running to the door.

"Wrong house!" he shouted. "I drove to the wrong house."

After sprinting to the front porch, he bent down and pressed his palms against his knees, trying to catch his breath. I'm pretty sure we all thought the same thing: who the hell is this weird person?

"Hey guys," he said to the Moth clones. "I'll take this one. Do you mind if I take this one? That would be great. I'm just going to take this one. I think I should. Okay? Yes, I'm going to take this one."

The clones didn't respond. They just looked at him funny, like he was an unwanted guest at a birthday party or Halloween party.

Any party, really.

Have you ever been to a party? I went to my first one a few days ago. It was insane.

"Hi, hello, hi," the painfully awkward man continued. "I'm Adam Shipley, Public Order Division officer in training. It's a great pleasure to meet you all. As part of my training, I've been on a ride-along of sorts with these fine gentlemen. We're here on orders from the Maudlin Authority."

I ended up living with this guy for six months.

The clones blushed in response to Adam's introduction. One of them made a gesture with his hand, urging the trainee to shut up.

Adam is a lot like glitter. You can try to get rid of him, but he never really goes away.

He bowed to Gertrude.

"I just want to say, miss—may I call you 'miss?' I think it's okay. It's okay, right? Maybe 'ma'am' instead? Should we stick with 'miss?' Let's do that. Yes. I just want to say, miss, that it's a very great pleasure to serve you and your children in this town. This is a great town. I believe we can do some great things with this town. Great things, I tell ya. Just great."

Christ.

He didn't have many words in his vocabulary. His compulsion for repetition exhausted the living hell out of me.

We all have our things.

I know what "compulsion" means. I have a few of those.

Adam waved his arm in a circular motion around Autumn like he was casting a spell on her.

"Our orders, ma'am, are to make sure that this young lady finds her way into your home. Additionally, you must acknowledge that you have received and read the documents sent to this address. Her documents—the documents pertaining to her situation—have you read them? Also, did I just call you 'ma'am?' I think I did. Yep."

Gertrude responded with a dumbfounded look.

There was something about him. The way he talked, the way he looked at you. His bright blond crew cut. His massive, square jaw. Even the way he dressed.

I couldn't help it. I had to bring it up.

"What's with the trench coat? It's summer."

My question struck a nerve.

"First of all, I don't know you. Second of all, I don't owe you an answer. Third of all, it's for appearances, okay? When I'm out on the streets, I want to be respected, okay? I want to appear in a manner that is, you know, demanding of one's respect. Does that make sense? Besides, all the great detectives wore trench coats. Sherlock Holmes. Dick Tracy. Fox Mulder. Bru—"

Bill chimed in.

"Technically, Mulder is a Special Agent, and you are neither a detective nor a Special Agent."

"Oh, what do you know!"

Autumn was dressed in the same clothes from two days ago. At first, I almost didn't recognize her. It was the rain—the way it soaked her hair and dissolved the makeup from her face, revealing pale skin. She looked like a skeleton. Everything about her seemed slightly different than I remembered, including her behavior. The confident, outspoken side of her didn't show. She tucked it away and replaced it with silence and a tired smile.

"Ma'am? Miss? The papers. Did you read the papers? Do you read the papers?"

Gertrude woke up.

"Are you asking me if I read the newspaper?"

That question included a heavy dose of whiskey breath.

Mystery solved.

"Uh, um, no. No, I did not. If and when you read the newspaper is your business. That isn't my business. I said 'papers' as in 'documents.' Yes, the documents. Did you read them? Did you? Did you read the documents?"

I read the documents.

Gertrude stood there in a daze but managed to bob her head and whisper a small "yes."

She appeared agitated and confused. She did that thing where she stared at nothing and didn't speak, like falling into a trance.

Well, she used to do this. She doesn't do it anymore, obviously.

It's horrifying to watch someone lose control of themself.

"Are you okay, ma'am? Everything okay, miss?"

I had enough of this guy.

"Do *you* think she's okay? Do you think *anything* is okay? What are you even doing?"

"I wasn't talking to you, sir. To be honest, I forgot you were even standing there."

Bullshit.

Adam refocused on Gertrude. Gertrude's focus puzzled him.

"Ma'am, why are you staring off like that? What are you looking at? There's nothing there."

At this point, you should be aware that whenever Gertrude shot a blank stare at the sky or a wall or seemingly nothing at all, she saw something no one else could see.

"Ma'am, I can't proceed unless you cooperate. I—*we* have some questions for you. It would be really great if you looked at me instead of behind me. Please and thank you. Thank you, please."

The clones looked over their shoulders but found nothing out of the ordinary, all things considered. I didn't see anything either.

"Can you get her attention?" Adam asked me. He snapped his fingers in my face.

I had a real smart-ass answer for him, but I didn't respond. Not that I didn't want to. I literally couldn't respond. It's like those nights when I would wake up paralyzed, unable to speak, but this felt different. I hadn't just woken up, obviously, and I wasn't greeted by a black shadow with red eyes. Still, this felt hauntingly similar to that.

I felt hot and cold and prickly like a confused cactus. Nausea stormed my stomach. Was I getting sick? The last thing I wanted was to puke my guts out in front of Autumn. But I wasn't getting sick. Not like that.

A sharp chill caressed my spine.

I knew what was going to happen next: my first blackout in years.

I was too busy feeling stupid to feel scared.

I had never felt embarrassed about my blackouts until Autumn became a thing in my life. Hyperawareness and self-consciousness crawled around the inside of my skull. I had never felt anything like this before; I hated it to death.

Adam's voice reduced to distant muffling in my ears. Barely audible, but audible enough. He looked at me with the most confused look I've ever seen on a person's face. He probably thought Gertrude and I were flying high on something.

That means he thought we were on drugs.

I didn't know what drugs were back then. After the orphanage, I made their acquaintance. We became good friends.

Oxycodone is my favorite. I want it all the time.

Like right now. I want some. Do you have any?

A tunnel formed around my blurred vision. My blackout hourglass flipped over. The countdown to my collapse had begun.

I expected Autumn to laugh at me or look at me funny, but when I saw her through the tunnel, I found a sympathetic smile.

Neither Moth statue offered Autumn an umbrella. I wanted to punch them in their faces, and I would have, but I was preoccupied with slipping into a time coma.

Autumn followed her smile with a nod as if to say, "I understand. Don't be afraid. You can go now. I'll wait for you."

I felt free to slip away.

That was a stupid thing I made up in my head. Autumn didn't know what was happening or what I was going through, but it didn't stop me from believing in my delusion. Faith is an overwhelmingly powerful thing, for better or for worse.

Add it to my list of drugs.

Place it on the shelf next to denial and ignorance.

Is that a "no" on the oxycodone?

The moments leading up to a blackout feel a little like getting put under for surgery. I had to get surgery when I was three. I didn't know why, though. My parents never explained it to me.

I still remember the experience.

A man wearing green, garbage-bag-looking clothes put a rubber mask on my face and made me count to ten. My consciousness faded halfway through the count, and the next thing I knew, I was somewhere else. It was over. I missed the fun part.

There's one minor difference between blackouts and surgery: On the operating table, I didn't see a tall, thin man staring at me from the corner of the room, grinning with a broken-glass smile.

A tunnel tightened around my periphery as I looked out the front door. My world blurred and feathered away, but I could make out shapes on the front porch.

I counted the forms in my head or whatever was left of my head.

One.

Two.

Three.

Four.

Five.

Everything went quiet. I faded faster.

My conscious mind prepared for a departure to another place. I wasn't allowed to follow.

I know; it doesn't make sense.

I held on just long enough to spot the fifth shape at the door.

The Grey Man stood directly behind Autumn.

He placed his hands on her shoulders.

There's a pattern here. Whenever the sickly, strange man from the rest stop graced me with his nausea-inducing presence, it triggered a blackout episode. There's a connection between these events.

Regardless, discovering a connection between the Grey Man and my blackouts fails to answer a few critical questions.

Why?

Why me?

Why was this happening?

What was even happening anyway?

What was the point?

It's funny. I've asked myself these questions before, but then I stopped. I forgot about the Grey Man. I shrugged him off. It's like when you see a ghost. It's real when it happens, but after a while, you convince yourself that you made the whole thing up.

It blows my mind how easily I let life happen without exercising self-awareness. I play the role of a silent witness to my existence.

In my defense, I stopped asking questions because he stopped showing up. Years passed. It's easy to dismiss something after time buries it. Things get lost and lose their place in life.

Take my sister, for example. I used to spend every day with her.

But now, I wouldn't recognize her if she stood right in front of me. Not like I'd ever get that chance, but you get what I'm saying.

Time takes everything from us, including us.

Before I slipped into nothingness, Gertrude's voice cut through the dark and held me. We crossed paths at the Consciousness Hotel. She checked in as I checked out.

"I thought you were dead," she said to the Grey Man. "I thought I killed you."

I fell backwards.

Billions of humans have walked this planet, or so I've been told. Gertrude was the last one I'd call a killer. I've read her *Sojournals*—no mention of murder. However, half the pages in the final journal were cut out. A perfect square cut inside the middle third.

I haven't told you this yet.

Inside the hollowed-out section of the book, I found an 8mm film reel. It was labeled *Alexander*.

I shined my flashlight through a few frames and found two distinct figures sitting at a table. Gertrude was one of them. The other was a man I had never seen before: Alexander Morris.

I stole the film reel and kept it under my mattress. It crossed my mind at the front door.

I spent my final conscious thought wondering who Gertrude killed or who she *thought* she killed, or why she would say anything about killing someone in front of these Moths. Once again, as usual, nothing made sense. I was left with no answers, no closure, nothing. The only thing left to do was fade out.

In that last second, before losing consciousness, someone slipped something into my back pocket.

And then—nothing. I remember nothing.

I need you to keep me awake. Shake me. Slap me in the face or something. If I fall asleep, I probably won't wake up.

Do you know what a concussion is?

Can you please hold me?

Hold me close. Embrace me.

Then shake me like the devil's inside.

I'm not ready to go yet.

Don't touch me.

I woke up in my bed. That's where I always ended up after a blackout episode. I'd like to thank whoever kept putting me there. It was a nice gesture.

No one enjoys waking up on the floor.

My head felt like someone shoved it in a vice and threw it in a washing machine. I never had such a violent headache before. I know I tripped on my shoelaces and slammed my face against the floor before the blackout, but it wasn't from that. Pain only partly describes the sensation. The inside of my head felt kinda muddy.

I don't know how else to explain it.

I'm not that great at explaining anything.

The corner of my eye caught a flickering light. It danced on the surface of the standing mirror in the opposite corner of the room.

The mirror was a recent addition to my room. It belonged to Gertrude. Before Autumn arrived, Gertrude rearranged everything in her room. She spent an entire day nervously putting things up, taking things down, bringing things in, and taking things out. I minded my own business, listening to *Play This at My Funeral* repeatedly, when she barged into my room with the mirror.

The damn thing must have weighed a hundred pounds, at least. She dragged it across the floor, placed it in the corner, and walked away. No exchange of words; it was a weird time.

When is it not a weird time?

The flickering light in the mirror's reflection came from a candle on the nightstand next to my bed. Talk about a fire hazard.

It seemed like someone wasn't thinking too clearly, but there was a reason behind it.

The flame danced with a purpose. It drew attention to the message scribbled on the mirror's surface:

It has been nine days.

I must be dreaming, I thought.

It's like when you wake up from a long nap in the middle of the day. Your body feels heavy—*really* heavy—and nothing feels right. You forget where you are. You forget when you are. You might forget who you are. Some small part of you wants to get up and shake it off, but you ultimately submit to it. You fall back asleep. Next thing you know, it's morning, again. You look at the clock, realizing that you just woke up from a twenty-two-hour nap.

It was something like that.

The words on the mirror were written in red. I thought it was from a permanent marker, and I panicked. Sure, it was Gertrude's mirror, but it was in *my* room. You can't just waltz into my room and run a permanent marker across my mirror.

I don't like it when people mess with my stuff. I don't have much, but that's not the point. I just don't like anyone touching my things or "borrowing" them or whatever. Things always get lost, misplaced, or broken. I can't handle it. I just can't.

Don't touch my stuff.

Sometimes, maybe less than sometimes, I'd let Charlie read my comics. On a good day, I'd give him a piece of paper from my sketchpad. But that's different. Charlie was my best friend. Everyone else could go to hell.

I hope he's okay.

I saw him this evening. He looked at me like I was someone else.

I could tell he was worried about me, as he should be, but it didn't stop him from talking to me like everything was okay.

"I'll save you a spot at Lola's," he said. "Tomorrow morning. Same time as always. See you then?"

"I don't have time for this."

That's the last thing I said to him. Then I drove off in the cop car I had stolen, completely consumed by rage. Blood all over my face.

I stared at the message in the mirror for a while. But for how long? It was hard to tell.

The strangest thing happened.

As I stood there, the *nine* became a *ten*. Dead serious.

The message changed before my eyes.

It has been ten days.

Time skipped a day.

Okay, time didn't *actually* skip a day. Something was just really, really wrong with me. It had been that way for weeks. I would lose track of time. Most days, I felt dizzy. Oh, and I had this nasty ringing in my ears. And brain zaps. Oh, the brain zaps, like tiny power lines snapping and jolting inside my head. They made my teeth vibrate. I could hear my eyes move.

Figure that one out.

I have a lot of problems. I feel sick all the time.

For our own protection, we weren't allowed to see a doctor when we got sick. Gertrude knew enough about Sacred Dark to make that judgment call. Lucky for us, she specialized in herbology, reiki, crystal healing, all that stuff. She had a concoction or tincture for just about any sickness.

These are all real things, I swear. I'm not making these words up.

Who's to say if any of it helped? Better than a body bag, I guess.

Bill argued that Gertrude's approach to medicine was "a bunch of hocus-pocus."

"These are not suitable alternatives for western medicine."

He was the closest thing we had to a real doctor.

He knew everything.

A few days before my blackout at the front door, I shared my symptoms with him. He spent some time digging through dozens of books, most of which were medical journals and nurse's handbooks. After many uninterrupted hours of obsessive reading, he returned to me with a diagnosis.

"Elliott, based on the symptoms you presented to me along with the various medical references I have in my possession, I have concluded the following: you either have temporal arteritis, or you are being followed."

"Wait, what? I'm being followed?"

"Excuse me?"

"You said I'm being followed. What are you talking about?"

"I am confused, Elliott. Is that what you think I said?"

"Yes, because you *did*. I just heard it. You said I have temporary arthritis or—"

"Tem-por-al ar-te-ri-tis. Shall I say it again? Slower, perhaps?"

"Don't be a dick. Repeat the other thing you said. The thing after the arthritis thing."

"I said you either have temporal arteritis—not arthritis—or an anxiety disorder. Your nausea, dizziness, headaches, et cetera, fit the description. I have a book about anxiety disorders if you—"

"That's not what I heard you say."

"Such a lack of gratitude. Such dismal comprehension. I am done. Goodbye for now."

When Bill was done, he was done, and no one could sway him or convince him otherwise. He was a man of his word.

I always respected him for that.

I looked closer at the message in the mirror. When I placed my fingers on the words, a sense of relief swelled in my stomach. No permanent marker. It smeared like lipstick.

Autumn.

I wanted to believe she left the message, but then I remembered something: Gertrude also wore red lipstick.

Gross.

If Gertrude wrote the message, it meant she was looking out for me. It meant her grudge against me was dissolving. I could live with that. But it also meant that her handwriting dramatically improved overnight. Not likely. I removed her from the list of possibilities.

I pulled focus, staring at my reflection in the mirror.

My face, my eyes, my skin—they disgusted me. I don't even know why. Whatever this feeling was, it had been buried for a long time and somehow reached the surface. I started to cry. I just looked in the mirror for a little while and watched myself cry.

How pathetic.

How pathetic.

But you couldn't help it, could you?

I bet you feel like crying now, don't you, you pathetic child.

Am I right?

I am.

I *am*.

I—I'm—wait, what am I saying?

I feel like I'm losing you.

According to the mirror, it took ten days, but I finally dragged myself out of my room. The darkness lifted, but it had been replaced by a sense of urgency.

James and I had a score to settle. He wanted to hurt me. By extension, so did the rest of the Vultures.

The Grey Man was on my list. He and Gertrude shared a connection. She saw him at the door and spoke to him, swearing that she killed him.

Oh yeah, Gertrude was on my list too.

She wasn't herself anymore. She hadn't been herself for a few weeks. Most of the time, she locked herself in her bedroom. She wouldn't come out for days at a time. It made me wonder how she went to the bathroom, which I found out the hard way. I don't want to talk about that.

During the infrequent hours when she left her bedroom, she stayed silent, tending to her isolation at the kitchen table. She just kept staring at the table's surface and drawing invisible pictures on it with her finger. Once or twice, she looked up at me only to look back at the table, like I was no one, nothing, nonexistent.

Decision fatigue wore me down. My list overwhelmed me. I didn't know where to start. I wished someone would tell me what to do. I've never been good at following my own lead.

Luckily, I didn't have to.

I remembered that someone slipped something into my back pocket before I blacked out at the front door. When I reached into my pocket, I felt folded paper, another message:

Find me when you wake up. I will guide you.

— ∀

The handwriting matched the mirror. The signature looked like an upside-down "A." The only "A" I knew was Autumn. Yes, "A" is also for "Adam," but he doesn't count.

Whatever. Mystery solved. Moving on.

I checked every room in the house, except for Gertrude's. She locked herself in her room, and I figured Autumn knew better than to dive into that dumpster fire. Then again, who's to say? I didn't even know her, yet here I was, chasing her around the house.

Why? Because she told me to. She wanted me to.

I wanted to.

Blind trust is my greatest weakness, my downfall. I'm always quick to trust certain people that enter my life. I believe in them. I give them the benefit of the doubt. You could say it doesn't always end well.

That was a joke.

I mean, look at me. Look at what they did to me.

I don't even know you, yet here I am rambling on about some bullshit that probably won't even matter a few days from now. I'm so quick to trust you.

Oh well. No sense in stopping now, right? It doesn't matter. I'm already fucked.

I didn't bother asking anyone if they'd seen Autumn around the house. I don't like asking for help. Even if I asked, I doubt anyone would have an answer. Everyone scattered and wandered off into their own parts of the universe.

Gertrude remained locked away in her bedroom prison.

Charlie spent the entire day sitting on the front porch. This wasn't uncommon for him. After all, that's where his mother left him before she went off to die.

I wish I had the guts to be brutally honest with him. He'd spend most of his days just sitting there feeling sorry for himself. He wore his sorrow like a badge of honor. I wanted to tear it off. We were all dealt an unfair hand.

Life happens.

Let's look at Anna Quinn and Delilah Hayward for a minute. I don't talk about them very much, but they had sorrows too.

Anna was left on the same porch when she was three days old.

Her mother dropped her off with the intention to return after finding her missing husband. She never came back.

Delilah was barely a year old when she became an orphan. The Moths found her resting peacefully next to her parents' teeth and wedding rings. The serial killer spared her.

I don't know if Anna and Delilah had excellent coping skills or internalized everything or what, but I never saw them moping around the house or feeling sorry for themselves. Not once.

During my search for Autumn, I peeked into their shared corner of the universe. I caught them kissing and whispering to each other.

Bill was where he always had been—sitting on the couch, his face buried in a book. He was reading something called *Battle Royale*.

"It came out earlier this year," he said as I entered the living room.

"Wait, what? How did you get your hands on a book that came out this year?"

Maudlin gets nothing new. We're cut off from the rest of the world. We don't even have the Internet. I hear it's pretty cool, though. Have you ever heard of Myspace? It's a real thing, I swear.

"Technically," Bill continued, "it came out four years ago, but the English translation was not published until this past February."

"Doesn't quite answer my question, Bill, but thanks anyway."

"Happy to help," he replied, void of emotion.

I liked Bill.

The Vultures sat in a circle in the backyard, holding hands. The twins, Devon and Darcy, said some words. The others remained silent, keeping their eyes closed. I felt deeply disturbed by this scene.

"It's a séance," Bill said.

"A what?"

"Say-onts. It is a meeting of sorts."

"Why are they holding hands?"

"The Phoenix brothers claim to be mediums."

"Mediums?"

"Do you always repeat words that you do not understand?"

Bill had a way of making everyone around him feel like an idiot. Myself included.

"A séance," Bill continued, "is a meeting or ritual where those involved attempt to communicate with an entity from beyond our physical realm. It is a way of opening doors to the paranormal."

"So right now, they're out there talking to dead people."

"I did not say that. You are a poor listener, Elliott Avenue."

"So they're *not* communicating with dead people."

Bill exhaled the greatest of sighs.

"They have no idea what they are doing," Bill replied. "They are kids, and kids like looking for trouble. Even if the twins possess psychic abilities, they likely do not know how to wield them. Therefore, they do not know who or what awaits them on the other side."

"I don't understand."

Bill slammed his book shut, stood up with clenched fists, and approached me until our noses nearly touched. I could feel the vibrations from his trembling. He was never good at making eye contact, so I took this seriously.

"Look out there. You can see it, can you not? The brothers are speaking. I have been eavesdropping. I try to keep to myself. You know this, Elliott. But I cannot help myself now. Something is amiss with those kids. I have seen this before. I have seen him before."

"What? Who? Where? When?"

"Ender Forest. 1988. I remember."

"What happened?"

"They spared me, but why? What was the point? I am still here, but a meaningful reason for my existence has not been found. It may never be discovered. It may have never bloomed, to begin with."

Nonexistence.

"Purpose awaits, even in a place like this, but what if I never find it? Am I doomed?"

"Are you okay?"

I didn't know what else to say.

Bill's eyes glistened. A tear fell down his cheek. I had never seen him cry before. I don't think anyone ever had until this moment.

"I have sworn an oath to maintain a balance in our universe. I have to go back, Elliott. I have to go back to the woods."

"Why? What's in the woods?"

"You cannot die if you were never born. We are not the only forms of consciousness taking up real estate beyond the door."

"I don't understand."

He laughed and shrugged his shoulders.

"Forget it, Elliott. I am talking nonsense. I read too many books."

He walked back to the couch and continued to read *Battle Royale*.

"Is that book any good?"

"It is a fantastic read, but it hits a little too close to home."

12 — Surrogate Monster

I KEPT SAWING LOGS.

That's a real expression, I swear. It means I kept falling asleep. Sometimes for a few minutes, sometimes longer. These weren't blackouts, though. I know the difference. I didn't dream before; I was dreaming now.

Not "now" as in "right now." The "then now."

Am I dreaming now?

You must think I've had wild, vivid dreams doubling as premonitions. Maybe some poor soul from beyond the grave visited me in my sleep with signs and sentiments. Omens and such.

What a load of garbage.

Am I right?

Oh. I'm sorry.

I didn't believe you actually thought I've had dreams like that. You know, the future-predicting dreams. The dreams where we encounter dead friends and family. To tell you the truth, I also believe in those kinds of things. Something like that happened to me once or twice.

See what I did there?

I was trying to be like you.

I'm just trying to fit in. Even as I lie here, I'm trying to fit in. I thought you were one of those people who don't believe in anything, and I want you to like me, but I don't think it worked. I didn't read you right.

I don't know what I'm doing anymore.

Please be patient with me as we move along.

I know; we don't have time for patience. I could make a long story short, but you're not the type of person who wants to be spared any details. The more you know, the better. You also invested your time in this. Maybe your money too. I don't know. But you made it this far. I better make it worth your while.

Bill liked me less and less. I felt his frustration with me. He disagreed with my opinions, challenged my thinking, and corrected me nearly every time we spoke. He argued for the sake of arguing. It didn't help that he knew everything. I swear, he knew everything. He made sure we were aware of it too. All those damn books. Spouting random nonsense about Tsetse flies and sudden ionospheric disturbances. Hinduism and Dadaism. Johnny Unitas and Joni Mitchell.

What a weirdo.

"Where do you get these books from anyway?" I asked him once. More than once. I didn't forget his answer; I was just trying to be his friend, but Bill wasn't in the business of making friends.

"I found them."

When I asked him about *Battle Royale*, I felt like a truck hit me. It's like when you get a sudden urge to vomit, except in my case, it was sleep. It kept happening after Autumn showed up, but she wasn't the reason. That wouldn't make any sense. Maybe it was something she brought with her. Something that followed her.

I've always been allergic to cats and shadow figures.

Humor is not my thing, obviously.

I went from small-talking with Bill about his book to waking up with my face pressed against the cold, metal kitchen table.

Congratulations, Elliott Avenue. You've successfully fallen asleep in every room of the house.

I never liked hanging out in the kitchen. I barely used it. If anything, I'd pass through it a lot to get to the back door. The kitchen was just a hallway from my point of view.

Bill disagreed.

"According to the traditions and behaviors of the average American family, the kitchen is the most common area of the home. It is where family members congregate and bond the most."

"I think you're forgetting something," James shouted from down the hallway as he sharpened his nails.

James sharpened his fingernails all the time. That was his thing. He would lean against the wall, remove a nail file from his back pocket, and shape his nails into razor-sharp triangles.

"What am I forgetting, James?"

"We're not the average American family. We're not even a fucking family. You keep talking, but your words mean nothing."

Stop. Fast forward. Play.

The kitchen hadn't aged very well over the years. I could tell by looking at the wallpaper. Gravity, humidity, and time had their way with it. The way each sheet hung loosely near the ceiling reminded me of palm trees.

I've never seen a palm tree before, but I know what they look like. Bill had a stash of *National Geographic* magazines.

It's quite sad, really, now that I think about it. The closest thing to a palm tree I've ever encountered was sad, saggy, striped wallpaper. The white stripes yellowed as the years passed, but the pale green stripes remained untouched, seemingly unaffected by the slow death of time.

That morning, or afternoon—whatever—one of the wallpaper sheets hung lower than the rest, nearly falling off the plaster wall. Only the bottom third held on.

Not the strangest thing ever—the house had been in a slow, steady decline over the years—but the visible crack in the plaster wall didn't make sense to me. It was a perfect, vertical slit running from the ceiling to the floor. Nothing falls apart *that* perfectly, I thought.

I had never seen this slit in the wall before.

Keep in mind, I had just woken up. I have twenty-twenty vision, but it's always blurry in the morning.

I don't get why people rub their eyes when their vision blurs or deceives them. It doesn't work. The same goes for squinting unless you're translating a dream.

I felt like I weighed a few thousand pounds, but I managed to lift my face from the table. Leaning forward in the chair, I made a poor attempt to get a better view of the exposed plaster wall. Sure enough, it was still out of focus. However, through the blur, I noticed something strange. The perfect slit in the wall was glowing. A pale yellow light flickered on the other side.

I leaned in closer until it was an arm's length away.

I leaned in even closer.

Closer still.

I almost touched it.

Thump.

Something took a hard fall on the floor down the hallway. A shattering noise and a shrill cry of pain followed it.

This sudden, startling string of noises caught me off guard; I fell out of the chair. On my way down, my flailing right hand slammed into Gertrude's crystal vase. For as long as I'd been living there, the vase remained untouched, until now. It broke into a million sparkling pieces. I fell on the pieces and screamed bloody murder on the floor.

It's funny how things work, sometimes.

After the initial shock wore off, I thought about lying on the kitchen floor forever and feeling sorry for myself. I'm just going to stay on the ground, I thought, and drown in self-pity over my broken life, my sad little world. It didn't last long, though. Not because I felt I deserved better or anything like that. I just couldn't leave a mess of smeared blood and glass on the floor.

Cleanliness overrides self-worth.

Either way, they yield the same result.

I didn't look at my cuts. I didn't check to see what the glass did to my arm. I left the blood on my skin. We didn't have a first-aid kit, but that didn't matter. Something else drove me. I felt it then as I feel it now. I always feel it: time running out.

I didn't have time to take care of myself.

I never did. I never do.

Time is a fading memory, like a Polaroid developing in reverse or a moth I can't catch.

Feel free to chime in with your own shitty, poetic metaphors.

Yeah, sure, you can tell me there's a difference between *having* time and *making* time. Blah, blah, blah. I don't want to hear it.

I made time to clean up the floor—shut up—but not myself. Someone else needed my time, my help.

I didn't need to guess who it was. I already knew.

Gertrude was the crash that caused the crash.

I flicked some glass from my elbow and started down the hallway. Destination: the last door on the left, across from mine.

Well, it was Charlie's door too.

I hadn't talked to Charlie in a while. I hadn't talked to anyone, actually, except Autumn and Bill.

I had that standoff with James, but I'd been out for over a week after that. Can't do much talking in the blackout dimension.

Dissociation likes to pop in and say hello from time to time.

As I walked down the hallway, I remembered something my father said to me a long time ago.

His mother was dead or dying—one of the two. He was on the phone for a while, gripping the receiver like it had wronged him in some way. He ended the call by smashing the phone against the kitchen table. Shards of plastic flew like confetti.

This explains the scar under my left eye.

I know what confetti is.

He didn't check to see if I was okay. Instead, he stood up, punched the table—I think the poor table had had enough at this point—and gave a speech.

"This is what happens, Elliott. *This* is what happens."

Allow my father to explain what happens:

"You grow up. You get old. Then one day, your body fails you. That's right. You'll be walking to your sitting room from the kitchen because you *have* to water your fucking geraniums. The watering can you're holding weighs more than you, and your sense of balance ain't what it used to be. So guess what? You fall. You fall down and break your hip.

"Do you know what happens when you get old and fall down and break your hip? You die. You fucking die."

As far as I know, there wasn't a funeral. I never met the lady. My father's mother lived somewhere beyond the Wall. That's all I know about her besides the story about her geraniums and her broken hip.

It doesn't sound so bad; better than bleeding out on the pavement after the worst night of your life, am I right?

Still too soon for jokes?

When I got to the door, I was shocked to find Gertrude's wreath had been vandalized. Someone crossed out the Latin words around it and carved a new message:

Nigrum umbrae sunt non receperint in hoc domum.
CONFRACTUS EST CIRCULUS.

The black-stone amulet that once rested at the center of the wreath was gone.

Gertrude's door was unlocked, but I still couldn't get it to open. Something blocked it from the other side. I made the awful mistake of trying to kick it open. A shrill moan vibrated through the door. Gertrude's body blocked it from the other side. She writhed on the floor in the fetal position. I should have been more cautious.

Sometimes, I don't think. It's a fatal flaw.

I'm not even sure if I feared for her safety. I knew she was going to die. Soon. I mean, she was—I don't know—two hundred years old or something. The morning I met her, back in 1992, she already looked like she was on her way out.

As Gertrude writhed on the floor, she made sounds I've never heard before. Bone-dry vocal cords reacting to broken brain signals. Unfiltered misery. Anger, loss, and ferociousness.

The beginning and the end.

Her screams. Her crying. The groans and growls. They revealed something: the strongest woman in the universe had finally given up.

"Oh shit, I'm sorry!" I didn't know what else to say.

Even in her misery, she found it in herself to reprimand me.

"Lan...guage, boy."

This woman was incredible.

In the end, we didn't have the healthiest relationship or understanding of each other. I betrayed her trust to satisfy my interests and curiosity. She started drinking—heavily. Not because of me. Well, in a way, it was because of me, but not in the way I thought. I don't expect you to understand.

I stood by her door, consumed by guilt.

It triggered my emotional defenses.

Castle walls, activate. Vulnerability, take a hike.

I crawled inside myself. I was there, but at the same time, I wasn't anywhere.

In the nothingness, I thought about my mom.

She died inside the buckled steel and concrete of Sacred Dark Hospital. My father found the decency to let Annabelle and I visit her every day that week.

Her room smelled like piss. The thick, humid air made it hard to breathe. Black mold grew on the ceiling above her hospital bed. It spread a little more each day. I noted the pattern: black, tube-like branches sprawling out in circles.

My mom watched me as I watched the mold. I couldn't look at her, or at least not right away. I was afraid. After a small eternity, I forced my eyeballs in her direction.

She smiled. Her eyes glossed over with tears. It confused me.

It's okay, child. It's alright. I'm right here.

I looked at the mold again, too scared to confront my feelings. I tried my hardest to focus on the clusters of black circles, but the harder I fought, the worse it got. As my castle walls came crashing down, I felt the saddest, most peaceful thing ever experienced by any human being ever.

"Mom, help me."

I looked at her one more time; she was dead.

She left her smile behind.

"Gertrude! Are you okay? Oh, Christ. Did I kill you? Did I kill you?! Say something, damn it!"

This was it, I thought. I just ended her life. Death by a door to the chest.

How depressing.

"Language," she whispered. "Mind your tongue in this house."

"Gertrude? I'm coming in. I think I can squeeze through if I push the door just an inch."

It took more than an inch. My forced entry did more harm than good. The last time I forced my way in, I lost her trust.

But I had to get in there.

The sight and smell of her room stunned my sensory organs. The pungent odor of I-don't-know-what hit my nose hard. The curtains were open, but not a single sliver of light cut through the window. Layers of newspaper covered the glass. Coffee mugs, aluminum cans, and glass bottles littered every surface: the bed, dresser, everywhere. I couldn't see the floor. I couldn't even feel it beneath my feet. I only felt a sea of trash.

Through the dark, I spotted insects taking up residence, claiming cracks in the floor. A colony of tiny crawling things marched single file over Gertrude's legs. It was the closest thing to order I had seen in a while.

"Glamorous, isn't it?" Gertrude asked, noting my amazement. "Last time you were in here—*snooping around*—I'm sure it looked much different. Such is life, I suppose."

I crawled inside myself. She lay on the floor, but I felt cornered.

"Never mind that, child. All is forgotten. It must be. You have a good heart."

"I'm not a child."

"Oh, but you are."

This wasn't going the way I expected.

"It sure sounds like you're feeling better," I grumbled. I leaned against the bedpost; used toilet paper and a dirty ceramic plate slid off the mattress. Gertrude remained on the floor. The bugs explored her neck and arms.

"I thought—you—well, I thought…"

I'm used to being the one on the floor, so to speak. After all the times I felt lost or broken, she knew how to handle me. Now that we switched places, I realized I couldn't do the same for her. Instead, I focused on myself. I made it about me.

I waited for Gertrude to interrupt me and tell me what I was trying to say; it didn't happen this time. The faint flicker of energy she emanated just moments ago had disappeared. Labored breathing replaced her slanted remarks and old lady speech. She sank with every breath, deflating into the earth after each exhale.

She found it in herself to breathe.

I found it in myself to speak again.

"Gertrude, talk to me. *Talk* to me. I heard you fall. I heard you scream. What's happening? Look at me. What's happening to you?"

I already knew.

The placement of her hands told me everything. Her left hand gripped her chest. Her right hand clutched her hip.

It's all in the details.

"I—I—my hip, and my—my—and my—they—oh no. Wow."

She broke her hip and cracked some ribs for good measure.

Do you know what happens when you get old and fall down and break your hip?

You die. You fucking die.

This ship just lost its captain.

I dropped to my knees and held out my arms.

"Sacred Dark. I can take you there. I can carry you."

My idea hit her like a shot of epinephrine.

"You want to take me *there*? My boy, if we go there, I'll surely end up in the dumpster. You know what I'm talking about. You've seen it. I know you have. The torturous things they do there—we would not be safe. *You* would not be safe. They'll throw you in too."

She had a point.

"Okay, fine! We're not safe out there. I get it. But are we even safe *here*? What do you suggest—hang out on the floor until you *die* and leave us to fend for ourselves? Do you want to leave me with those psychos out there? James and those freaks? They're up to something. They are *up to something!* They spend all day just sitting in a circle. Staring at the sky. Chanting together. Hurting and hazing each other for the hell of it. They mark their skin with safety pins. Like, what the hell? What's it all about? What's it all for?"

I waited for answers, but she didn't speak. So I kept going.

"I'm running out of time. I'm going to be eighteen next month, and then what? I'm not prepared for this. I didn't sign up for this life! Why don't I just go into the bathroom and hang myself? Why not? That would be the end of it, *thank god*. No more living in fear. No more missing my mom. No more wondering where my sister went. No more fantasies about murdering my father for what he did to us. No more! I can't do this. I was doing just fine in my nonexistence before I got thrust into this bullshit life. Where am I going to go? You never prepared me for any of this! You did this to me! I don't want this anymore!"

I imagined a lemon-yellow extension cord hanging from the exposed pipe beneath the bathroom ceiling.

"Did I ever tell you that I knew your mother?" Gertrude asked.

"What does that have to do with anything I just told you?"

She paused until I realized what she said.

Wait for it.

"Hold on. What?"

Wait for it.

"Did you just say you knew my mother?"

There it is.

"Yes, I knew your mother."

My mind flew at a speed that my voice can only dream about.

"You knew my—what? When did you—how? I don't understand. Why didn't you—no. I didn't know. Why are you telling me this now, after all this time? Why did you keep this from me?"

"To protect you."

Gertrude started hacking her lungs out before she could utter another word. Thick, wet coughs. Violent coughs, over and over, until blood shot out of her mouth.

The sounds she made reminded me of *Evil Dead*.

I grabbed some used toilet paper from the floor and wiped her lips with it. The blood matched her smeared lipstick perfectly. Even in her suffering, misery, and madness, she never went a day without putting on that blinding, red lipstick.

The blood-to-toilet paper ratio was not ideal, and she kept coughing up more blood. I had to use my hands. As I wiped her lips, she started to cry.

"Help me, Elliott."

She curled into a fetal position. I held her on the floor. She cried for a long time. I don't know for how long. We didn't speak. My arms were open.

For a few seconds, everything felt fine. Her crying and coughing stopped. No screaming, no shaking, just steady breaths. The silence and darkness consumed me. It calmed me. It calmed everything.

Do you know what sensory deprivation is?

It's a real thing, I swear.

"I was there," Gertrude said out of nowhere, stirring the stillness in the room.

"Where?"

"Your mother. I was there when she was born."

My mind danced along the threshold of derealization as it often did, as it often does.

"Gertrude, what are you saying? Where is this coming from?"

"Patience, child," she answered, drawing a slow breath.

"For you," I replied, "all I have is patience."

"For you," she replied, "all I have is love."

That was nice.

"I brought Heather May Avenue into this world," she continued.

"You're my grandmother?"

"No, I'm afraid not. I wish I was. I want to be. I once convinced myself that I am, but Elliott, sweet child, we do not share blood."

I looked at the blood on my hands. I even went as far as showing them to Gertrude. She just shook her head.

Is any of this making sense to you?

I didn't think so.

This is my life.

She looked away with fear in her eyes, struggling to say something she didn't want to say. I knew in my heart that I didn't want to hear it, even though I had no idea what it meant.

I whispered to myself.

No. No. No. Please, don't. Oh god. Please. Please, don't.

"She's waiting for you."

And the hits kept coming.

"You've been through so much, Elliott, but I'm afraid it's going to get worse. It's only just begun."

I stopped asking questions. I didn't try to understand. I just sat there as she coughed up blood and hard truths. I didn't want to know anything anymore.

"The boy from the West is a man now, but he is no man at all."

Cough.

"He has waited *so long* for you, as he does every time you arrive."

Cough.

"He longs to open the door. But you can't let him, Elliott."

Cough.

"When we start over again, we will try harder."

Cough.

"I will wait for you."

Cough, cough.

Gertrude opened her eyes.

Her cough stopped. She was…dancing? She appeared to be, at least. I watched her attempt to rhythmically move the unbroken parts of her body.

"I want to hear music again," she said. "Put on a record, Elliott, would you?"

On a black, wooden nightstand in the far end of her room, I found an old Crosley record player. Unlike everything else in her room, it was in pretty good condition. I couldn't find her records, but I did spot an 8mm film reel hiding behind the nightstand. It looked similar to the one I stole, but this one had a different label: *Elliott.*

"I can't find your records," I said, quietly slipping the film reel into my pocket.

"There should be one in the player already. Play that one. Turn the dial. Put the needle on. Let's dance, or at least pretend."

We both lay on the floor, covered in blood, and we danced.

As I looked into her eyes, tears fell from mine. I cried so hard. This is it, I thought. This is the end of everything I ever loved.

"I will wait for you," Gertrude said. "We will try again."

The man on the record sang in an otherworldly voice.

He kept asking if there's life on Mars.

13 — Palm Trees

WE DANCED ALL NIGHT.

We fell asleep on the floor.

I woke up; Gertrude didn't.

Was she dead? I had no idea. I wanted to check, but I couldn't. I don't know. It's hard to explain what happens to me right after I wake up. My mind goes to an odd place.

Yours does the same thing.

You wake up. Not completely. Only just a little bit. In the waking, your conscious and subconscious reunite like old friends. One clocks in as the other clocks out. They exchange pleasantries and acknowledge each other's existence. Maybe share a waltz. Who knows. The point is that they're both present at the same time for a few seconds.

At this conjunction—I know what "conjunction" means—you don't know where, when, or who you are. The silvery paper falls into the solution, but the picture hasn't developed yet. You become this.

Blank.

Covered in a silver emulsion.

Photo-sensitive.

Waiting for the picture of your life to appear.

Until it does, my friend, you are no one.

I was no one.

Identity erased.

The date and time escaped me. My eyes were open, but I saw nothing. I heard a faint hiss coming from somewhere. My conscious mind hadn't clocked in yet. Until it did, I was a vessel. Not quite human. Attributes include breathing, sluggishly reacting to stimuli, and nothing else.

I dragged paper across the solution. Silver salts in motion.

Here comes the picture.

Darkness filled Gertrude's room. I studied the plastered sheets of newspaper on her window, saturated in moonlight.

From the cold, hard floor, I skimmed the front pages.

The headlines. The headlines. The headlines.

Marlowe Acquires 86 Hotel

Sacred Dark Opens Psych Ward

Maudelyn Magdalene Builds Her Wall

'Mass Suicide At Lola's Diner

Katerina Rist Seen Leaving Ender Forest

At the time, I didn't know what newspapers were. My parents didn't read them. Gertrude never talked about them. The closest thing I had to the news was a rooftop and a TV.

I hated the TV. I preferred climbing onto the roof and studying Maudlin's crooked-smile skyline.

The rooftop was educational.

It's how I found out about the Sacred Dark body dumpsters.

It's how I found out that functioning cars are a rare thing along these roads—if you could even call them roads.

Most cars in town don't move. The rest are stolen every night. I'd bet every working car in Maudlin has been stolen at least twenty times.

It's how I found out about the traveling pharmacist, the man who slinks around town with his rusted ice cream cart filled with drugs. I get most of my pills from him. I'm just not sure where he gets them.

He goes by many names:

Doctor.

Ice Cream Man.

Mr. Medicine.

Angel.

Devil.

Gallipot.

An unrelenting itch pulled me back into my waking life.

My conscious mind clocked in. I felt ants marching on my arms in search of I-don't-know-what. They explored my face, neck, ears, everywhere. Their fibrous legs played my skin like a piano, but I didn't dance. I didn't say a word. Hell, I didn't even care that I had bugs crawling all over me; I welcomed them. Take me, I thought. Just take me and get it over with.

How did it come to this?

The smell of brown liquor hung in the air.

Flies swarmed overhead. Their flight sounds overpowered the hissing record player. The record spun, but no music played.

As I lay there, I found something I didn't expect. I couldn't see or hear it, but oh, I felt it.

Darkness, a void, an emptiness, a heavy black hole. It started to consume me. I didn't quite feel like myself. Something about it felt so familiar, even comforting. Yes, comforting.

I don't like talking about this part, but since I might not make it through the night, it doesn't matter.

I'm not sure if anything matters anymore.

Through the darkness, I glimpsed a shred of light in the form of a choice: kill myself, or get up from the floor, start a fire, burn it all to the ground—this home, these people, everything I thought I enjoyed in my life—*then* kill myself.

I was a fool for thinking I would eventually get to live some kind of normal life. I spent my entire life wearing blinders.

It was time to come down from a years-long trip on one of the worst drugs of all time: hope.

My mom used to take this drug. My father kept trying to take it away from her. At the orphanage, Gertrude took frequent hits of hope and asked me to try it. I hesitated but eventually got hooked. Over time, though, I developed a tolerance, so I laced it with denial to chase the high.

It reminds me of the feeling I get when I mix hydromorphone hydrochloride and diphenhydramine. When I take both at the same time, I sink into the floor.

They intoxicate me.

It took me a while, but I managed to lift my body off the floor. I knelt there with my palms down, looking down in disgust.

I call this yoga position "downward-facing dissociation."

Scanning the room, I thought I had died and gone to hell, if there is such a place. An old, possibly dead woman lay in her own filth on the floor. Tiny creatures crawled on every surface. Piles of garbage and rotting food sickened the air. Dried-up vomit coated the dresser. The top of the dresser, which once held Gertrude's most prized possessions, had become a graveyard for liquor bottles. She filled them all with her urine.

As I rocked back and forth on all fours, I had this sinking feeling.

A voice in my head spoke to me.

You did this.

236 | Thomas Smak

I did this. All of this.

The room, this house, Gertrude's half-lifeless body on the floor, my prolonged isolation, the years-long, slow decay of my life, this unrelenting voice in my head—they collectively swelled and crashed, producing a violent, angry wave. I felt like a demon.

I laughed, laughed, laughed like a broken record.

I punched the floor until my fist was wrapped in blood. Then I punched it again, ten more times.

Laughing and punching. Laughing and punching.

My voice shifted into a higher pitch. It kept going higher and higher, mutating into a scream.

I proceeded to smash my skull into the floor.

Words spilled from my mouth. I didn't know where they came from or why I said them, but I said them.

I didn't have a choice.

I traded back and forth between violent screams and shouting unfamiliar things. Jet-black rage consumed me. I felt a crushing desire to break the light around me. No, not just around me, but around everyone, everything, everywhere.

My insides burned, but I wanted it. I writhed in the insatiable desire to self-destruct.

"You took everything."

I took everything.

"You will burn for what you did."

I will burn for what I did.

"It's my turn."

Go ahead. I give up.

"I'm taking you with me."

Take me.

"Grab the blade from the floor."

I don't care.

"Drain yourself."

Nothing matters anymore.

"Do it!"

"Are you okay?"

Autumn's voice drove the entity out of my mind, just in time.

The dark cloud dissipated; I felt like myself again.

But it wasn't a pleasant transition. Like the moments after waking up from surgery or a night of heavy drinking, my body hit a certain threshold that can only be reset through violent, massive, projectile vomiting. This went on for a few minutes. I made a generous contribution to the bodily fluids already splattered around the room. I don't think I ever felt so sick in my entire life.

Sick but relieved.

Does that make sense?

I believe Bill referred to this as ambivalence, but I might not be interpreting that correctly. Don't believe everything I say.

Relief is a scarce thing for me. I've only experienced it a few times in my life. It has a power greater than any drug I've ever put down my throat, through my lungs, or under my tongue.

It's the warmest embrace, like the open arms of my dead mom.

The whiplash from maniacal rage to sudden relief gave birth to an unfamiliar feeling. Was this…euphoria? I mean, I've felt euphoria many times before, but not without help from opiates. This time it happened organically, unassisted.

Something about it felt like love—if there is such a thing.

Autumn waited in silence as I took a moment to gather myself, but I felt her presence. I used the remaining thread of strength in my breathing bag of bones—I'm so poetic—to lift myself off the floor.

I turned around, and there she was.

I wanted to cry—really hard. I wanted to cry and hug her.

But I kept my tears inside.

I wanted to impress her, and crying isn't impressive. Crying isn't cool. Only losers cry. That's what my father used to say. Even now, I hear him in my head.

In light of recent events, it's probably not a good sign.

Forgive me, Father, for I have sinned, but you know that already.

Autumn broke her silence.

"Should we say a few words?"

I couldn't keep from smiling. Her voice had a grip on me. It made my cheeks hurt. It brought me back to sanity, if there is such a thing.

But I didn't understand her question.

"What do you mean?"

"That's what you do when someone dies. You say a few words."

I never heard of the whole say-a-few-words thing. I've witnessed it before, like at my mom's funeral, but I didn't know it was actually a *thing* or whatever.

An idiom. That's what it is.

Right?

"Is she dead?" I asked, eyeing Gertrude's body.

"You tell me, kid. You were here first."

"Yeah, but—I don't know what I'm doing. I don't know anything."

Making the smallest decision, or doing *anything* for that matter, was impossible. I forgot how to do everything. I mean, I could still breathe, but even that was a little shaky.

Autumn showed up at the very moment I needed someone.

I assigned her as my guide. I barely knew her, but it didn't matter. Desperate times or something like that, right?

Right?

"Okay, calm down," she commanded. "Put two fingers over her carotid artery and let me know if you feel a pulse."

"What—what's a carrot artery?"

She tried so hard not to laugh at me, but it was a losing battle.

Her wavering laughter frustrated me. At the same time, it hit me like a drug. Infatuation cut through me. It only lasted for a second, but it felt so good. This must be what happiness feels like, I thought.

I was wrong.

Infatuation isn't happiness. It's just a thing that tricks your body into producing dopamine and procreating. I can't help but wonder if the choices we make are really our own. They're just a product of our biology. We're on autopilot. Humans seem confused about what part of the body is in charge.

Follow your heart.

Go with your gut.

Use your head.

Check your dying foster mother's pulse.

"I'm being serious!" I shouted.

"I know, dear, and it's perfect."

I couldn't let her know how I felt, so I didn't show my hand. The panic card is the easiest card to play; I pulled it from my deck.

"Perfect? Please, show me what's so perfect about it. Show me what's so perfect about *anything*. Look at her! Look at me! Look at this place! It's all falling apart! I can't—"

I felt it coming on again—the stupid crying—so I turned away and pinched my leg as hard as I could.

My three-step method has proven successful whenever I don't want to cry in front of someone.

Step one: shut up.

Step two: look away from the person you're talking to.

Step three: pinch yourself as hard as you can.

Give it a try sometime. Let me know how it works for you.

She put her laugh away. I felt pretty awful about it.

"Jesus, just touch the left side of her neck. Check for a pulse. You do know what a pulse is, right?"

"Oh, shut up."

I didn't know what a pulse was.

This was our first fight.

I know; I'm stupid.

I pushed my fingers against Gertrude's neck. It reminded me of this one time when I opened the refrigerator and touched raw meat to satisfy a curiosity. It felt the same: cold, damp, elastic.

Beneath her skin, a faint, rhythmic tapping pushed back.

"I feel something!" I shouted. "So, what do we do now?"

Autumn didn't seem entirely convinced.

"Is she still breathing?"

I tilted my head and put my ear close to her face.

"I don't know what I'm doing. Here, you do it. You're better at this than me."

"How can you be so sure?"

"Because I don't know what I'm doing. I can't do *anything*."

I wanted her to feel bad for me.

Gertrude circled the drain, and I made it about me.

Me, me, me.

I'm so important.

Autumn traded curiosity for displeasure. She slipped her hands into her back pockets.

"Figure it out."

That was one of her things. Whenever she got upset or irritated or whatever, she put her hands in her back pockets. I consider this a weakness. She gives herself away when she does that. She shows her cards. I don't think anyone ever noticed that about her.

But I noticed.

I moved my ear closer to Gertrude's face—big mistake.

In a massive cough, blood, mucus, and god-knows-what-else spewed from her mouth, coating half my face in a thick, sticky mess.

I tried to play it cool and act like nothing happened.

"Well, I think she's breathing,"

"I see blood doesn't creep you out," Autumn noted, hiding her second-hand embarrassment.

The dusty hand mirror on the floor next to Gertrude caught my attention. I saw myself again; I looked even worse than I did the day before.

I didn't recognize my body. I shrunk inside my clothes, which I hadn't changed in weeks. It's disgusting, but it's the truth. I couldn't remember the last time I changed my clothes. This includes my underwear, socks, everything. That should give you an idea of the last time I had bathed myself.

My eyes sunk further inside my skull. Broken blood vessels spread like vines across them. The surrounding skin swelled with overlapping reds and blues, forming swollen, purple bags. The rest of my skin held a hint of yellow.

Do you know what jaundice is?

I had grown in reverse. I appeared to be shorter. It looked that way at first, but then I noticed my posture. Gravity had its way with me and my crooked, curled spine. As it turned out, a hunch is more than a feeling based on intuition.

I stared at the person in the mirror—horrified.

Who are you?

My eyes fell down a tunnel again, just like they did at the front door. Everything surrounding the mirror faded to black. I thought about something I read in one of Bill Dweller's medical books—it's called peripheral vision loss, or tunnel vision.

As I fell further and further down the tunnel of haunting self-reflections, a voice echoed from above, pulling me out from the black.

"Did you show him?" Gertrude whispered to Autumn.

Fluid gurgled in her lungs as she took a breath.

"Not yet," Autumn replied, "but I'm about to. Right now, actually. We're going."

"We're *going?*"

They knew something that I didn't. It birthed a feeling I had never felt before.

There was a lot of that happening—all these new feelings.

I'm having a hard time finding the word for it. I mean, I felt left out, excluded, blah, blah, blah, but that's not it.

What the hell is the word?

Oh, wait. There it is:

Territorial.

Do you understand why? Do I need to explain? Can you see what's happening here?

All these years, I thought I had an exclusive connection with Gertrude. We acted on behalf of an unspoken contract with each other, or so I thought. She had her secrets, obviously, but I assumed she only shared them with me. The last thing I expected was to walk into a secret she kept with someone else, let alone someone new.

Autumn was new.

Right?

I gave Gertrude my best squinty-eyed look.

"You broke the contract," I grumbled.

"What?"

"Never mind."

She was on her deathbed—floor—whatever. I dropped it as soon as I picked it up.

"Shut up, let's go," Autumn demanded.

"*Where?*"

I turned to Gertrude and asked the same question, but she couldn't answer. Only blood came from her mouth. She painted the floor with it.

It's funny; even though she was dying and I was being taken somewhere against my will, I wondered how we were going to wipe the blood off the floor. All the towels were dirty. Gertrude always did the laundry. I didn't know how.

Just to clear any confusion, I know how to do the laundry now. In hindsight, I feel like an idiot. Washing clothes is the easiest thing to do. Technically, no one washes clothes; the washing machine does all the work. We take all the credit.

The things I think about, man.

"Didn't you get the note I slipped in your pocket?" Autumn asked.

"That was you? I didn't know."

I knew.

"Did you not see my 'V' in my note? That's my signature."

"You mean the up-side-down 'A?'"

"It's a 'V.'

"How am I supposed to know that was you?"

"Who else could it have been?"

"Why didn't you just wake me?"

"You don't think I tried?"

"How would I know? I was asleep!"

"You're hopeless, kid. A true-blue idiot."

"What does that even mean—true blue?"

Gertrude cleared a wad of clotted blood from her throat.

"Leave—now."

Autumn grabbed my hand and took me away. The feeling of her hand in mine turned my legs to jelly. My entire body went numb. My head nearly detached and floated away.

I thought I was going to die. It was the best thing ever.

We flew down the hallway, making our way toward the kitchen.

I thought about palm trees.

At the intersection of the house, we ran into Bill.

Autumn let go of my hand.

Something didn't seem right about him—he was in a hurry.

An oversized, brown canvas bag rested over his shoulder. It over-flowed with books; he carried just as many. The tower of non-fiction literature in his arms blocked his view of Autumn and me, but he sensed our presence and quickened his pace to avoid a collision. Un-fortunately, he lost his balance in the process. The tower fell to the floor. I wanted to help him, but Autumn wasn't in the mood to stop for anyone.

"Do we have time to help him?" I asked.

"Whatever," she griped, shrugging and sighing.

Everyone seemed to be in a hurry. I didn't know why.

Bill broke ground on the reconstruction of his book tower. By the time I started helping him, he was already halfway done. I picked up a few books, but he didn't need my help.

"Bill, what's up? Where are you going?"

"I don't want any part of this," he replied. "You two are mixed up in something you do not understand. I do not want to be around for what happens next. If you will excuse me, I must get going. I feel as if I am running terribly late from something."

Autumn corrected him.

"You mean you're running late *for* something,"

Bill gave her the dirtiest look of all time.

"No."

I didn't bother trying to understand him.

"Don't forget these." I handed him the last of his books.

I felt a warning sign that my blood sugar was about to drop.

His choice of books distracted me:

The Feynman Lectures on Physics by Richard P. Feynman.

Familiar Trees, Volume One by G.S. Boulger.

Man's Place in Nature and Other Essays by Thomas Henry Huxley.

Hostage to The Devil by Malachi Martin.

One of them stood out among the rest.

The Stand by Stephen King.

"You read fiction?"

Bill never read fiction.

"I do now."

I had never known Bill to read anything other than scholarly articles or various works of non-fiction about plants and bugs and weather patterns and quantum mechanics and whatever.

"Why?"

I didn't know what else to say. After waking up from a ten-day nap, I had the worst time stringing words together. I felt my brain breaking. My lips were numb.

"I underestimated it. Fiction, Elliott. It is coming to life."

He ran out the front door like a monster chased him.

Before he disappeared out of view and into the night, he shouted a familiar request.

"Don't forget the binoculars!"

The house suddenly felt less safe.

Autumn grabbed the sleeve of my hoodie and pulled me into the kitchen. I couldn't help but laugh. All of this felt fake or like it wasn't happening. I couldn't take anything seriously. I reached my limit. Nothing mattered anymore.

Nothing matters anymore. Nothing is real.

There it is again.

I've become the poster boy for derealization.

I have no idea what I'm talking about.

The kitchen was falling apart, much like the rest of us.

Blood-soaked glass crunched beneath our feet. It made the floor quite slippery. My shoes turned into ice skates.

I've never gone ice skating, but I imagine this was how it felt.

The glass beneath my shoes pressed against the tile floor, allowing me to slide and spin around.

This had become the only thing I cared about. All I wanted to do was stare at the floor and spin around in my new ice skates. I watched the half-clotted blood spiral into thin, red ribbons.

"Wow," I said over and over.

"Wow."

"Wow."

"Wow."

"Wow."

A disembodied voice interrupted me.

"Look at you go, Angel."

It triggered a feeling—something nostalgic and disturbing.

The voice wasn't a sound but a memory.

"Mom?"

I started to black out, but Autumn intervened and pulled me up. The fog over my eyes cleared a little. She clenched my wrist and threw me against the refrigerator.

"Christ, kid! What the hell is your problem?"

I didn't know what to say. I could barely speak. I mean, if I put my mind to it, I could have told her that something strange came over me as soon as I saw the blood and glass on the kitchen floor.

I could have told her the blood came from my body.

I could have told her I fell after reaching for a sliver of light beaming through fake palm trees on the wall.

I could have told her that spinning in circles summoned the memory of my dead mom.

I could have told her that I used to know what it meant—what it truly meant—to be happy.

But I went in another direction.

"I'm fine."

Autumn whispered to herself.

"Oh, Gertrude, what have you gotten me into?"

I kept staring at the floor, enchanted by my bloody Rorschach painting: a rabbit eating a snake. My mom kept talking to me from somewhere inside my head.

"Keep spinning! You make such wonderful circles."

My eyes went black; I hit the floor. Autumn, once again, caught me and picked me up.

"Momma? Where are you? What are you doing?"

Autumn sat me in a chair.

"I'll tell you what I'm doing," she shouted. I heard biting anger in her voice, but it left as quickly as it came. She took a deep breath and put her hands on my shoulders.

"To be honest, Elliott, I have no idea what I'm doing either. I'm just following orders, which is something I never, ever do. But I made a deal. I made a promise. I got what I asked for, and now I have to give something in return. It just so happens that you're involved in holding up my end of the bargain. I don't know what else to say. Gertrude didn't explain. I don't even know you, yet here I am, and here we are. Now, we have to go. Come on, get up."

"Following orders?"

"So, you did hear me! For real, though, I thought I lost you for a second. I've seen some pretty repulsive shit in my life, but I've never seen anyone make giant spin art with blood before."

"What's spin art?"

"The whole calling-out-for-your-mom-while-spinning-in-circles thing was really something too. I don't know why you're such a big deal, but Gertrude seems to think so. Can you get up now?"

Autumn stepped away, leaving a clear view of the refrigerator. Someone must have pulled it away from the wall. Once again, I stared at the thin strand of pale yellow light beaming between two tired sheets of wallpaper.

I was about to ask my next question, but my stomach spoke first, reminding me that I hadn't eaten in almost seven days.

I powered through it.

"What did she do for *you*?" I asked.

I wanted to feel upset that Gertrude helped her and didn't tell me about it, but I reminded myself that nothing mattered.

Defeatism is a cozy blanket.

"None of your goddamn business."

I didn't pry any further. I couldn't. Hypoglycemia wouldn't let me.

"I should probably eat something."

Her eyes lit up. Her energy changed.

"Oh, hey, I can help with that!"

"Please."

"Don't bother looking in the fridge. There's nothing there. I took everything, even the expired stuff."

Like Bill, Autumn had a canvas bag. She did this incredible magic trick where she flung the bag around from behind her, caught it in mid-air, and pulled an apple from it. You should have seen it. She could make anything look like magic.

"I always have snacks in my bag. Here, take it."

As she tossed the apple toward me, the stenciled words on her canvas bag caught my attention.

Property of the Maudlin Authority

She noticed me noticing it and threw the bag over her shoulder.

I didn't catch the apple in time; it landed on my foot and rolled across the floor, slipping through the wallpaper, disappearing beyond the yellow light.

Clunk

Clunk-Clunk-Clunk

Clunk-Clunk

Clunk

Clunk-Clunk-Clunk-Clunk

Clunk

It's funny; I'd never heard that sound in real life before, but I still recognized it.

"Did the apple just…fall down a flight of stairs?"

"Abracadabra," Autumn replied, flashing a pair of jazz hands.

"What does 'Abracadabra' mean?"

"Nothing. Let's go."

If Bill were there, he would have told me.

I have to admit, I was heartbroken when she didn't grab my hand and pull me along with her.

Sometimes, I enjoy tachycardia.

She may have excited me, but I was still afraid to follow her. What choice did I have, though? It was either that or starve to death. After all, she had all the snacks. I still wanted that apple.

"After you, Elliott Avenue."

I spread the wallpaper sheets like curtains and stepped into the light. This must have been what Dorothy felt like when Toto revealed the Wizard.

What a letdown.

In my world, the Wizard was a hundred-watt, yellow-tinted, incandescent light bulb.

It didn't match any of the things on my list of possibilities:

An alien.

A ghost.

A time machine.

The afterlife.

Charlie.

I thought maybe he found a new hiding place.

I hadn't seen him in a while.

No supernatural discovery here. Just a lousy light bulb.

The stairs were interesting. They didn't stand out from a standard set of stairs, but I had never seen a large flight of stairs before.

"Are you coming, kid?"

"I don't like this."

"Well, you made it this far. Might as well keep going, yeah?"

"This is weird. Where are we?"

"Just come down, and I'll try to explain."

"I want to go back to my room."

"If you come down here, I'll hold your hand."

"Okay."

That's all it took.

I began my descent, crawling backwards down the stairs with my eyes closed. Fear and hunger kept me from walking down them like a normal person.

I counted twelve steps before my hands and knees felt cold concrete. At the bottom, I found relief—and the apple.

Endorphins and adrenaline cycled through my brain as I bit the apple and held Autumn's hand.

Probably the best moment of my life.

She used her free hand to pull a string dangling in front of her. It turned on a light, revealing the basement.

All this time. We had a goddamn basement.

"Where are we?"

"This is where Gertrude keeps all her stuff."

"Stuff?"

"Secret stuff."

I let go of Autumn's hand and fell into a state of disbelief.

"By the way," she continued, "Gertrude asked me to tell you something. She said you'd know what it means."

She looked me in the eyes. It burned my insides.

"Happy birthday, Elliott."

14 — Sub Terra

MY MOM HAD A MINT GREEN, DUCK CANVAS DRESS.
White lace trim bordered the sleeves. She pinned a tiny bronze plate just below the collar. It had her name engraved in white. Glossy plastic earrings dangled from her ears, pretending to be diamonds. A white satin headband tamed her wild, frizzy mess of hair.

I saw this version of her every evening before she left the house.

She worked as a waitress at Lola's Diner, across the street from The 86 Hotel. Twelve hours a night, six nights a week behind a counter, serving coffee and listening to humans talk about their problems. That's how my father put it, at least. He wasn't in any position to talk, though, given his many failed jobs.

Before my mom left for work each night, she spent half an hour with Annabelle and me. During the summer months, she took us on walks up and down Gainsborough Street, where we lived. She would tell us how she used to take walks by herself before we were born, and even though we weren't around yet, she missed us dearly.

I heard this story every time we went on a walk. My six-year-old brain didn't understand it.

"How could you know me, Mom?"

"What do you mean, dear?"

"How can you know me before I was borned? Before I existed?"

I had a decent understanding of what it means to exist.

I'm not sure if I do anymore.

She stopped walking and knelt down to face us at eye level.

"You have always existed. I have always known you. I have always loved you."

As we eased into November, we spent our half-hour ritual indoors. It's not that she minded the cold. West Carolina weather is comfortable all year. The shorter days and earlier sunsets disheartened her more than anything.

Maudlin's body count goes up after the sun goes down.

My family had a tiny house—it was less than half the size of the orphanage—but it still made for a decent place to play hide-and-seek. Floor-to-ceiling pillars of random junk stood like monoliths in every room.

Cardboard boxes crammed with carbon paper.

Leather-bound suitcases stuffed with neglected button shirts.

Weird metal boxes attached to buttons and switches.

A stack of newspapers here.

A mountain of notebooks there.

Empty water bottles labeled with duct tape.

Empty medicine bottles labeled with duct tape.

So many empty bottles. So many strips of duct tape.

All of this was normal to me.

Annabelle and I liked hide-and-seek for different reasons. Her favorite part was getting found, but not me. I enjoyed the thrill of never being found. Outsmarting the seekers makes the game far more exciting. It only got better the longer we played.

I don't know if you've ever played hide-and-seek before, but it turns into a game of wits. You have to evolve your strategy after all the good hiding spots have been used and used and used.

Every time we played, I made it my mission to stay in hiding longer than before.

"You'll never find me, Mom."

One evening, not long before she got sick, she threw on her mint green dress and told me to go hide. Usually, she gave me until the count of one hundred before seeking me out. This time, she only counted to thirty.

Annabelle didn't play with us. She developed severe anxiety problems around that time. Hiding made it worse. She followed me to my hiding spots sometimes, but that was too much for her after a while.

Twenty-nine.

Twenty-eight.

Twenty-seven.

I fled to my father's room.

Usually, this would be a bad idea. It was my *father's* room. That evening, though, he wasn't home. I mean, it was a stupid idea either way, but that's exactly why it made the perfect hiding spot. My mom knew I avoided his room out of fear. She did too.

Technically, it was her room too, but she only used it to store things. My parents didn't sleep in the same bed. She took to the couch instead.

Twenty-three.

Twenty-two.

Twenty-one.

The far-left corner of the room had a closet with two folding doors. The door handles were handcuffed together with a plastic child-proof device, but I knew how to disable it. My parents put these things all over the house; they didn't work.

I failed to realize that disabling the device on the closet door handles would give away my hiding spot. It couldn't be reattached from inside.

Eighteen.

Seventeen.

Sixteen.

Something about the closet didn't feel right compared to the rest of the house. For one thing, I could actually see the floor. No empty bottles or newspapers or weird metal boxes. Just a single wooden box resting on the dark green nylon carpet. The clothes hanging overhead were perfectly spaced apart by one finger width.

More mint dresses. I hid behind them.

Eleven.

Ten.

Nine.

Once again, I had found the perfect spot.

I took a moment to lean back, catch my breath, and celebrate. Victory was mine! But the moment passed as soon as it arrived.

The wall behind me moved.

In a desperate attempt to keep my balance, I grabbed the dresses. The clothing rack snapped in half; I fell through the wall and landed in an unfamiliar place.

Where am I?

Three.

Two.

One.

Cold wind lashed at my skin. Heavy moisture hung in the air. A deep, vibrating hum resonated from far away.

"Hello?"

My voice echoed and bounced. This place didn't feel like home.

As my eyes adjusted to the darkness, I spotted something from the corner of my eye: a clothing rack. This one didn't have more mint-green dresses, unlike the one I had just broken. It held six white garments. They kind of looked like dresses, but they had long sleeves and felt scratchy.

When I had my surgery, the doctors wore similar clothes.

Years later, I found similar clothing worn by a handful of gentlemen in one of Bill's medical journals. They posed for a picture.

"Who are these people?" I asked him.

"Physicists. They are physicists."

Before I could investigate any further, my mom's hands reached through the opening in the wall and pulled me out. I turned around to get one last look at the cave room before she shut the closet doors. Beyond the clothing rack, I spotted a small flight of stairs leading down into a tunnel.

From that day on, the bedroom remained locked. My mom installed a deadbolt. She stopped playing hide-and-seek with me.

"I'm just so tired, honey. I think I need to lie down."

I thought this was some excuse to keep me from finding more secret tunnels or other strange things. It ended up being cancer—the beginning of the end.

At her funeral, I couldn't stop thinking about the cave room. When the church people closed her casket, I replayed the memory of her closing the closet doors. It was the only time I had ever seen her afraid. She feared the discovery of her secrets more than cancer or death. When she died, she took those secrets with her, or at least she tried to. Inside the crumbling church, I put the pieces together.

You think you know someone. You're confident that you know them well—better than you know yourself. As time passes, you learn things from them: how to trust, how to love, how to play, how to fall, how to get up. They become more than just a part of your life. They become a part of *you*.

In Maudlin, you're lucky to have this experience once in your life.

Unfortunately, that luck goes south when the person you "knew" dies and you find out they were someone else the entire time.

I refused to trust anyone after my mom died. I swore I would never trust again. I was so sure of this. Then I met Gertrude. She helped me feel safe. She took me in and helped me remove pieces of my armor.

But not all the pieces. That will never happen.

She showed me trust with her time, words, and actions. I gave in and opened myself up.

But not completely. That will never happen.

If only I had known the same thing would happen again.

My biological mother had a secret closet. My foster mother had a secret basement.

"How's the apple?" Autumn asked.

"Good."

Chewed-up pieces fell out of my mouth—not my most graceful moment. But goddamn, when you're starving, who needs grace?

Speaking of food, have you ever wondered where our food comes from? It's a testament to the strangeness of Maudlin. We're surrounded by a massive wall, but we don't starve. In fact, food is hardly a worry. Doesn't that seem a little suspicious to you?

It's not that nothing grows here. We have the forest. Maybe the apple came from there. Maybe it came from somewhere else. Either way, it was damn good. It brought me back to life.

I sat on the bottom step of the stairs, removing bits of apple skin caught between my teeth. Autumn stood in the middle of the basement, tapping her foot while staring at me. I could tell this wasn't her first time down here. She didn't scan her surroundings.

She had been surrounded by them before.

I felt that nerve in my chest twitch again.

Betrayal.

Not caring about anything was harder than I realized.

"What are we doing down here?" I asked. "Why are you in such a hurry to show me this place? How did you know it was even here?"

"Jesus, kid. You're easily riled up, aren't you?"

"*I'm* asking the questions!"

The crippling wave of hypoglycemia receded back into the ocean. The sugar in my blood brought me to my feet and resurrected anger. Cue the explosion.

"There's a fucking basement!" I shouted.

"That's not a question, but yes, there's a fucking basement."

Her response ignited more rage inside me. With clenched fists and teeth, I unleashed a barrage of screams and profanity. Every bad word in the English language shot past my lips. I think I charged at her too. It's hard to remember. It felt automatic.

All reaction, no thought.

This proved to be a great lesson in getting to know Autumn. The moment I got too close, she grabbed my shoulders, dug her nails in my skin, and let me have it.

"Listen here, kid. I haven't slept in three days. Don't even ask when I had my last shower. I'm exhausted, just like you. I'm a mess, just like you. And I'm pissed off, just like you. I'm on your side, but I swear to God, if you cross me, I will end you."

She didn't blink or break eye contact. I shrunk in her presence; I was six years old again. It's like she knew eye contact makes my skin feel like it's burning.

She tapped into my weakness in the most paralyzing way.

Still, it wasn't enough to hold me down. Curiosity got the better of me as it often does.

"Autumn?"

"Ugh, what?"

"How long have you been living down here?"

Under the dim light of the low-hanging bulb above, her cheeks turn red. They almost perfectly matched the color of her hair.

"A little while," she nervously replied.

"Autumn."

"Three weeks, maybe? I don't know. Maybe a month. Maybe longer? I don't know what day it is."

"What? I don't understand. Why do you live down here? Where did you come from?"

"I'll tell you sometime, but that's not important right now. That's not why we're down here."

"Why are we down here? Please tell me *something*."

"Honestly, I have no idea. Gertrude told me to bring you into the basement and wish you a happy birthday. She said you'd know what that meant. She said you'd do the rest after that."

"Do *what*?"

"No idea, but whatever it is, please do it already. I want to leave."

"What's stopping you from leaving?"

"I told you, Elliott. I made a promise."

"What kind of promise?"

"The kind I'm not telling you about."

I couldn't get anything out of her. She seemed just as clueless, but she also knew things that I didn't.

She held her cards close to her chest. I couldn't even find my damn cards. Neither one of us understood the rules of the game. We just knew that folding wasn't an option. All the poker games I played with Adam at the hotel really got into my head, I guess.

"Well, the least you can do is show me around." I insisted.

"The least I can do? Wow, you've got some nerve, kid."

She pulled on another string hanging from the ceiling. Several tube-shaped fluorescent bulbs flickered and buzzed over our heads. Dim, yellow light struggled to illuminate our surroundings.

"I feel like I'm in a nightmare episode of *MTV Cribs*," she said.

"What's *MTV Cribs*?"

"Never mind. Let's start here."

Autumn summoned a flashlight from her snack bag and pointed it at the floor near the stairs. We started there and moved clockwise around the basement.

"Nothing special here," she said. "Just a pile of old journals.

"Hold up."

I knelt down to get a closer look. One journal had *Sojourn* written on the cover.

"Did you go through these?" I asked.

"I didn't go through anything. That's part of the rules. Gertrude let me crash down here, but I'm not allowed to touch anything."

"You expect me to believe that?"

"I don't care what you believe, kid. Can we keep going?"

I reached for one of the journals and opened it.

"Apparently, that rule doesn't apply to you," she grumbled.

October 29, 1952

The village gathered in droves. Alexander dragged us from the forest into Sojourn—every man, woman, and child. He threw Darwin's corpse in the middle of Charon Street. The sight of his unrecognizable body inspired no reaction from the crowd. They watched intently as I wept. Not a word nor a flinch. Just eyes.

Alexander remained beside me, standing tall and proud as I fell to my knees. His cold, wet hand caressed my hair. This act was undeniably a part of his theater. Every move: a calculation, a manipulation, a sleight.

He gave a speech to his people. Darwin's nearly lifeless body consumed my attention. I do not fully recall what Alexander said—only pieces. He spoke of an impending miracle and a new incarnation. "The next phase."

As an outsider, I saw the truth: his village was inhabited by a herd of sheep in human skin. I must give Alexander credit. He was the most cunning shepherd.

The remaining pages were ripped out. I tossed it aside, grabbed another one, and flipped to a random page.

"Anything worth mentioning?" Autumn asked.

I didn't respond.

April 17, 1966

I received a letter from Katerina today. Somehow, after all these years, despite fleeing a thousand miles away, she found me. Her birds must be nearby. They are seemingly everywhere, all the time.

She knows that I took Maddie with me. She knows about Maddie's daughter; Katerina claims she belongs to the Enders. She demanded that I give her up. I fear what will happen if I don't comply, but my heart won't listen. My heart won't let me.

Perhaps it is about time I return to Sojourn. I hear it goes by a different name these days.

"Elliott, come on, we have to keep moving."
I tossed the journal into the pile and grabbed another one.
"You said I'm supposed to look around. That's what I'm doing."
"Yes, but there's a lot to see, and we're running out of time."
"Hold on, one more."

August 1, 1985

The day I was born.

> *Heather's colleague, Eloise, ran through the labyrinth until she found my house. Upon catching her breath, she informed me that Heather's water had broken. I fetched some towels and a pail of water.*

> *When we arrived, we were too late. My heart sank as I witnessed the grief in Heather's voice, on her face, and in her arms. Eloise consoled Heather in an attempt to suppress her echoing cries. Who knows who or what might have heard them.*

> *We sat with Heather as she lay on her back with the dead child, umbilical cord still attached. I asked her if she had a name in mind. She looked up and smiled.*

> *"Elliott. I was going to name him Elliott."*

> *After saying his name, the symbol on the door lit up behind her.*

I threw the book halfway across the basement as if it were on fire.

"Jesus, what happened?" Autumn asked.

All I could do was stare at the pile of journals and try to comprehend what I had just read. All these years, Gertrude had been sharing a wild story with me about Maudlin's history. I wasn't even sure I believed it. At most, it was a cheap birthday present. Imagine my surprise as I read my part in the story—*my* part.

A sinking feeling pulled me down. I felt like a sweaty, confused cactus. My stomach churned. As I bent over, waiting to puke, I realized Gertrude was still trying to tell me something. She wanted me to know where the story left off. After that, it would be mine.

She couldn't tell me how the story ended, but not just because she was dying.

The story was still happening.

"I just want a normal life," I whispered.

"What did you find?"

"Nothing."

"Elliott."

"I thought we were running out of time. Let's go."

"Fine."

Autumn knows how to read people. She didn't press me further. I appreciate that.

We left the journals behind and crept further into the basement.

I couldn't believe what we found next.

"Holy shit!"

Autumn looked at me, confused.

"What, these?"

She pointed her flashlight at a sea of books. Shelf after shelf after shelf of them. Thousands and thousands.

"Bill, you son of a bitch."

This explained where Bill got all his books, but it left me with more questions.

"Who else knows about this place?" I asked.

Autumn shrugged. "No idea."

"Have you seen anyone else down here?"

"I haven't seen anyone, but sometimes when I'm lying in bed, I hear footsteps. Maybe it's just that tall, weird kid getting books. Maybe there were others. I didn't want to look. I didn't want them to know I was here. That's all I can say."

I stopped paying attention as soon as she mentioned the bed.

"You have a bed? What bed? Why?"

Autumn pointed her flashlight at the far end of the wall, past the millions of bookshelves. Sure enough, there it was.

"Well, it isn't *my* bed. I just sleep on it. Is that really what you're focused on right now? All this random junk in the basement, and you're fussing about my bed?"

"It's not your bed."

"Whatever."

The bookshelves demanded my attention. I counted seventeen of them—eight rows on each shelf and roughly forty books in each row.

The books were color-coded. White books on top, followed by red, orange, yellow, green, blue, purple, and black. I stood in front of a shelf with golden yellow books at my eye level. At the very center of the row, an old, weathered book with a frayed spine rested between two *National Geographic* magazines. When I pulled it off the shelf and read the cover, I thought I was dreaming.

A Violent Dance: Essays on Parasites and Parallel Reality Shifting by Gertrude Morton.

"Did you see this?"

Autumn squinted at the cover, unimpressed.

"Doesn't mean anything to me. Sounds like a bunch of gibberish. And no, I didn't see it. I already told you I didn't touch anything. That's the rules."

I laughed.

"You don't strike me as someone who follows the rules."

"You don't know a goddamn thing about me."

"Well, I know your name. Ha!"

My attempt at being playful covered up the fact that I knew many goddamn things about her. I read them all in her file.

"My name isn't Autumn."

"Wait, what?"

Okay, so I didn't see that coming.

"Well, it is—it's my real name—but no one calls me that anymore. Just—just don't call me that, okay?"

She struggled to finish her sentence, tripping over the words. I felt her self-consciousness. She couldn't talk about her name without looking back at an unwanted memory. I watched her get lost in it.

"Okay. What should I call you?"

After a small eternity, she pulled herself out of the memory, grabbed the golden yellow book from my hand, and stashed it away in her snack bag.

"Plenty of time to chat later, kid. Now's not the time."

"You want to chat later? I'd like that."

"I don't care what you like."

"Can I have the book back?"

"You can have it back when we're done. Keep looking around."

I couldn't get a read on this girl to save my life. That's exactly how she wants it.

"Where should I look next?"

"How about this?"

The beam of her flashlight landed on a hollowed-out, three-foot-tall tree trunk pretending to be a table or a cabinet. I've never seen anything like it before. The same goes for nearly everything on and inside it. I only recognized the handwriting on the vials and scraps of paper inside the hollow trunk. It matched the writing on all the notes I found in the freezer back in '92—the ones taped to all the plastic bags filled with plant parts.

All the words on these vials sounded completely made up.

"Cope—copelandia? Am I saying that right?" I asked.

Autumn laughed.

"Hey! Be nice."

"I'm not laughing at *you*, kid. I'm laughing at what's in that vial. I'm just a little surprised to know Gertrude has magic mushrooms. Pretty hilarious, if you ask me."

"Magic mushrooms? Like a magic trick? Do you do magic tricks with them?"

I didn't know what shrooms were.

Boy, do I know now.

"Yeah," Autumn giggled, "something like that. They might come in handy later."

She opened her snack bag, signaling me to toss them in.

"What about all these other things—they're just letters—LSD, DMT, MDMA. Should we take these too?"

"Yup. We can do plenty of magic tricks with those. You'll see."

I grabbed every vial and threw them in her bag. A smile stretched across her face. She was making fun of me, but I didn't care. Making her smile was all that mattered, no matter the reason why.

Autumn rifled through her bag.

"I'm running out of space. I prefer to travel light these days. Might need to let some things go."

She used the tree trunk table as a place for her discarded items: empty tin cans, mousetraps, dice, broken eyeglasses, chalk, three decks of playing cards, a pocket calculator, half a loaf of bread, a pizza cutter, and a handful of multi-colored wires.

"What are the wires for?" I asked.

"They're PC cables. I ripped them out of an old computer. I just figured they might come in handy someday. You never know."

"What's a computer?"

"Are you for real?"

"Yes."

Autumn laughed as she discarded a handful of salt packets from her snack bag.

"Kid, you need to go outside once in a while. You might learn some things."

"I go outside! You saw me in the backyard, remember?"

"Yeah, but that's not what I mean. You need to go *outside*. Explore the city. See what's happening out there."

"Is that where all this stuff came from?"

"Not everything. I found these in the house."

She removed the two 8mm film reels I had found: *Alexander* and *Elliott*.

"Which one do you wanna watch first?" she asked, tapping the reels together.

"Hey! Those are mine!"

"Are they? Because Gertrude asked about her stolen film reels. She didn't want them ending up in the wrong hands. I found one under your mattress and the other on the kitchen floor."

It must have slipped out of my pocket when I fell out of the chair.

"Gertrude wants you to watch them."

"Watch them? How? With what?"

"With that thing over there."

I followed the beam of Autumn's flashlight as it moved across the floor to the center of the basement, landing on a bizarre-looking metal object.

"This is a film projector. I've never used one before, but Gertrude told me how to set it up. I'll figure it out. Just give me a minute."

"I thought you weren't allowed to touch anything."

"She made an exception."

I reached out to investigate the projector, but Autumn slapped my hand away.

"Don't touch it! You're clumsy. You break things."

My castle walls went up. For a moment, I hated her guts to death. But I didn't say how I felt. I just crawled inside myself and stared at the machine.

"Here, give me some light while I do this," she continued, handing me the flashlight.

I wanted to ask how it worked, but I hated her for calling me clumsy. It didn't stop her from reading my mind.

"Think of it like a VCR for 8mm film. It's not as simple, though. You can't just throw the reel on there and hit play. There are switches, knobs, cranks, clamps, levers, blah, blah, blah, you get it. I think I'm supposed to pull this back."

She studied the projector's lens. It was attached to a hinge that swung open like a door, revealing two guides to place the film.

"Let's give *Alexander* a try."

She slid the film along the guides and hooked the end into an empty reel at the top of the projector. After swinging the lens back into place, she placed her finger on the "LAMP/OFF" switch.

"Don't look at the lens," she instructed me. "Look over there."

When she flicked the switch, a white, rectangle-shaped light appeared on a makeshift screen draped over the concrete wall.

The rectangle looked dim near the center, but not because of the light. There was something behind the screen—something dark.

I feel dizzy again.

You might need to take me somewhere soon.

I won't last much longer like this.

When she flicked the "START/STOP" switch to the "START"

position, the reels spun, sliding the film past the lens, revealing a black-and-white motion picture of a young woman sitting at a table by herself.

She appeared to be in her late twenties, maybe early thirties. She sat with her head down, hands folded, waiting for something. After ten seconds or so, she started talking to herself. She moved her lips, but I couldn't hear her voice.

"Where's the sound?"

"It doesn't have sound. Doesn't matter, though. Gertrude said you don't need sound. Just watch."

A dull, lifeless room surrounded the woman. Nothing in it but a table, two chairs, and a spotlight overhead. Not even windows. Just wooden planks for walls. She didn't want to be there. She didn't belong there. This wasn't home, but she couldn't leave. Not yet, at least.

The empty chair across from her implied company. Until that company arrived, she mumbled unintelligible words and hung her head beneath folded hands.

"I don't get it," I complained. "What are we waiting for?"

A shadow loomed from the left side of the frame, growing and growing until it touched the woman's face. When she looked up to greet the shadow, I almost pissed myself.

"Holy shit. That's Gertrude."

The shadow's owner entered the room—a tall, fit man wearing what I assumed to be a black, wide-brimmed hat and trench coat. His attire could have been brown or some other dark color. It's hard to tell in black and white.

"And that must be Alexander," Autumn presumed.

"What the hell is going on?"

Seeing Alexander with my own eyes after reading and hearing about him blew my mind clear out of my skull.

A part of me thought the stories about him were just fairy tales made up by a bored, unstable woman looking for a way to pass the time. After watching him enter a room and make contact with my foster mother, that part of me dissolved.

Alexander approached the chair but refused to sit. Instead, he used it to brace himself as he bent his body forward, getting a closer look at Young Gertrude.

His body language painted the picture of a man seeking dominance. To take a seat would mean to get down on her level.

As soon as he entered the room, Young Gertrude stopped moving her lips. Her prayer hands turned into fists. She tensed her shoulders and fired an unwavering stare. Every visible sign of weakness disappeared. The expression on her face made it very clear—every particle of her being loathed the man standing in front of her.

"Glad I brought this with me."

Autumn pulled a bucket of popcorn from her snack bag. I'm not kidding. "It's like we're at the movies!" she continued, shoving a massive pile of greasy popcorn in her face.

"I've never been to the movies."

"Jesus Christ. I swear to God, after we get outta here, I'm taking you to the movies. You're missing out, kid."

"There's a movie theater in Maudlin?"

"Kinda. I'll show you sometime. You'll see."

You can see it too.

This place has a movie theater. It's in the back, just around the corner from the *Mortal Kombat* arcade machine.

I pulled my focus from the projector screen and wondered if Autumn had just asked me out on a date.

The thought hypnotized me. My skin flushed. My heart thrashed around in its cage. My head nearly floated away. I felt closer to God. Who cares about all this stupid basement bullshit, I thought. I'm going on a date with Autumn Vester. Nothing else mattered.

I'm not sure how long I floated around in this trance, but it was long enough to get hit in the face by a handful of popcorn.

"Pay attention!" she shouted.

When I looked at the screen again, I caught Alexander mid-speech, performing a myriad of gestures and staring at the ceiling.

I have to admit: he captivated me. I couldn't hear him, obviously, but I didn't have to. Something about his eyes and movements drew me in. There was a magnetic charm about him. I bet Young Gertrude agreed with me. I saw it in her eyes on the screen.

Alexander slowly lifted his hands in the air, palms facing up, inviting her to stand.

"The priest did that in the church," I said. "He told everyone to stand up with his hands, and they listened."

"I didn't know you were the religious type."

"I'm not. I only went one time."

"Let me guess—Christmas? Easter?"

"My mom's funeral."

"Bummer."

I hate it when people use that word. It's the most unimaginative and insensitive way to express sympathy. I'd rather receive silence than a "bummer." Keep your stupid words to yourself.

Of course, I didn't say this to Autumn.

Young Gertrude accepted Alexander's offer. When she stood up, he extended his right hand toward her and mouthed five words: *Do we have a deal?* Her eyes fluttered as she contemplated her next move. She didn't need to consider his question; she already knew the answer. Something else was on her mind.

After much hesitation, she gave him a slight nod and shook his hand. Alexander grinned and nodded in return, but when he tried to complete the handshake and let go, Young Gertrude only squeezed his hand harder. Despite his towering height and unmatched strength, he couldn't release himself from her grip.

In one swift motion, she pulled him over the table, removed the knife attached to his belt, and repeatedly stabbed him. I counted six stabs to his upper back, then she thrust the knife into his neck and left it there.

Alexander bled out on the table. His killer didn't linger. She flew past the frame and exited the room. On her way out, she must have knocked over the camera—everything turned sideways—but the film kept rolling.

Autumn and I watched in silence as Alexander's blood dripped from the table and oozed past the frame along the floor. This went on for several minutes until the last frame flickered, and the screen turned white. I don't know how, given what we had just witnessed, but Autumn continued shoving popcorn in her mouth.

"So *that* happened," she said. "What the hell was that all about anyway? Care to enlighten me?"

I can't say I didn't see this coming, but holy crap, actually seeing it shook me.

All these years, I had been living with a murderer.

Ironically, she was one of the most gentle humans I ever knew. My brain broke as I fathomed the polarity between love and gore. It shattered me—the possibility that both could live inside her, or me, or anyone.

After the initial shock wore off, I re-examined the pieces of this convoluted puzzle:

Gertrude.

Alexander.

Darwin.

Autumn.

Charlie.

Bill.

The Grey Man.

The Moths.

The Vultures.

The underground door.

The blackout spells.

The disappearance of my family.

They all shared a connection to each other; I was at the center.

But *why?*

Despite all I had seen, heard, and felt, I failed to understand the reason behind any of this. I get that Gertrude wanted me to figure it out so I could finish what she started and whatever, but what if I didn't want to?

After watching Young Gertrude slaughter Alexander, I needed a break. I reached my limit. I preferred going on movie dates to unraveling the mysteries of the universe.

With all these people, places, and things swirling in my head, I answered Autumn's question to the best of my ability.

"I don't know."

The reel continued to spin on the projector, but no picture played on the screen. Just white flickering light. Once again, the darkness hiding behind the screen caught my attention.

"Let's see what's on this one," Autumn said, holding the *Elliott* reel in the air. "Aren't you curious? It has your name on it!"

"Wait. I'm curious about *that*," I replied, pointing at the darkness.

When I grabbed the edge of the white sheet, a cool draft brushed through my fingers. The air wafted out from a large hole in the wall.

It reminded me of a random fact Bill once told me:

"Your sense of smell is linked closely to memory, more so than any of your other senses."

I took a breath. My mind's projector played the memory of the evening when I found the secret cave in my parents' closet.

That was twelve years ago.

It smelled the same, like mold and metal.

"Flashlight!" I shouted.

Autumn beamed her light at the hole in the wall, revealing a long, narrow tunnel, just wide enough for a human to enter. The circular opening measured around three feet across and tapered further down. I couldn't see the other side; it faded to black.

"Hello!" I shouted into the tunnel. My voice ricocheted in every possible direction. I waited, hoping someone on the other side would respond, but I heard nothing.

"Should we check it out?" I asked.

"We still have another film to watch."

"Eh, let's watch it later. I want to see where this goes."

"There *is* no later. You're supposed to watch this."

Autumn's determination to follow Gertrude's instructions clashed with my curiosity to find out what waited for me at the other end of the tunnel. At the same time, my curiosity clashed with the desire to gain Autumn's approval. I wanted her to like me. I wanted to make her smile.

I wanted to go on that movie date.

"Fine!" I roared, putting my curiosity on hold. "Set it up."

Autumn lifted the lid from the *Elliott* film canister, revealing a worn, folded piece of paper resting on top of the reel. It slid out of the canister and fell on the floor. I picked it up.

"Is this yours?"

"Never seen it before. What is it?"

"Looks like a map."

Two maps, actually—one on each side: *Above* and *Below*.

The *Above* map showed two locations that I recognized: Sacred Dark Hospital and Our Lady of Sorrows Church. The twenty or so other locations scattered throughout the map were unfamiliar to me.

The *Below* map's scale matched the one scribbled on *Above*, but that was the only similarity. Aside from that, I didn't recognize a goddamn thing on it. All the lines, circles, and crosses looked like a bunch of nonsense.

Autumn didn't see it the same way.

"This really would have been nice to have a couple weeks ago."

I didn't understand.

"What do you mean?"

"The tunnels are—"

She cut her answer short and froze. Many footsteps thumped and creaked across the floorboards over our heads. They marched inside from the backyard, walked past the basement entrance, and kept going until they reached Gertrude's room. Muffled voices accompanied the footsteps, but I couldn't make out what they said.

After a brief gathering in Gertrude's bedroom, the footsteps continued until they reached the top of the basement stairs.

"We're out of time," Autumn whispered. "They're coming."

"Who?"

I figured it out as soon as I asked.

Here we go.

I waited a long time for this.

Silence surrounded us. Time slowed down. Shadows at the top of the stairs appeared and changed shape, leaning in and pulling back like ocean waves.

Their swaying motions triggered a memory.

I suffered from insomnia for much of my life, and I put my parents through hell because of it. I remember lying in bed, calling for help because I couldn't sleep. Half the time, my father would barge in and tell me to shut up and go to sleep. I longed for the other half when my mom walked in the room, held me in the rocking chair, and whispered songs into my ear until I crashed.

Every time, my mom planted an affirmation in my heart:
"We have the same shadow."

The shadows dancing back and forth at the top of the stairs gifted me with the rediscovery of this memory.

It all went to hell when the shadows at the top of the stairs tossed Gertrude's naked body into the basement.

Her legs hit the ground first, shattering on impact.

Her torso followed, slapping the concrete floor like a wet noodle.

Her head took the final blow; it cracked against the concrete.

Somehow, after being thrown down an entire flight of stairs, she was still alive, still breathing, but barely. Blood poured from her nose and ears. Her shallow breaths hissed from the fluid in her lungs. Her eyes twitched and scanned the room until they found me.

We looked at each other from opposite sides of the universe. I swear to God, she spoke to me. She sent me messages from her mind: *Don't be afraid. Let this happen. It's a means to an end.*

The footsteps filed down the stairs until five figures revealed themselves.

Johnny, Dallas, Devon, and Darcy entered the basement carrying large metal cans with fluid sloshing around inside them. They held one in each hand. James followed behind them.

"Douse it, all of it," he commanded as he crept down the stairs. Without hesitation, they removed the caps from the metal cans and splashed the fluid all around the basement.

Autumn took a deep breath. "Kerosene."

"What's kerosene?"

"It's what we're gonna use to burn this place down," James replied.

He leaned against the wall and tossed a black stone up and down in his hand.

"Can you believe it?" he continued. "This stupid thing's been keeping him out all this time. How does that even work? It's a *rock*."

"Shouldn't have thrown her down the stairs," Johnny interrupted. He took a deep drag from his cigarette and pointed it at Gertrude. "She's gotta say the words. Won't work otherwise. Can't get words from a dead lady."

I know Johnny flew with the Vultures. I know he wanted to burn the house down. But damn, he looked so cool doing it with his black, slicked-back hair, puffy blue vest, and cigarette. I wanted to be him.

James didn't appreciate Johnny cutting in the conversation.

"You know, I was gonna let you do it," he barked at him. "Nobody talks to me that way."

Johnny shrugged his shoulders and kept smoking. James passed the black stone to Dallas.

"Here—pry the words from her mouth."

Dallas frightened me, mostly because of his height. He towered over everyone. I wouldn't have been able to stop him if I tried. The gold butterfly knife sticking out of his back pocket would have stopped me too.

He circled his prey several times before falling to his knees. He retrieved his knife and flipped it around in his left hand a hundred different ways. His right hand held the black stone. He studied it closely until Gertrude interrupted his focus with a guttural moan.

"Sounds like you're ready," Dallas taunted. Gertrude responded with a whimper. He got down on all fours until both their foreheads touched.

"Break the circle," he whispered. "Say the words."

He rubbed the black stone against her lips, covering it in blood and spit. As he pushed the stone up against her gums, he smiled and giggled with satisfaction.

"That's not necessary," Autumn said.

James pulled a black tanto knife from his back pocket.

"Nobody said you could talk, bitch."

"I'm not afraid of you."

He pressed the tip of his blade against her neck.

"You will be."

Their standoff ended when Gertrude threw up all over the floor. Everyone backed away in disgust except for Dallas; he stayed on all fours, hovering over Gertrude.

"Say the words, or I'll cut his tongue out."

He pointed his blade at me.

I felt powerless. Less than powerless, if there is such a thing. It's like when you're dreaming. Everything happens around you, and you just watch. You don't move or speak or think. You don't react at all, not even emotionally. You're just there—a conscious nothing.

Dallas pressed the side of Gertrude's face against the floor. The black stone rested near her lips. Fluid in her lungs bubbled as she took a breath.

With the last shred of strength in her body, she muttered the words James wanted to hear.

"Ego haurire tua virtute.

"Ego dare clavem.

"Frange circulus est mecum."

She kissed the black stone. Her body went limp.

"Was that it?" Dallas asked James.

"Word for word. Now break it."

On his first try, Dallas smashed the stone with the butt of his knife. The stone shattered. All the lights in the basement went out.

I remained a conscious nothing, a shell of my former self.

Autumn reached for my hand—it didn't matter.

Charlie screamed for his life upstairs—I didn't care.

I inhaled the pungent stench of vomit and kerosene—whatever.

In the darkness, fuzzy, unidentifiable shapes danced in front of me, falling in and out of view. Tiny specks of blue light, like stars, flickered through the shapes. This visual mess swirled and spun to form a recognizable picture, a memory.

In a flash, I saw the massive wall of brochures inside the rest stop. I stared at the happy, normal lives depicted in each one, knowing I'd never have that for myself. I felt the absence of my father and sister, noting relief and unhappiness. I stared at the map of West Carolina and the big red dot: "You are here." Everything was just as I remembered, almost. The Grey Man wasn't there. I waited, but he didn't walk inside.

As I stood there, stuck in the memory, I recited the words he once spoke to me:

"One day—maybe not today, maybe not tomorrow, maybe not a thousand years from now, but one day—we will be together again. When we do, there will be others. Your world will not appear the same. Neither will mine. I have a plan for you, Elliott. I will see it through. Mark these words."

The basement lights flickered on again; the projected memory dissolved. Everything looked the way it did before the lights went out, except Autumn let go of my hand. We stood in the same places, quietly, waiting for something to happen.

Autumn laughed at the Vultures.

"Was that little show of yours supposed to scare us?"

I tried to get her attention.

"Autumn."

"Is the boogeyman coming out soon?"

"Autumn?"

"Please, I'm dying to meet him,"

"Autumn!"

A shadow stirred at the top of the stairs. It lingered there for a moment, waiting until it had our undivided attention. As it descended the stairs, I recognized the sound of its footsteps.

Halfway down, the shadow revealed its form: a tall, sickly-looking man with grey skin, dressed in black, showing his broken glass smile.

The Grey Man acknowledged me with his eyes and tipped the brim of his hat.

"Elliott, it's so good to see you again."

He turned toward the Vultures and opened his arms.

"Thank you, boys, for letting me in. Your loyalty over the years has paid off. It will not go unmissed, I assure you. I am in your debt."

When he noticed Autumn standing next to me, his demeanor changed. He slithered in her direction, sizing her up and down.

"Are you lost, darlin'?" he asked her playfully. "I don't recall sending you an invitation to our soirée."

Caught between fight and flight, Autumn backed away from him; her hip struck the film projector table. The *Alexander* film canister fell to the floor, rolled toward the Grey Man, and stopped at his feet. His smile resurfaced when he picked it up and read the label.

He clutched the canister to his chest and leaned over Gertrude's almost-dead body.

"Remember this, Gertie? You sure did a number on me. How long has it been—fifty years? Forgive me for losing track of time. When I jump from one train to the next, so to speak, the memories don't always transfer, but I do my best. I see you've seen better days. Funny how things work sometimes, wouldn't you say, old friend?

Pins and needles jabbed every inch of my body.

Cold sweat soaked my skin.

"You're not Alexander," I said to him. "I watched him die."

I'm surprised I had the mental bandwidth to speak, but it didn't get me far. My words only frustrated him.

He reacted as if I had just failed a test.

"Okay, Elliott. Let's ponder this for a moment. If I'm not Alexander, then *who am I*? What is my name? Can you tell me that much?"

I didn't know what to do besides stand there and stare at him like a goddamn idiot. I didn't know who he was, but he insisted that I did. Color me confused.

"Each time the hourglass flips, we find each other again, but you forget who I am. How long must we keep dancing like this, child?"

He took a step toward me.

"What about *you*? Do you remember who *you* are?"

He extended his arms. His palms turned into pale white fists.

"My dear Elliott—you are the key to my heart."

I didn't understand him, but I believed him.

Almost every morning, I wake up and forget all my dreams. But I know the dreams happened. My conscious mind clocks in; I feel like I just came back from somewhere, but I don't know where I went.

The Grey Man's words reminded me of that.

"You don't have a heart," Autumn interrupted, speaking for me. She felt less like a crush and more like a caretaker. But whatever. I didn't care. Nothing mattered anymore.

Derealization achieved—fully out of my mind.

The Grey Man tilted his head and examined her like a riddle he couldn't solve.

"I still don't know what you're doin' here, little lady, but you're right about one thing: I don't have a heart."

He darted toward her and grabbed her collar.

"It was taken from me."

I should have stopped him, but I didn't.

In a flash, his demeanor changed; his rage receded.

He straightened Autumn's sweater collar, patted her shoulders, and returned to his place next to Gertrude.

"Apologies, little lady. Matters of the heart—a sore subject! But you needn't worry. Just go back to your home. The rest of us will be on our way."

He turned to the Phoenix Twins.

"Do you have the lapis stones? Did you get *all* of them?"

"We found one more buried in the backyard," Darcy replied—or was it Devon? I couldn't tell them apart back then.

The other twin pointed to Gertrude.

"We searched all of Gertrude's possessions, including her body. Had to extract one of her teeth. Blood everywhere."

"How many does that make?" the Grey Man asked.

"Six," they answered in unison.

"*Seven*," he hissed. "I asked for seven. Why don't you have seven?"

I hoped the missing stone was stashed away in one of my pockets, but when I patted them down, I felt nothing. I couldn't remember the last time I had it on me. I figured I lost it a while back. But it's just a rock, I thought.

Sure, my mom said it was special, but it didn't matter. She's dead. No rocks could bring her back. I guess I cared about it a little more back when the Vultures took turns smashing it on the ground, but time changes everything.

Time has this funny way of setting your house on fire while you're asleep inside it.

The Grey Man signaled the Vultures to search the house, but there was no need.

Autumn fooled us all.

With a massive, shit-eating grin on her face, she reached into her snack bag and revealed the seventh stone.

It hung from a silver chain, fastened to an amulet.

"Because I have it."

Do you know what it means when someone "holds all the cards?"

There I go again.

The Grey Man eyed the stone. I expected desperation or fear from him, but he remained cool as a cucumber, peaceful as a dove, pacific as the ocean, or whatever godawful simile you prefer.

Sorry, I'm just trying to lighten the mood. I can only handle so much darkness at a time. I need more laughter—and blood.

I'm pretty sure no human is designed to bleed this much.

We might have to do something about it sooner or later.

I vote sooner.

Much, much sooner.

The Grey Man pointed to the amulet.

"You don't even know the object which you hold."

"Doesn't matter," Autumn replied. "You want it. I have it."

I caught a second-hand high standing next to her as she reveled in her power.

Dallas pointed his knife at her.

"Why don't I just slit her throat?" he asked. "Problem solved."

To be fair, he had a point. Murder seemed like a quick solution. Just end her life and take the stone. Problem solved.

He waited for the order, but the Grey Man resorted to rhetoric.

"Lower your blade, soldier. We needn't take this little lady's life. Superfluous!"

I saw it on their faces; nobody knew what "superfluous" meant.

Rather than speak in plain, relatable language, the Grey Man used complicated words to establish superiority.

This version of him did, at least.

I believed Autumn held all the cards until the Grey Man revealed the ace hidden up his sleeve.

I swear, I'm not doing it on purpose.

"Your place at our table makes sense to me now. You, Autumn Vester, have gotten yourself involved in something much greater than you can ever fathom, just like your mother did. Thus, you will attempt to take a life for the sake of self-preservation, just like your mother did. However, where your mother succeeded, you will fail."

I watched her body shake at the mention of her mother.

"I say this as a favor to you," he continued. "I wish to spare you from the mortification that will inevitably follow if you take this path. All you need to do, little lady, is place the stone on the floor in front of you and leave. That's it! Oh, one additional request: I ask that you take the stairs on your way out. The rest of us will take our leave through the tunnel."

"Bullshit—what do I get out of this?"

The Grey Man danced around the room—a waltz box step, if I had to guess. One hand clutched an invisible back, the other embraced an invisible hand.

"I'm glad you asked! First, you get to keep your life. Second, you get to keep whatever is left of your dignity. You'll need both if you ever want to find your father."

"He's still out there, you know. He waits for you."

His little speech targeted her greatest weakness.

She still hadn't found her father after he discarded her almost twenty years ago.

He finished the dance over Gertrude's body and took a bow. His voice shifted from playful to sincere.

"Nothing waits for you here, little lady. Gertie sent you along on a glorified fetch quest—for what? What have you to gain from it, or is it because you owe a debt? Either way, child, look at her. The curtains are closing on her life. She has nothing left to give. You have nothing she can take. Just walk away. Free yourself. Leave the stone and the boy behind. You don't want any part in this."

Autumn did as the Grey Man instructed and placed the lapis lazuli on the floor.

No witty response.

No clever comeback.

She didn't resist, and I didn't try to stop her.

I stood there like a mannequin.

It's not that I accepted my place in all of this. On the contrary, I was ready to turn in my key and check out of this unendurable existence. I had seen enough. I had nothing left to give. Nothing left to live or fight for.

This is it, I thought. I'm done with this nonsense.

Cash me out.

"Well, I guess that's it then," Autumn said. She looked at me with sad eyes and hugged me. During our embrace, she whispered to me.

"Au revoir, Elliott Avenue, until our next encounter."

She didn't let go right away. She only held me tighter, or at least that's what I thought. As it turned out, she was reaching inside her sleeve for something. She kept it hidden all this time, waiting for the right moment to use it.

Another ace, another sleeve.

In this case, the ace was a black stainless steel throwing dagger.

In one fell swoop, she consoled me, grasped the blade from her sleeve, and sent it flying into the Grey Man's neck, severing his carotid artery, killing him in a matter of seconds.

I had waited eleven years for this.

The Grey Man turned into a temporary sprinkler; blood spurted out from the hole in his neck. Autumn got sprayed the most. I took second place.

Imagine this is your life.

After the blood and dust settled, everyone just sort of stood there, waiting for something to happen.

I wondered: how does one remove themselves from this traumatic event and attempt a normal life—or any kind of life?

I didn't have to wonder for very long.

James pointed his knife at Gertrude's body.

"It's not over. Watch."

She looked the same: still dying, barely breathing, bathing in a pool of blood, vomit, and kerosene. Nothing remarkable.

Autumn lost interest after a few seconds.

"I think we've all had enough of this—whatever *this* is."

She stepped toward the Grey Man's corpse, removed her dagger from his neck, and slid it back into her sleeve.

"I'm gonna collect my things and head out."

As she placed lapis lazuli and *Elliott* film reel into her snack bag, Gertrude's body inflated.

I watched her chest.

Rising and falling.

Little by little, awakening.

Rising and falling.

Faster now.

Rising and falling.

Accelerated breaths.

Rising and falling.

So fast that I lost count.

Her breaths became moans. Her moans morphed into growls. In between her growling, she coughed and coughed until her coughs exploded into laughter.

She couldn't move her body—it was reduced to a bag of broken bones—but she had her voice. After clearing the blood and mucus from her throat, she spoke to Autumn, or rather, the Grey Man spoke to Autumn through Gertrude.

"You failed! Just like I said you would."

"He did it!" Dallas shouted. "Just like he said he would. Wow."

James stared at Gertrude's body with dead eyes.

"That's our cue, boys. Light it up."

The Vultures removed glass bottles from the hoods of their sweaters. Clear liquid sloshed around inside them. The Phoenix twins struck matches against the concrete wall and combined them into a single flame. They huddled around the matchstick fire and clinked their bottles together, igniting the strips of fabric hanging from them.

"Cheers."

Four bottles flew into the corners of the basement, exploding into massive fireballs. Flames followed the kerosene trails along the walls, floor, and Gertrude's legs. Her skin crackled and popped as the fire gorged away.

James shook his Molotov cocktail under his chin and locked eyes with Autumn.

"Are you afraid of me yet?"

Autumn stood at the center of the basement, avoiding the flames. James stood at the foot of the stairs, winding up his pitch.

No matter which way I turned, I couldn't escape the thick heat that surrounded me like a blanket. The dancing, unquenchable fire fed on the oxygen in the air, leaving little left for the rest of us.

Each breath drew me closer to the conclusion that this was the end of the line.

I might have been scared if I didn't want to die.

I welcomed this.

James blocked the stairs; Autumn dashed toward the tunnel. He flung his flaming bottle in her direction as she reached the opening in the wall. The bottle exploded against the back of her head, engulfing her red hair in a fiery blaze. But somehow, even with her head on fire, she kept running, running, running down the tunnel until her flame disappeared out of view.

The Vultures crowded around the tunnel entrance.

"Hunt her down," James ordered. "She has the seventh stone."

I took a seat on the floor and watched as they sprinted down the tunnel. After they ran out of sight, I lay on my back and waited for the house to collapse on me or the smoke to invade my lungs.

Both options raced to claim my life. It would have been so lovely, I thought, if I had the portable CD player with me.

Play This at My Funeral.

I breathed in; a thousand daggers pierce the tissues of my lungs.

My eyelids scratched like sandpaper when I blinked.

Noxious, black smoke swirled and swelled around me, so thick I couldn't see anymore.

Through the darkness, Gertrude's voice cried out to me, but it wasn't her.

"My dear child! Our moment has finally come! Crawl to me. Embrace me. I will do the rest. It won't hurt, I promise. You won't feel a thing."

I crawled on all fours and followed the voice toward the flaming bookshelves. When my dragging knuckles made contact with her seared skin, I collapsed into the fetal position and hugged the trunk of her body.

"Oh, I'm so proud of you, child. You're a good boy. Now, I must leave before you. That's how it works. I'll be there with the hourglass when you open the door. It will all be over soon."

She kissed my forehead with melting lips.

"See you on the other side, my heart."

I spent my last moments of consciousness listening to Gertrude's reanimated body bash the back of its skull against the concrete floor. Smashing it over and over and over until it popped.

Her body deflated in my arms. I followed closely behind.

As the world around me caved in, I let myself fade away.

"Goodnight."

I caressed the black blanket of death.

The curtains closed.

I didn't smell smoke anymore.

The sound of roaring flames dissipated.

A gentle warmth replaced their scorching heat.

My lungs didn't hurt because I didn't have lungs anymore.

I lost the corporeal pieces of myself.

But I was still *something*, lying in the dark. I can't tell you for how long, but *how long* doesn't exist in a place without time.

You may be wondering how one senses the absence of time.

Trust me, when you feel it, you'll know.

I could have rested there forever, spending eternity knowing nothing, feeling nothing, free from the burden of a body, but my reverie in the nothingness didn't last.

Another being entered the void.

I felt their energy like a magnet, attracting me as I attracted them. We pulled each other in until our proximities nearly touched.

The being struck a match and lit a white candle resting on the table between us. The flame revealed a beautiful woman in a mint green, duck canvas dress.

She smiled at me with tears in her eyes.

"Found you."

15 — Hypovolemia

MY BLOOD TYPE IS AB POSITIVE.

I'm a universal recipient.

I'm not telling you this for the hell of it.

This isn't fun fact time.

I still have so much say, but if you don't take me to the hospital *right now*, then forget it.

We can't let this happen.

Sacred Dark is my only option. Yes, they still pile patients in dumpsters, but I've been there before and left with discharge papers, not in a body bag.

I'm willing to take the risk if you are.

Please. We have to leave.

On the way, I'll tell you what my mom said to me in the place between places. She had been waiting for me there ever since she died, but when I got there, she told me I couldn't stay.

"I caught you before he had the chance, but I can't do it twice. I must send you back, my love. You still have some living left to do."

Caught and thrown back like a fish so that I may swim again.

On my way out, she asked me to tell Annabelle that her mom loves her very much.

"She's out there. She's looking for you. Find her."

Did I find her? If I did, would I even know?

I wanted to hug her and ask a billion questions, but I didn't have a body. No arms to reach with. No voice to speak from.

By that logic, how did I hear her?

Maybe my maum communicated some other way, and when I returned, I translated her messages into words.

I don't know the rules or how things work there. My human brain can't comprehend what I experienced there, wherevever "there" is.

Wherever and whenever. Time doesn't flow there.

Why is my skin so wet?

Do you see this?

What's happening to me?

I've never see anythimg like this before.

What?

Can I have some water? I'm so thirsty.

Can I have some water? I'm so thirsty.

Can I have some water? I'm so thirsty.

Oh. Oh wait. I just rememembered something.

What?

I should wait until we get to hospital.

I something read in one of Billl's books: orl hydration can be un-safe whem treating blood loss resulding from injinury.

Yes. Yes. Yes. Yes. The book. The book. I remember the book.

Shock Paarthathogenenisis and Therapy: An Internationananananal Symposum by Klaus Dieetrch Bach.

Yes. Yes. Yes.

Best options ar eintravenious fluids and blodplama transfision.

I should wait fer IV.

Jus get me there. Hopstable. Hostable. Please help me hospal.
Hard to talk now. Try again. Hospital. I did it. Hospal. Take me.

Take. Take take to scared dark

Two one zero three. Two one zero threee.

Wait for IV. Wait for ive. IV. Wait. Pleas. IV. Wait. Wait for me.

Plee please.

Waait. Wait. Anna.

Anna will await for me wait for me will wiat for me w

Some baut to too you feel

Feel. I feel you. Feel feel feel feel. I feel.

Momma. Mmma. Mma.

Mommmmmmmmmmma.

Fifonfndanna. Ifnderifodnna.

Momma.

I dt wnt th isanymo re

hell

help

help

help

help

water

help

momma

help

To be continued…

ABOUT THE AUTHOR

Thomas Smak is a professional UX writer living in the Detroit Metropolitan Area.

While sitting by himself at a National Coney Island in January 2004, he pulled out his journal and started brainstorming ideas for what would eventually become *The Myths of Maudlin* series. 17 years later, he finished his first novel, *Where the Sky Children Fell*.

Along with writing fiction, he enjoys *Peanuts* comics, synthesizers, video games, Settlers of Catan, making friends with bees, studying existential dread, hunting ghosts, and gardening with his wife.

Made in United States
North Haven, CT
20 March 2023

34348068R00182